PROTECTING HER HEART

THE SONOMA SERIES
BOOK FOUR

SHELBY GUNTER

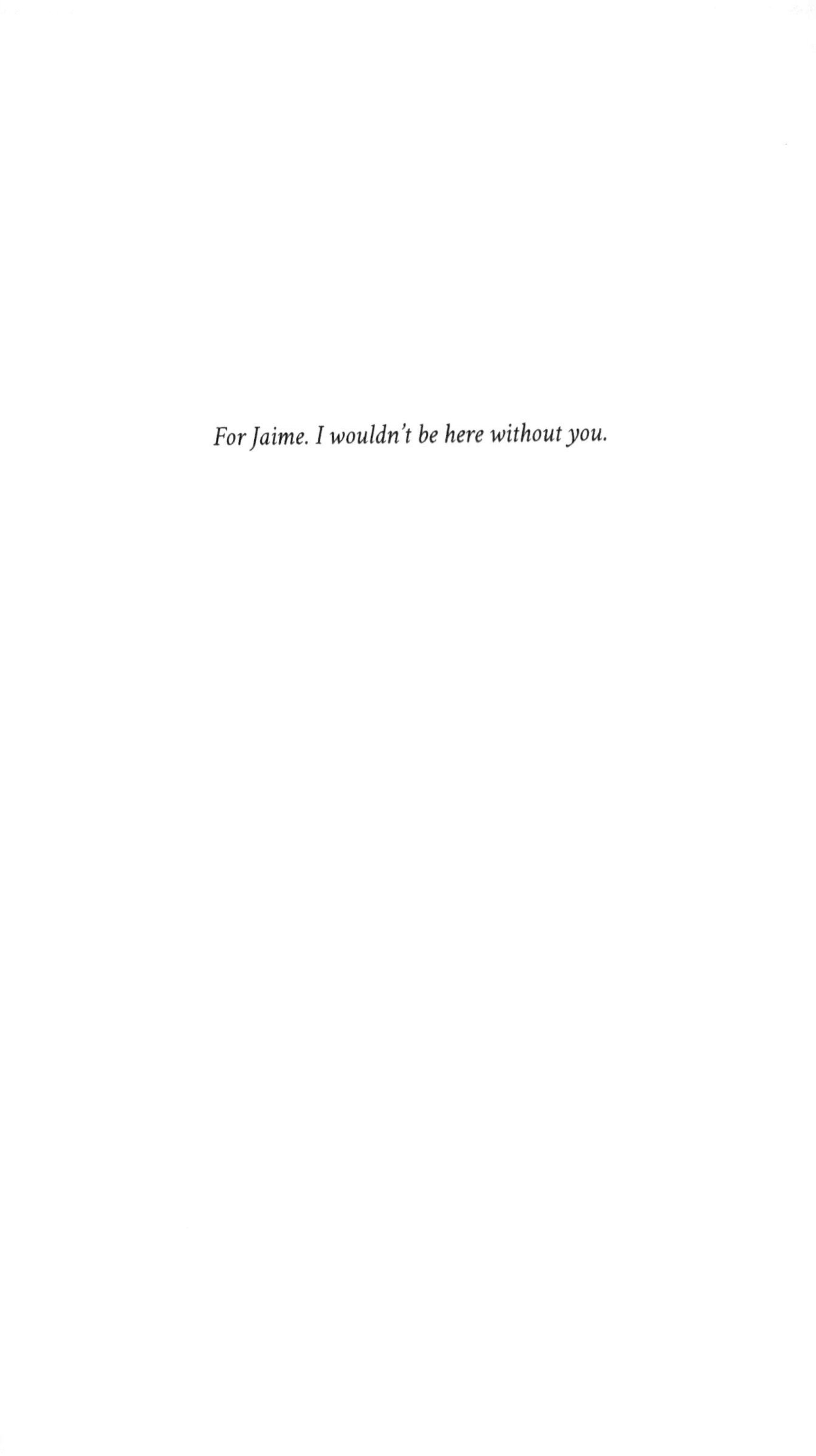

For Jaime. I wouldn't be here without you.

PROLOGUE

UNKNOWN

She's so pretty. Soft, ivory skin and long, brown hair so shiny I bet it would feel like silk against my fingers. I can't wait for the day I can touch her whenever I want. When I can show her how much I love her. For now, I know I can only watch.

I hate it.

The shadows of night conceal my body. With the forest surrounding me, she has no idea I'm here. I can see her through the window of her house. She's playing with her animals, laughing when they're being silly. I laugh along with her, happy to be sharing in her joy. The gentle touches she gives them have jealousy slithering through me like a snake in the grass. What would it be like to have her hands on me like that?

I can already feel her tender embraces.

She'll love me just as much as I love her.

There's no other option. I'm hers forever.

And she'll be mine.

SARA

"Oh, shit." The words slip out of my mouth before I can shut them down.

"Literally." Dr. Charles chuckles as he adjusts his hold on the squirming Pomeranian. The poor thing is so scared she just crapped all over our exam table. Luckily, the owner isn't in the room with us. It usually creates exponentially more drama when they are.

"One last shot, then little Lulu can go get a bum wash," Dr. Charles says with a grimace. Despite the very smelly room, being a vet tech is my absolute dream job. Caring for animals is something I've been obsessed with since I saved a baby raccoon when I was six. Mom was none too thrilled, but I'd fallen in love with the little guy.

And any other wounded animal that came my way.

The Sonoma Animal Clinic handles mostly dogs and cats, however, there are plenty of other types of animals in our small town. We've got a few hamsters, a couple of lizards, and we even have a little garter snake that comes in for regular checks. We also handle some of the bigger livestock outside of town, but for the most part, we only help with challenging births and vaccines for the farms. There's a vet in Westlake that handles any of the major issues.

Dr. Charles Crawford, our fearless leader, started the animal clinic when his family moved here almost twenty years ago. I remember the very first interaction I had with him when I was a distraught sixteen-year-old. My youngest brother, Nolan, accidentally kicked my hamster, Millie, and I was terrified she was going to die.

The way Dr. Charles soothed my nerves while taking the best care of my pet set me on the path to becoming a vet tech. For a long time, I debated becoming a veterinarian myself. It was a tough decision, but I ultimately decided I wanted to be hands-on as quickly as possible without incurring all the debt vet school would have brought.

When little Lulu is finished with her shots, I carry her to the sink in the back of the clinic. Our large building gives us the space to offer multiple services outside of just everyday visits. We've got crates of various sizes for boarding, a room outfitted for any type of surgery, as well as three exam rooms for our regular checkups.

Setting the squirming Pomeranian into the deep sink, I work quickly to rinse off Lulu's butt, then do my best to dry her off. At this point, she is done with her vet visit, and I have very little hope of continuing to hold on to her without her trying to snap at me.

After I return Lulu to her owner, I set about cleaning up the exam room. When I step in, the smell of cleaning products hits my nose, telling me it's already been cleaned.

"I handled cleanup for you," Michelle says from behind me. Her icy blonde hair is in her typical messy bun while her gray eyes are sharp and focused. At thirty, she's only a few years younger than me, so we've become pretty good work friends over the last few years.

"You didn't have to do that, but thanks."

"Sure. We've got the staff meeting right after we close, so

I figured if I got a jump start on the closing checklist, we could get the meeting started right away."

"Good thinking!" I grin at her.

She goes off to finish closing down the clinic while I head up to the front for our last patient. The front desk is a long counter that separates the waiting room from the rest of the clinic. Susan, our clinic manager, handles all the office tasks like a drill sergeant. She's organized, meticulous, and will cut you if you mess with her system. I love her.

She hands me a file for Toby, an overweight tabby cat we've been monitoring for obesity concerns. Once I get him back to the exam room, I go through all the normal checks, making notes for Dr. Charles. Once I'm done, I let him know it's his turn and head back to the front of the clinic to help Susan and Michelle finish closing up. It's six o'clock, and we're all eager to get the meeting over with.

"You have any idea what Dr. Charles wants to talk about?" I ask when I step up to the desk. Not surprisingly, Susan has most of the end-of-day tasks completed.

"Not a clue. He only told me about it yesterday so I could put it on everyone's schedules." Her pinched expression tells me exactly how she feels about the last-minute update.

"So, it's a full staff meeting?"

"Apparently."

We have seven employees at our clinic. Susan, Michelle, and I are the full-time techs. We also have two part-time techs, a high school intern, and, of course, Dr. Charles.

We make our way into the break room at the back of the clinic. It's small but has your basic necessities: fridge, microwave, a few cabinets, and drawers holding paper cutlery. The six of us chatter, filling the space with noise, until Dr. Charles comes in a few minutes later, a serious expression on his face.

"I apologize for the last-minute meeting and appreciate everyone being willing to give up their time for me. I'll try to make this quick." He runs a hand through his silver hair, his face lined with worry. Usually, Dr. Charles's brown eyes are lit up with humor, a smile never far from his handsome face. Right now, a joke seems about the furthest thing from his mind. It makes my gut twist.

"You all know I had to take a couple of months off for my health a while back, and I appreciate everything you guys did to keep the clinic going while I was gone. I figured I'd bounce back and be fine to continue working, but it doesn't seem like that's the case. My heart is giving out on me. The doctors say I need to do everything I can to reduce my stress to keep it going."

"What exactly does that mean?" Susan pushes when Dr. Charles doesn't continue talking.

He clears his throat and makes eye contact with everyone in the room. "It means I have to retire."

A chorus of confusion arises at the declaration, my own questions drowned out in the mix of noise. A sharp whistle from Susan has all of us shutting up. Dr. Charles nods at her in thanks.

"I will not be shutting down the clinic," he starts when we're all quiet. A collective deep breath is released at his words. It seems I wasn't the only one worried about it. "My son, Benjamin, has moved here from Greensboro to take over for me. He was a vet at a large animal hospital there and has a lot of great experiences I think will truly benefit the clinic."

That's an interesting development. It's common knowledge among our team that Dr. Charles has always wanted Benjamin to take over for him when he retired. According to Dr. Charles, Ben has been very vocal about having no interest in living here or taking over the clinic, deeming it entirely too small for his abilities. I wonder how he feels now that it's happening.

"When can we meet him?" Michelle raises an eyebrow,

mistrust lining her features. We're all unsure about how this transition will go.

"He's just arrived in Sonoma this week. I'm hoping he'll be ready to start learning the ropes on Monday."

That's a quick turnaround if he only just arrived.

"Are you going to be okay, Dr. Charles?" I ask. With the shock of him leaving finally abated, the reason why this is all happening in the first place pops back into my head.

"Oh, yes, I will be fine. I'm just having to bow down to my old, decrepit body a little sooner than I was planning." He winks. The twinkle is back in his eye, telling me he really is going to be okay. He's been the best mentor and boss I've ever had the pleasure of working with. I'll be sad to no longer work for him.

Change is one of those things that sneaks up on you when you're least expecting it. Sometimes you can prepare for it, like when you move or get a new job, but the impactful changes are the ones that come out of nowhere, dropping into your life so suddenly they create a ripple effect, disrupting your life forever.

To me, that's true change.

I have a feeling this bomb is about to create a ripple so strong my life will look nothing like the one I had before.

I'm not sure I'm ready for it.

2

BEN

The brown fan blades spin round, creating the familiar whirring breeze from my teen years. It's been a long time since I've laid on my childhood bed, sulking at the unfairness of my life. Memories of doing this same thing at seventeen filter through my mind. My senior year of high school, my parents moved us to this shitty small town, where I had no friends and no choice in the matter.

Needless to say, I was pissed.

Those feelings are resurfacing now, even though I'm thirty-six instead of seventeen. I thought I had everything figured out. I had the career, the fiancée, a fancy downtown apartment, even a dog to round out the successful checklist. Now, I have a fiancée who lives an hour away...and a dog. Which, admittedly, makes up for a lot of the shit that's been heaped on me.

My head falls to the side as I stare at Sadie. Her soft coat gleams in the sunshine coming from the window across my room. The golden retriever has been in my life since I started my job in Greensboro six years ago. We've been through many things together over the last several years. This is just another bump in our road together. The only difference is, this time, the bump could last forever.

God, that's depressing.

"Come on, Sades." Her head lifts. "Let's go pretend like we aren't miserable."

I walk out of my bedroom at my parents' house and head downstairs, Sadie's nails clicking on the wood floor as she dutifully follows behind me. Walking through the living room, I step to the back door to take her out. Watching her play always puts me in a better mood. I know she's enjoying having the space to run free in the backyard. Living in an apartment didn't leave much room for her to play like she loves to do.

We play fetch until we're both tired. Sadie would continue until she physically couldn't move anymore. I usually have to be the bad guy and make her stop so she doesn't get hurt. Instead of going back inside, I sit in the outdoor seating area on the deck. The weather is perfectly mild today, which helps my mood significantly.

If I were home, I would probably be getting lunch with Rebecca or just leaving the dog park with Sadie. I used to spend my weekends catching up on everything I didn't do during the week or doing whatever activity Rebecca had planned for us. I don't even know what she's doing right now. Things have been strained between us since I came home. And every time we do talk, it's like she's a different person. She hasn't exactly been the supportive partner I expected, which has put pressure on our relationship.

When Mom called to tell me Dad's health was declining, I immediately came home to help her take care of him. There was a short period when I wasn't sure he was going to get better. It was a scary couple of months.

Rebecca didn't come to Sonoma one time when things started to turn dire. At the time, I thought it was better that way. I was too focused on my dad's health and wouldn't have been able to give her much attention. Looking back now, it would've been nice to have someone in my corner.

After Dad recovered, I went back to Greensboro, fully expecting things to go back to normal, but they never did. There was this uneasiness in my life that never seemed to go away, even though I was back to my regular routine.

Then Dad told me he was being forced to retire if he wanted his heart to stay strong. He pleaded with me to take over his clinic until he could find someone else. I agreed, despite having no desire to move here. I have no idea how long it'll take, and it's not going to be easy to find someone willing to live in a small town or run a family-owned business. Especially if they're not even a part of the family. If I'm honest, I sort of hate the idea of letting a stranger run our family clinic despite not wanting to do the job myself.

Rebecca and I talked about doing the distance thing until we could find a better alternative. Greensboro is only an hour's drive from Sonoma, so it's doable for the short term. Rebecca Smyden, daughter of the finance mogul Jeffrey Smyden, would never move to this Podunk town. The idea of her spending any time in Sonoma is laughable. She's a city girl through and through. Between her daily Starbucks and her constant need for being seen out and about, she would never survive here.

I just hope the search for someone new doesn't take too long. If this tension between Rebecca and me gets any worse, I'm not sure how we'll survive.

The patio door opens, pulling me from my thoughts. Mom steps outside with a tray of food in her hands that looks large enough to feed an army.

"I made us some lunch," she says, setting the food down on the table. There are two plates on the tray, both with ginormous sandwiches.

"Thanks, Mom." I grab a plate as my stomach growls. I

didn't even realize how hungry I was until the food was in front of me.

"Of course. Can't have my baby starving."

I roll my eyes at her. Being an only child was great in some respects, but now that I'm older, my mother still treats me like I'm twelve. It makes living back at home inordinately worse.

"Are you going to get out of the house today?" she asks. Her attempt at an innocent question is as subtle as a freight train. She's been pushing me to explore, to get to know the town a little more. She keeps telling me it's changed a lot in the twenty years I've been gone. I'm not sure how that's possible since it's still a small town, where people gossip for sport.

"What would I do? Stroll down Main Street with Mrs. Holliday, gabbing about whose kid is a shithead?" I raise my eyebrow.

"If you did that, she'd be talking about you." Mom's eyebrow raise is even better than mine, and I can't hold in the laugh that bursts from me. She's got me there.

"Touché."

Mom runs her hand through her shiny blonde bob that looks the same as when I was a kid. I got both my blue eyes and blond hair from her, but my facial features match my dad's, to a T.

"I'm not trying to force you to love this town; I know that's a losing battle. I just want you to get out of the house so you'll stop thinking of this place as the dump you've made it in your head. There's so much more to it, and if you want to do well at the clinic, you should keep your disdain to yourself."

I sigh, knowing she's right. It won't do anyone any good if I let my anger bleed out into the clinic. Making enemies isn't my goal here. I just need to focus on finding the right candidate to run the clinic, and then I can attempt to piece my life back together.

Mom and I finish our lunch without any more arguing, except when she slips Sadie some leftover pieces of lunch meat. Mom enjoys spoiling Sadie, to the point where I'm afraid she's never going to want regular dog food again.

My phone rings as we clean up, and Mom shoos me to answer. She grabs our dishes, then heads inside with Sadie at her heels.

"Hey, Rebecca," I answer, a little knot of hesitation setting up camp in my gut.

"Ben, I'm so glad I caught you." The sound of the city in the background is loud, telling me she's walking somewhere.

"What are you up to?"

"Heading to lunch. Listen, are you still planning on coming back next weekend?"

"Well, I actually need to talk to you about that."

"So, that's a no," she says without any inflection. I can't tell if she's pissed off or okay with it.

"No, I'm not going to make it back next weekend. We can try for another day, or you could come here instead."

"Hi! I'm so glad we got to do this!" Rebecca's voice is far from the phone, so I'm guessing she made it to her lunch date. She continues to talk for a few minutes while I just sit here, waiting for her to remember she's still on the phone with me. "Hang on a second. Ben, are you still there?"

"Yeah, still here," I huff.

"I'm at lunch now. Can we talk again later?"

"Sure." The phone goes dead without a response. There are moments when Rebecca's life is moving one hundred miles an hour, and she only stops to give me a sliver of her time when it's beneficial to her. I can understand, especially since I had a similar view of our relationship when I worked so much at the animal hospital. I always thought that if we got married, it would be easier because we'd live together;

our lives would be fully entwined. But I'm not so sure anymore.

Coming home has given me a lot of time to think about my relationship with Rebecca. Over the last several months, it feels like she has been pulling away from me little by little. I know she's busy with her life. She has a lot of responsibilities because her family is one of the more influential families in Greensboro. I just imagined she'd be a little more supportive of this upheaval.

But is it fair to ask her to give me more time just because I suddenly have an abundance of it to spend on her? I don't know.

I guess we'll figure it out eventually. Until then, I should probably start learning everything I can about how to run Dad's clinic.

3

SARA

The cork comes out of the wine bottle with a satisfying pop. I dump the wine into the two glasses sitting on the bar, listening as a heated debate over romance books rages on. Tonight is book club night at Quinn Jackson's house. She and her husband, Cooper, have a sweet basement with an oversized sectional, a projector screen, and a fully functional bar. It's the perfect place to hang out.

I take the full wine glasses back to the couch, handing Quinn her glass before sitting in my chair again.

"I say the dirtier the better. Without the steam, how are you supposed to understand the deeper connection between the characters?" Natalie asks. Her cheeks are flushed, which isn't a surprise. She has her red hair pulled back in a messy bun, and she's wearing leggings and a long-sleeve shirt despite it feeling like a million degrees in the room. She's still not quite comfortable with her burn scars after an arsonist tried to set fire to her house with her still in it.

"But there's always so much to the plot and character development; the sex is just a bonus," Quinn responds. Her brown hair hangs loosely around her shoulders tonight. We're all in comfy clothes since we decided a movie marathon was in order, even if we're here for book club. Quinn also has these blue eyes that hold so much compassion in them; you feel like the only person in the world when she gives you her whole attention. It's one of the reasons she joined our group so seamlessly.

"I agree with you, Quinn; the plot takes the cake over the sex scenes. However, I would enjoy the books less without them," I say, adding my two cents. We started a book club to give us another reason to hang out with each other more often.

As everyone has started pairing off, we've gotten so busy that it's hard to have time to hang out with each other as often as we used to. I'm the last single person in our group. Even Levi, Cooper's brother, has started dating Hope, which came as a huge surprise to us all. He used to be the stereotypical bachelor, always hanging out with different women. We never expected him to settle down with anyone, let alone the sweetest woman ever.

I don't mind being the last single one of the group. None of my friends have ever made me feel left out, and I really do enjoy being alone. I've honestly never given much thought to who I'll end up with. I figure, one day, he'll come into my life when he's supposed to, and until then, I'll just date when I feel like it. I'd rather wait for the right man to come along than settle for just anyone.

"How's Dr. Charles doing, Sara?" Quinn asks.

"He just told us he's retiring."

Surprise shows on all the girls' faces at my words.

"Is he okay? What does that mean for you?" Lucy asks. Sitting next to Megan, the two of them look like sisters with their sleek blonde hair. Their only difference is Lucy has brown eyes while Megan has blue. We tease Lucy and Megan that their husbands, Max and Todd, are the only ones who can tell them apart.

"He's okay. Apparently, the stress of running the clinic

was becoming too much for him to handle, so he's retiring. I guess his son is going to be taking over for a while. None of us have met him, though, so I have no idea what that will be like."

"At least the clinic isn't closing down," Megan says.

"Wait, is his son Benjamin Crawford?" Natalie asks, an odd look on her face.

"Yeah, he was a few years older than us. I don't remember him from school, even though he was a senior when we were freshmen," I respond. How Nat can remember some dude who was only around for a year, I'll never understand.

"You don't remember the hot blond that used to hang out with Adam and Matthew?" she asks, referencing the eldest two of my four brothers. "He always had this broody, dark cloud parked on his forehead."

Adam and Matthew—and even Carter and Nolan, to a lesser extent—were part of the popular crowd growing up. They were athletic, intelligent, and, unfortunately for me, attractive. They're still this way today, only they're more selective about who they're friends with.

"Holy shit." An image of an angry Ben suddenly pops into my head. I had the biggest crush on him back then. I can't believe I didn't remember that. I'm pretty sure I even attempted to flirt with him. And he looked at me like I was an alien. I must've blocked out that particularly embarrassing time in my life.

God, my little fourteen-year-old heart was shattered when he didn't give me the time of day.

"I completely forgot he used to hang out with Adam and Matthew. They had so many friends growing up it was hard to keep track sometimes," I say, trying to cover my reaction. I'd rather not share my humiliation at trying to flirt with the hot guy who was so far out of my league that it wasn't even funny.

If Ben is as resistant to running the clinic as I think he'll be, I can almost guarantee he'll be just as broody as he was at eighteen. I wonder what his scowl looks like now that he's all grown up. It's probably bad form to be picturing how hot your new boss will be when he starts tomorrow.

"That's totally accurate. Your brothers were super popular in high school," Nat responds.

The conversation turns to our reminiscence of high school, telling Quinn about all the shit we used to do. Even though it feels like she's been a part of our friend group from the beginning, Quinn only moved to Sonoma a year ago. The rest of us have been friends since we were in kindergarten.

As the evening winds down, I decide to head home before it gets too late. I'm missing my little zoo, which means they're probably missing me just as much.

My drive home is quick, a perk of living in a small town, and I walk up the steps to my tiny cottage. There's not much to it, with only two bedrooms and one bathroom. One side of the house has the living room that's open to the kitchen; the other side has the bedrooms with the bathroom in the middle. It's perfectly cozy for me and my animals. I have the second room set up as a gym. All the people in my life live in town or close to it, so there wasn't any need for an extra bed.

When I go to unlock my front door, I notice a flower on my doormat. I bend to pick it up, confusion running through me. It's a single red rose. No note, no indication of who could've left it. It's a little odd, but maybe it was left here by mistake. Someone could've had the wrong address, leaving it for the wrong person.

I unlock the door, taking the rose with me. No reason to waste a perfectly beautiful flower. As I step into my house, Koda and Luna jump up from their dog beds and race toward me. Koda sticks close to Luna's side, making sure she doesn't run off course. Luna is blind, and the minute I brought her home, Koda took her under his wing, making sure she could find her way around the house.

All my animals have little quirks to them, which is why I took them in. Koda, my black lab, is missing most of an ear. Luna, my little white husky mix, is blind. Minnie, my black-and-white cat, is missing a leg. Lizzo, my lizard, is missing her tail, and Bruno, my hamster, has a large patch of skin on his head that never grows fur. If I'm honest, he looks a little like the stereotypical monk you'd find in a movie.

Each one was dropped off at the shelter because of their quirks, which is exactly why I brought them home. I wanted them to know they deserved love, no matter what they looked like.

They're my babies. "Yes, you are. You're my little squishes." I smoosh Koda's cheeks, scratching his head as his tail swishes back and forth.

I greet all my animals equally, then let the dogs out in the backyard to do their business. Once everyone has been loved on, we settle into the living room to watch TV until I'm ready for bed. Tomorrow is going to be interesting with Benjamin starting at the clinic.

His broodiness will be easy to ignore. I just hope he's not an asshole about it.

4

BEN

The red brick building before me feels both familiar and completely unknown. I never imagined I'd be walking through those doors as an employee. I spent so much time here when I was a teenager, watching my dad work through the monotony of regular checkups. I knew I wanted to be a vet, but I never wanted to work in a place so boring. I couldn't understand what my dad enjoyed about weighing fat cats whose parents can't stop giving them treats despite knowing they're putting the animal at risk.

My job in Greensboro was exciting. There were complex surgeries and rare disorders to study. I never knew what my day would involve until I got there. I loved it.

Now, I'm about to walk into this building and complete wellness checks all day. It's not what I wanted for my life, and finding someone to take over won't be easy. I highly doubt the pool of interested candidates is going to be great. How many top doctors are going to want to move to the middle of nowhere? And I'm not going to pick the first vet who applies, either. I want them to understand what they're taking on and what this clinic means to my family. Which means the search for the right person is going to be tedious.

Thankfully, my boss at the animal hospital in Greensboro allowed me to take a leave of absence while I get things sorted here. She's been very supportive of me helping my dad get back on his feet, but I don't want to take advantage of the time she's allowing me to have. Maybe the first few candidates who apply will be perfectly qualified.

And I'm officially delusional.

With a huff, I get out of my car to walk inside the clinic. The lobby has several chairs lined up along the wall facing the desk. Susan, the clinic's office manager, looks up at me through her cat-eye glasses. She's been around since Dad started the clinic. As a teen, she scared the holy hell out of me. All she had to do was raise an eyebrow, and I'd straighten my shit out immediately.

It doesn't seem like much has changed over the past twenty years when she glares at me behind the desk as I greet her. "Good morning, Mrs. Engles."

"Benjamin."

I scurry through the pass-through door to head back to Dad's office. He's spending mornings at the clinic this week to help ease me into the flow of things while not over-working himself. It's not like I can't handle doling out vaccines. I could do those in my sleep. I want to focus on the admin stuff since running the business side of things isn't quite in my wheelhouse. Mostly so I don't piss off Susan if I ruin her system. Being her intern in high school was scary.

I gently knock on Dad's open office door, making him glance up. His smile stretches wide when he sees it's me. It makes my chest ache knowing how much it disappoints him that I don't want to take over the business.

"Hey, son. I was just getting logged into the system."

I pull a chair around his desk to sit next to him while he goes through the ins and outs of his normal morning routine. It's all pretty straightforward, nothing too compli-cated. I'd imagine Susan takes care of most of it since she doesn't trust anyone else—especially not my father, who is technologically challenged on a good day.

"I think I can manage that."

"It's probably easy for you tech-savvy kids." Dad laughs. He's always been the kind of person who sees the best in any situation, taking whatever life throws at him with a smile on his face. It makes his disappointment in me even harder to stomach. We used to have a great relationship until we moved to Sonoma. Then it felt like there was nothing I could do right. Every time I turned around, I was making the wrong choices.

The straw that broke the camel's back was when I chose to go to Cornell for vet school instead of Dad's alma mater, North Carolina State. Passing up the opportunity to go to a prestigious school like Cornell seemed monumentally stupid, but I think Dad took it as a slight against him. It created this weird relationship between us that I've never been able to navigate.

"Let's go meet the team. Everyone should be here now." Dad stands from his chair, and I follow closely behind.

We walk out of his office, rounding the corner into the break room. It feels a little like an ambush when I see the entire team of employees crammed into the tiny space. They all look like they're watching a zoo exhibit. Their eyes are curious, wanting to get closer, but unsure of what I'll do if they move too fast.

I just stand next to Dad, keeping my face neutral. I don't recognize a single person here except for Susan. How are these people going to feel about me taking over for my dad? I won't run this place like he does. I tend to be a little more exacting and a lot less fun.

In Greensboro, it wasn't a problem. We weren't there for a fun time; we were there to take care of people's pets. It was a different atmosphere than Dad's clinic. Fitting in here isn't going to be easy, even for the short time I'll be around. Just another reason why I don't think this job is for me.

"Everyone, meet my son, Benjamin. I'm excited to be putting the reins of this place into his capable hands. He's got a lot of experience from the animal hospital in Greensboro, and I know his expertise and knowledge will be extremely beneficial to our clinic." Dad's face is beaming with pride, which only makes the brick in my stomach multiply. He's so happy I'm here.

All I can do is nod at the group in front of me, my throat too clogged with emotion to speak.

An awkward silence ensues while we all try to figure out what to do next. Finally, Dad says, "Right, well, I'll let you guys get introduced as you go. Ben, we've got the whole crew on the schedule this week to give you an opportunity to get to know everyone individually."

I clear my throat. "Sounds good." I glance at the people in front of me. Each one has a look of concern on their face. Except for Susan, of course. She just looks disappointed, which is how she's always looked at me. She knew all about my behavior growing up and has never been my biggest fan.

Everyone sits there for another moment until Susan shoos everyone back to work. I walk back into Dad's office with a defeated sigh. I didn't expect this to go over super well, but I also didn't expect them to look at me like I was an unqualified kid coming in to wreck the entire clinic.

Dad slaps his hand on my shoulder. "Let them get to know you, son. Then they'll see what I do."

"Sheer disappointment? That's not exactly what I was hoping for."

Dad freezes, his hand still on my shoulder. Without saying a word, he closes his office door, then gestures to the seats in front of his desk. With his elbows on his knees, he stares at me for a moment. I feel like a teenager again, waiting on him to reprimand me for whatever stupid thing I did.

"You honestly believe I'm disappointed in you?" he asks, looking me dead in the eye.

"I know you are, Dad. I see it in your eyes every time I come home. Look, I don't want to have this conversation right now. I'm going to get out there and do my job." I stand before he can say anything else, opening the door and stepping out of his office. I walk up to the front desk, where a couple of techs are whispering with Susan.

"I wonder what crawled up his ass. Did you see how serious he was?" the dark-headed tech whispers.

"Yeah, but he's hot, so it works for him."

"Michelle!"

"Ladies." Susan's voice carries over the two techs, making them both straighten, realizing I heard what they said. They turn at the same time; the one with blonde hair is smirking at me like she couldn't care less that I heard her. The other one's hazel-brown eyes are wide with worry. Her dark hair is pulled up into a messy bun, a few tendrils falling out around her face.

"Who do we have first this morning?" I ask the room, deciding not to address their gossiping. There's no point in acknowledging it, anyway.

"We've got Buster, a nippy chihuahua, here for his yearly vaccines, then Gunner, a pit bull who ate his Mom's wedding ring and has yet to pass it," Susan responds.

"Lovely. Let's get to it, then."

The techs scurry around me, heads bent together as they pass.

"Great start to the day, Benjamin." Susan's tone is dripping with sarcasm.

All I can do is sigh. Again.

I have a feeling I'll be doing that a lot over the next several weeks.

5

SARA

"There's still shit on the floor in exam room two," Ben snaps out.

I grit my teeth to keep from snapping back. It has been a frustrating day, to say the least. Ben has been less than nice since the first patient arrived, constantly expecting us to do all the dirty work while he barely talks to the owners about their concerns.

In all honesty, he's been a real asshole.

"I'm getting to it now." I try to keep the bite out of my voice, but after an entire day of getting barked at, it's hard. Once the floor is cleaned, Susan hands me the next patient's chart. I step out to the waiting room to see little Danny trying to wrangle his three-month-old puppy from under the chairs.

"Hey, kiddo. Do you need some help?"

"Yeah, he won't come out. I think he's scared," the eleven-year-old tells me, his body almost fully under the chair at this point. I glance at Danny's mom, Tara, as she grimaces, exasperation lining her face.

"Here, let's try this." I squat down next to Danny, pulling a treat from the pocket of my scrubs. Danny wiggles his way out from under the chairs, allowing me to see the beagle pup laying on his belly. I hold the treat out to the puppy, letting him sniff it. Before he can eat it, I slowly move it so he's following the treat out from under the chairs.

Once he's out, I pick him up from the floor, letting him eat the treat.

"Wow. We'll have to try that at home, Mom!" Danny says, his smile wide on his face.

"Sure, honey," she responds, shaking her head. We head back to an exam room as the puppy squirms in my arms, trying to get down so he can explore. Once we're in the room, I start my routine for a wellness visit, making sure everything looks okay.

"We are desperate for some training," Tara says while I work.

"Is this little guy giving you some extra trouble?" I scratch the puppy's ears when I'm done checking his temperature.

"Like you wouldn't believe." Tara grabs Danny around the waist, pulling him onto her lap to keep him out of the way.

"Susan has some pamphlets for a couple of great programs. When we're all done here, I'll have her talk to you about them."

The beagle pup lets out the cutest little howl as I finish up, making us all laugh. "It doesn't seem like little Bowie likes the idea of training," I tease. "I'm going to step out and grab Dr. Crawford. I'm not sure if Susan told you, but he's going to be taking over for Dr. Charles now that he's officially retiring." The fact that Dr. Charles preferred us to call him by his first name whereas Ben prefers his last says a lot about how different the two of them are.

"She did. I'm looking forward to meeting Dr. Charles's son."

Don't get too excited.

The words are barely contained in my head as I nod at Tara before stepping out of the room.

"Dr. Crawford, we're ready for you in exam room one."

Benjamin is standing next to our supply closet, a frown marring his handsome face. His unruly blond hair is sticking up on the ends as if he just ran his hands through it. God, I hate how handsome he is. His muscles are shown off by his tight button-down shirt stretching across his wide chest. I'm pretty sure those buttons are close to bursting. An image of me ripping it open pops unbidden into my head.

"Why is the closet organized like this?" Ben's scowl deepens as he looks at me, his tone yanking me out of my daydream.

"Because we've never taken the time to change it." In all actuality, reorganizing this closet would've made Dr. Charles incredibly confused. I'm pretty sure it's been this way since he opened the clinic. Changing it now would have caused more problems than it solved.

He harrumphs, then shakes his head. I have no idea what that was about, probably him coming up with another reason to hate this place.

When he turns toward the exam room, I follow dutifully behind.

"Hello," Ben says as he steps into the room. Without waiting for a response, he starts checking out Bowie. The vaccines are already prepped on the counter, allowing Ben to begin administering them.

After a long, awkward silence, Danny's mom speaks. "Sara said you're taking over for your father. That's great. I'm sure he's happy about that."

"Yes, I believe he is," Ben responds.

Tara looks at me, and I just shrug my shoulders. Ben's tableside manner is pretty lacking. He's been nicer to Tara than most of the other people today. He scowled at one owner when they asked about not giving their cat flea and tick medicine. Another owner, he stared at for a second, then walked out of the room without a single word.

To be fair, they asked about dinner treats right after Ben demanded they stop giving their dog extra food.

"I'm done. He should be good to go." Ben walks out of the room, not bothering with a goodbye.

"Well, that was interesting," Tara says, making me laugh.

"Yeah, he's talented, though, so he'll be great to have around in an emergency." I feel the need to defend Ben in the hopes no one gets too pissed off and leaves. There aren't any other animal clinics in town, but Westlake is not that far away.

"Can I pick up Bowie now?" Danny asks. He's been waiting so patiently this whole time.

"Sure, I'll even give you a treat for him." I hand Danny another treat from my pocket, then help him get Bowie down from the counter.

I lead them all out of the exam room and back to the front lobby before saying goodbye. When I finish completing Bowie's chart, I put it in the correct box for Susan, then take an enormous deep breath. Bowie was our last patient for the day. I'm grateful we're done. I don't think my shoulders could manage any more tension.

* * *

"GET OUT OF HERE, ASSHOLE," I growl, making my brother, Matthew, laugh. I sneak an elbow into his ribs, allowing me enough room to kick the soccer ball from his feet, taking off down the field.

"Cheater!" Matthew yells, racing after me.

I pass the ball to Carter before Matthew can catch up. Carter does some fancy footwork, tripping up Nolan, allowing him to score a goal.

"Yes!" I yell, running to Carter and jumping on him. He spins me around before placing me back on my feet.

The five of us have been playing soccer together since

Adam decided he wanted to play at eight years old. Twenty-eight years later, he's still leading the pack with Matthew right behind at thirty-four. Matthew also trails Adam in bossiness, much to my annoyance, but he makes up for it when he helps me train for the occasional triathlon.

Carter, who's thirty, is a literal genius with computers and is the quietest of all of us. Nolan, the youngest at twenty-six, is our resident goofball. Half the stuff that comes out of his mouth will make your eyes roll, but the other half will have you rolling with laughter.

I sit right in the middle of all of them, a year younger than Matthew.

Being the middle child and only girl was interesting growing up. I always leaned towards being a tomboy because I didn't have another option. If I wanted to play, I had to do whatever the boys were doing. I didn't mind too much. It's not like the things we did were boring, and I was able to play on all the same teams as my brothers for a long time, which made it fun. I do enjoy my independence now, though. Handling shit on my own is kind of my forte.

I was lucky enough to have my best friends to help balance out the testosterone I lived with back then. It gave me a pretty good idea of what having sisters is like. When Natalie's dad passed away when we were twelve, she and her mom leaned into our family, and I gained the sister I always wanted. She spent every afternoon and weekend at my house since her mom worked a lot.

I loved every minute of it. Almost as much as I loved showing up my brothers on the soccer field.

"You're such a little cheat," Matthew says, grabbing me in a headlock. I spin my way out of it, punching him in the arm for good measure.

We're all sweaty and breathing hard from the game as we gather around in a circle. "How's everything at Sideline? Tessa doing okay?" I ask, stretching out my tired muscles.

Adam and Matthew own Sideline Sporting Goods, a very successful chain of sports equipment stores. They sell every kind of sporting equipment you'd ever need. They've made a killing from it, too. I couldn't be prouder of them.

"Things are fine." Adam shrugs. "Tessa is good. I wish she didn't have to go on maternity leave, though."

"Mister perfectionist over here is worried the temp agency is going to send a moron who has no qualifications to replace his secretary," Matthew teases.

"No, I'm just used to how Tessa works. Trying to get used to someone new is going to suck."

"That explanation isn't any better, dude." Nolan grins at Adam. I agree with him. Adam tends to be a perfectionist, and he expects his employees to be the same. He can be kind of a grump about it, actually, which is why I am so glad I do not work for him. I pity the person who will be filling in for Tessa. They're in for a treat.

Adam rolls his eyes, turning to me instead. "How are things at the clinic?"

"Disastrous. My new boss started, and his tableside manner sucks. He acts like he doesn't have any desire to be there." I'd be surprised if any of them remember Ben since he was only around for a year.

"That's a tough situation to be in," Matthew responds.

"There's a chance he might hire someone to replace him, which could be good. His brand of management will be tough to get used to if he stays."

"You can handle it, sis. You put up with Matthew and Nolan." Carter elbows me.

I laugh at the indignation on their faces.

"Hey! You and Adam were just as bad," Nolan argues.

"Nah, you two were the worst," I rib them.

Matthew glares, taking a step toward me. I take off running before he can grab me, squealing as I go. The rest of the guys get in on the chase, making it a game of who can catch me first. This was exactly what I needed after the stupidly long day I had.

With my brothers' help, I'm reminded I can put up with a lot of bullshit. Eventually, Ben's behavior won't get on my nerves anymore.

Hopefully.

6

UNKNOWN

The spotlights shine brightly on the field, cloaking the surrounding area in darkness. I live my life in darkness. It's the place I'm safest.

Watching her gives me comfort. Makes me feel like home. I wish I could get closer. To feel her under my hands. I bet her skin is as soft as it looks. One day, I'll have her arms wrapped around me, holding me close. One day soon, if the plan comes together. There have been too many obstacles recently. Too many things standing in my way to get to her.

I watch her run across the field, her smile lighting up the whole place. It feels like that smile is directed right at me. I know she can feel my presence here. Why else would she be so happy?

Then those assholes start chasing her.

A growl rumbles in my chest. They're touching her. I should be the one touching her. No one else. I don't care if they're her brothers. She's mine. I want to run over there and take her away from them.

But then she laughs.

It brightens her entire face, making my fists unclench.

I love when she laughs.

I don't think I can wait any longer to take her. She needs me to protect her, to keep her safe from anyone wishing her harm. We're going to be a family soon; why would I want to wait to make that happen when she could be mine right now?

Moving the timeline up will be okay. It'll still work out how it's supposed to, and she'll finally be mine forever.

It's all I've ever wanted.

Her.

7

SARA

The gravel crunches under my shoes as I walk toward Donna's Bar. The building looks like an old cabin was plopped right in the middle of town with its log siding and dark-stained front porch.

This is the only decent place to get a drink in town, which usually means weekends are packed. Tonight is no exception. The rowdy crowd is loud enough to hear in the parking lot. I hurry my steps since I'm late enough as it is. I lost track of time playing with the dogs. The mild weather has made it more fun to be outside.

The noise only increases when I walk through the doors. Country music blares through the speakers, but the music will shuffle through the major hits of every genre. There's always a little bit of everything for everyone. It's one of the many reasons it's so popular.

I finally spot Michelle through the crowd, sitting at a high-top table, scrolling through her phone. After the exhausting week of dealing with Benjamin, we decided a drink was in order.

Pushing my way deeper into the bar, I get stopped no less than six times by people saying hello. Friday nights are usually the busiest, with Saturdays being a close second. Hell, even Thursdays can get crazy. And in a small town, where everyone knows everyone, there's no way you won't see someone you know.

"I didn't think you'd ever make it over here," Michelle says when I get to the table.

"No kidding. Everyone's out tonight." I hook my bag on the back of the chair, taking out my wallet. "I'm gonna go grab a drink. Do you need another one?"

"No, I'm good. I put in an order of onion rings a bit ago, as well, if you want to share."

"I'm starving, so I'll get my own. And a burger. Maybe an order of wings, too." I grin.

After another round of two-stepping my way across the bar, and mentally cursing myself for not having done this first, I finally have a drink in hand.

"Remind me why we decided to come here on a Friday night?" I ask Michelle when I'm back at the table.

"Because we both wanted onion rings, and this is the best place to get them." She crunches down on said ring, a teasing glint in her eye since I don't have my food yet.

"Maybe we should open a food truck. Offer all the bar food without the wait." My stomach grumbles at the thought.

"When would we have time to do that?"

"Never." If I didn't think Michelle would slap my hand, I'd steal some of her food.

"Plus, we'd miss out on the entertainment at the clinic." Michelle laughs.

"True, although Dr. Doom and Gloom is going to be hard to deal with for eight hours every day. This week has been brutal."

"He's so pretty to look at, though. Kind of makes up for it." Michelle grins.

"He does do broody really well. If only he'd keep his mouth closed the whole day, it wouldn't be so bad." My food is brought out to me, and I dig in with unladylike aggression —bad habits carried over from my childhood and having to compete for food against four teenage boys.

Michelle turns her nose up at my behavior but doesn't say anything. I am what I am. There's no changing that.

"He is kind of a jackass, isn't he?" Michelle continues. This week with Ben has been...long, to say the least. Grumpy doesn't even begin to cover his mood, not to mention his inability to be polite about anything. He makes a demand, then expects it to be followed. I can't believe he acted this way at the animal hospital in Greensboro. He would've been fired on the spot.

He's so talented, though. That's what drives me crazy. If he'd lose the chip on his shoulder, he would be an incredible doctor.

"Do you think he's going to hire someone new to come in and replace him?" I don't want to go through another change, but if this continues, I might welcome it.

"I can't imagine why he wouldn't. He doesn't want to be there, so finding someone new would solve all his problems."

"I can see that. Let's hope he either comes around or finds someone quickly."

"Cheers to that." Michelle holds up her glass, and I clink mine against hers. "How are your brothers?"

"Pains in my ass, but good. Adam was complaining about having to get a temp assistant while Tessa is out on maternity leave the other day. The dude is entirely too high-strung."

"You should just leave them and come be my family instead." Michelle smiles.

"You know I already love you like a sister, but I kind of love my brothers, too." I laugh.

"Even though they don't deserve it." She rolls her eyes.

I shrug. My brothers can be overprotective assholes at times. I sort of love them for it, even though it drives me crazy. "How's your brother doing?"

"Fine, I think. I haven't talked to him in a couple of months." Michelle's brother lives in South Carolina and doesn't visit her very often. They lost their parents when they were teenagers, so it's just been the two of them for a long time. I don't know much beyond that. Michelle doesn't like to talk about her past, which I can understand after going through something so tragic.

"That's such a bummer."

"It's okay. He has his own life. I'm just glad he checks in sometimes."

"Why don't you come to Mom and Dad's when we have family dinner?" I hate how bummed out she seems.

"Nah, that's okay. I'm having family dinner right now. We'll just create our own family one day." She winks at me.

I laugh, even though I wish she'd just come with me. A few minutes with the Ellis clan would cheer her up in a heartbeat.

We finish our drinks, chatting about everything while commiserating about having to deal with Oscar the Grouch come Monday. I plan to relax as much as possible this weekend so when the workday comes around again, I'll be better suited to deal with the grump.

When it starts to get late, Michelle and I say goodbye on the front porch. Her car is parked on the opposite side of the parking lot from mine, forcing us to go our separate ways.

I take a deep breath as I walk to my car. The tepid air feels refreshing after being inside the packed bar for so long. I love going out and socializing with people, but sometimes, I revel in these moments of quiet solitude. There's a certain satisfaction in being by myself. It makes me feel strong, capable. Like I can handle anything that comes my way. And I know I could.

Unlocking my car, I start to get in when the hairs on the back of my neck stand up. I look around the lot, scanning all the cars around the building. There's no one else outside.

Even the noises of the bar have gone quiet in the back of the lot.

Despite all my assurances, it still feels like someone is watching me right now. There are a million places they could be hiding, which doesn't make me feel any better. In fact, that makes it much worse. My gaze flicks to every shadow and corner a person could be hiding.

Now I'm just freaking myself out even more. With one last scan, I get into my car, shaking my head. That was weird. I try not to speed out of the parking lot with my fear running rampant. There was probably someone walking down the street who happened to look over at the bar.

I highly doubt someone would be watching me.

8

***

BEN

What a fucking week.

I knew working at Dad's clinic would be hard, but I didn't think it would be this bad. I haven't helped the situation with my shitty attitude either. I've been pretty hostile to the techs, which I do feel bad about. They don't deserve my ire. But it's been difficult not to let my mood carry over to them.

I do admire their ability to respond with sass when I'm being exceptionally angry, despite how much it further pisses me off in the moment. Sara has gotten especially sassy in her retorts. Remembering her jab about me deserving the bite from a rather pissed-off hamster makes a smile break on my face. If I hadn't been bleeding, I probably would've laughed at her comment.

"What are you smiling about over there?" Mom asks from across the table.

I glance up at her, then at Dad, who's been oddly reserved this whole week. It's not like him to be quiet for an extended period of time. I figure he's struggling with having to retire sooner than he wanted. I don't blame him. If my body started telling me I had to retire before I was ready, I'd be livid.

"I was just thinking about a mean little hamster I worked with this week."

"I will never understand you and your father's love for the mean ones."

"It's a switch from the monotony of doing the same thing over and over again."

"Are things going okay? Susan said it was a little tense this week." Mom's grimace tells me Susan was a little more colorful with her description of how the week went.

"They're not great, but things will settle. Dad, have you put out the ad for a new vet yet?"

"Not yet. This week has been hard. I'll try to put it out next week." He glances at me, then at Mom before turning back to his dinner.

If he didn't look so disheartened, I'd be mad at him for not doing what he said he would. Instead, I feel like there's a hole opening in my chest. It's all I can do to finish my dinner before I make my excuses to leave the table. Sadie dutifully follows behind me as I step into my room. Her constant companionship is about the only thing getting me through this whole fucked-up situation.

Grabbing a book, I sit in the wingback chair in the corner of my room, hoping to get my mind off the look on my dad's face when I asked about the vet ad. I don't know what the right answer is in this situation. No matter which path I choose, I'm going to end up hurting someone.

The ringing of my phone pulls me out of the story I'd fallen into, making me realize it's been a couple of hours since dinner. Rebecca's name on my phone has me perking up a bit. I've been trying to reach her all week, but she either doesn't answer or is too busy to talk when she does.

"Hey, Becks. How are you?"

Silence hangs on the other end of the phone, so I pull it away from my ear to make sure it's connected. She must have pocket dialed me or something. I repeat her name to see if she'll realize she's on the phone with me when I finally hear voices.

"So, you're sure he's not coming tonight?" a guy says. His voice is deep and unfamiliar.

"I told you, I confirmed it. We're fine," Rebecca responds.

She has no idea I'm on the phone with her. I don't have any idea who she's talking to, but I'm pretty sure she's talking about me.

"Good. I'll have plenty of time to dirty you up, then," the man growls. Rebecca giggles, and my stomach drops at the implications of what this conversation means.

I knew things between us weren't great, but I didn't think they were this bad. I figured we were both just stressed about this upheaval in our plan; I didn't think it would make her turn to someone else. God, how could I have been so stupid?

I listen for a few more minutes, solidifying that Rebecca is, in fact, cheating on me before hanging up. This is not what I needed after such a shitty week. Who does something so horrible to the person you were supposed to love unconditionally? She was supposed to be my forever, and now, I have no idea what to do.

Anger floods my system at the injustice of this whole fucking mess. I've given up everything to do the right thing. My apartment, my job, my life, and now, the one person who should've had my back throughout all of it has betrayed me.

I stand from my chair, grab a duffle bag from my closet, and start throwing clothes into it. Greensboro is only an hour's drive from here. I will not be a bystander in the explosion of my life anymore. I'm going to finally take back the reins, starting with my cheating fiancée.

* * *

THE DRIVE to Greensboro took less time than it should have due to my angry driving. When I left the house, Mom tried to squeeze the details out of me. The truth tasted like ash on my tongue, so I just told her I needed to go back to the city for the weekend.

As I drive through downtown, I take in the flurry of activity of a Friday night. Would I be out and about tonight if I were still living here? Maybe Rebecca and I would be out at a bar, getting a drink, instead of ending our three-year-long relationship. Although, if I think about it, we probably wouldn't have gone out tonight, even if I were still living here. Rebecca would've been out with her friends at some club while I would just be getting back from another shift at the hospital.

Is that why she did what she did? Because we stopped making time for each other? Our relationship started like a movie. I saw her across the bar, our eyes met, and after that, we were inseparable. We spent all our free time together, going on adventures and exploring new places. Somewhere along the way, we must've stopped putting each other first. But it doesn't justify what she did. We were going to get married. If there was a problem, she should've talked to me about it.

I feel like such an idiot. I should have seen the signs before now. She'd been pulling further away from me ever since my dad first got sick. At the time, I chalked it up to us both being too busy to make our relationship a priority. That should've been an indicator that something was wrong. When life gets stressful, you need a partner who is going to help you through it, not do their own thing while you figure it out alone.

When I pull into the parking lot of Rebecca's apartment complex, a weight settles into my gut. Despite being the world's biggest asshole this week, confrontation is not something I enjoy. I am not looking forward to this exchange. If I'm honest, I don't even know what to expect from Rebecca. She could potentially make a huge scene, playing up the drama she enjoys creating, or she could be completely indifferent. I'm not sure which option I'd prefer.

Turning off my car, I step out onto the sidewalk and make my way into the building. I still have my keys to her apartment, so getting inside is simple. I get into the elevator, trying to figure out what to say before I get there. I figure showing up at all will be saying enough.

Walking down the whitewashed hallways of her apartment complex feels worse than when I walked into the clinic Monday. The dread that swirled in my stomach on my first day is nothing compared to the dread I feel now.

Stepping in front of her door, I debate about using my key, but the idea of walking in on her while she's in the middle of... No thanks. I take a deep breath, then raise my fist to knock.

And I wait...

Several minutes pass with no answer, so I knock again, significantly more aggressive this time as my anger at the situation burns through me. I know exactly what's happening behind this closed door. It only makes me seethe with the knowledge of Rebecca's betrayal.

Finally, the door opens to Rebecca in a black silk robe. Her eyes grow wide when she sees it's me.

"Surprise," I say, keeping my voice neutral.

"What are you doing here?" she asks, her gaze darting over her shoulder.

"Thought it would be good to see you. Aren't you happy to see me?" Sarcasm drips through every word.

"Um, of course I am. I actually can't hang out right now. Could you maybe come back tomorrow?"

"No, I don't think I can." I walk through the doorway, forcing Rebecca to move out of the way. She splutters, trying to get me to stop, but I don't listen.

"I don't know who you are, but you can come out of

hiding. I know you're here," I say, raising my voice so whoever else is here can be a part of this little conversation.

"No one else is here, Ben," Rebecca denies. Her arms are crossed, a defensive line to her stance as she stares at me.

"Right, and I'm a unicorn."

Rebecca scoffs as a man I don't recognize comes around the corner in only pajama pants; his dark hair is disheveled for reasons I don't want to dwell on. I nod my head at him while he just stands there, a wary expression on his face. Standing in the middle of Rebecca's fancy-ass kitchen with the hum of the refrigerator buzzing in the background, I deflate. All the anger I had brewing inside of me dissipates with the knowledge that no matter how mad I am, it won't change a fucking thing. At this point, I just want to end it and be out of here.

I turn back to Rebecca. Her black hair is a mess around her shoulders, while her skin is as pale as snow. If she didn't normally look that pale, I'd think this situation is affecting her. Instead, her facial expression is neutral, maybe even a little annoyed. There's no guilt or shame because she got caught. Nothing.

It's as if the last three years of our life didn't mean a goddamn thing to her.

"I have one question." I stare at her, unable to reconcile the person standing in front of me with the person I used to know. "How long?"

"What do you mean?" she asks, confusion lining her face.

"How long have you been seeing other people? How long have I been a blind idiot?"

Rebecca's jaw clenches. "Since January."

Jesus.

Instead of being by my side while Dad was sick, she was getting her kicks somewhere else.

"Say something," she demands.

I heave out a breath as bone-deep exhaustion begins to

settle in the place of my anger. "Give me the ring back and send anything I've left here to my parents' house."

"That's it?" Rebecca looks at me as if I'm crazy.

"Yeah. I don't care anymore. You clearly don't either, so let's not turn this into an argument when it's apparent you don't want to fight for our relationship." I stare at the woman I thought I'd be with for the rest of my life and feel nothing. I don't know if I'm just numb to the shit heap of a life I've been thrown into or if she didn't actually matter to me as much as I thought she did.

I guess I'll find out when I've had more time to process.

Rebecca turns from the room in a huff, returning several minutes later with the black velvet box I gave her almost a year ago. She sets it on the counter, staring at me like she's waiting for me to break down into tears or something.

I grab the box, then turn back to the front door of the apartment. "Have a good life, Becks." The door closes behind me with a deafening click, ending yet another part of my life here in Greensboro.

9

SARA

"You can do this, Sara. You can handle another week with the asshat extraordinaire." I feel like the song "Eye of the Tiger" should be playing in the background as I pump myself up to go into the clinic this morning.

I made it through a whole week of Ben's constant grumbling; I can make it through this one, too. I even managed to get in a couple of good jabs that I swear made his lips twitch. If he wasn't such a broody bastard, I think he would've smiled.

Let's hope he's taken the weekend to untwist his panties and chill the fuck out so I won't run the risk of my head exploding when he pisses me off. Is that selfish? Maybe. Do I care? No, not really. We all have to deal with shitty life experiences at some point, and taking it out on others is not the way to handle your shit pile. He has the right to be pissed about his life, sure, but does that mean he gets a free pass to be a dick? No, it doesn't.

Taking a deep breath, I leave my bathroom wearing my poodle scrubs. The little dose of happiness they'll give me throughout the day will go a long way in helping me keep my cool. My babies are already in their beds, knowing I'm leaving for the day. I say a quick goodbye before jumping in my car to drive to the clinic.

The late spring sun is shining bright, which helps bolster my mood. I seriously hope Ben is in a better mood today. Maybe he'll have gotten laid over the weekend. That makes every man happy.

I wonder if he's any good in bed. He's sexy as hell with all his muscles. The shaggy blond hair does it for me, too. And as much as I hate the broodiness, it does offer a certain level of sexiness. I wonder if that carries over into the bedroom.

What am I thinking?

I don't want to have sex with him! I hate him. Oh, god, what if his naked image pops up in my head today when he's standing right next to me? Why did I have to think about him like that?

I pull into the clinic parking lot, mentally shaking my head, and force myself to focus on the goal of today. Don't piss off the new vet; don't let the new vet piss *you* off.

Simple.

As I get out of my car, Ben pulls into the parking lot. He catches my eye, and a frown immediately lines his face.

Lovely.

Off to a fantastic start this morning. Instead of acknowledging it, I walk inside to start the day. We're on call to handle a German shepherd momma about to have her puppies. They could come any day now, so we've been working to keep our schedule open. We don't want to put anyone in a bind if we end up having to cancel the appointments to help the momma with labor.

Michelle is already here, so after I store my stuff in the break room, I find her in the back, going through supplies. She's wearing cat scrubs that have hearts in their eyes.

"Apparently, it's funky scrub day," I joke.

She turns, taking in my scrubs. The poodles have speech

bubbles over their heads saying, *"Oy, Vey!"*. "Indeed, it is. Bets on how pissy Dr. McHottie will be today?"

I lightly tap Michelle's arm in admonishment. "Don't call him that, and by the frown I got when he pulled into the parking lot, I'll let you slap me in the face if he's whistling a tune this morning."

The gleam in Michelle's eyes tells me she'd be willing to take that bet. Two seconds later, the front door chimes, indicating Ben's entrance. As he walks through the clinic toward the office, he pauses, taking in mine and Michelle's scrubs.

He squints, then rolls his eyes mumbling, "What the fuck's wrong with normal scrubs?"

The minute the door to the office is closed, Michelle and I burst out laughing. "I told you he'd be pissy," I say through my giggles.

"What's wrong with our scrubs? I thought they were fun."

"Oscar the Grouch doesn't do fun. That's the problem." I head back to the front of the clinic with Michelle's laughter flowing behind me. At least I have her to make the days a little less hostile.

* * *

THE BEEPING of the microwave pulls me from my daydreams. Now that the weather is warm, I need to take Luna and Koda to the dog park. I've got a decent fenced-in backyard at my house, but sometimes, they enjoy having a little more freedom to run and play.

As I sit down to eat, Ben walks into the break room, his lunch box in hand. *Please let him take his lunch somewhere else.*

He's stayed tucked inside his office for most of the day since we haven't had many appointments. It's been a nice reprieve, not having his doom cloud hanging over the whole clinic.

I track his movements as he gathers his lunch together

until he sits down at the table across from me. His wavy blond hair is pushed back off his forehead today, matching the white button-down shirt and gray slacks. He looks very city slicker. And annoyingly sexy.

I hate how everything about him appeals to me. I shouldn't enjoy his surly attitude or his moody stares. Even his frown lines do stupid things to me. They make me want to do whatever it takes to make a smile crack across his face. Which is irritating because all he's been to me is an asshole. He doesn't deserve for me to make him smile.

"Did you need something?" Ben's voice whips across the table, making me realize how long I've been staring at him. Shit.

"No, sorry. I was daydreaming. Didn't mean to stare."

He nods his head, returning to his lunch. I want to ask him what his deal is, but it doesn't take a genius to know he'd rather be back in Greensboro than here. Should I try to make small talk? I don't want him to bite my head off no matter how uncomfortable the silence is between us.

"How's Dr. Charles feeling now that he's getting to rest a little more?" There, a safe topic that hopefully won't be triggering.

"He's better. Mom's been making him eat a lot of fish."

I grimace. "I'm sure he's none too pleased. I know he loves a good steak."

Ben's lips quirk up in a smirk, completely disarming me. "He does, but he also knows he won't ever win an argument with Sybil Crawford." He's beautiful when he's not scowling. Although, he's pretty hot when he is.

"She's a force to be reckoned with for sure."

We both lapse into silence again, only this time, it's a little less tense. Maybe we can make headway on un-grumping this grump.

Michelle strides into the room to grab her lunch. She

quirks an eyebrow at me, flicking her eyes toward Ben, silently asking what's going on. I shrug my shoulders. I don't know any more than she does despite sitting across from him. She leaves when her lunch is ready. Not that I blame her for wanting to leave the slightly thawed tundra that is our break room right now.

When we're finished eating, Susan comes striding into the room to tell us the German shepherd momma is in labor. "Gina said she's worried the momma is in some distress, so she called to see if you guys could go over and help."

"Sure. Let me grab my kit," Ben says, striding from the room. I finish cleaning both mine and his lunch, then put our lunch boxes away.

"Let's go, Sara. I'm waiting on you." Ben huffs like it was obvious he wanted me to come, too, and I was deliberately holding him back from leaving. I knew I should've left his lunch box out. I was trying to be nice, and look where it got me.

One step forward, two steps back. Grabbing my purse, I follow behind Ben as we walk out of the clinic. "Can you drive? I don't know where they live."

Surprised by his question, I nod my head, unlocking my car when we get close. This is going to be an interesting afternoon.

"When we arrive, wait for my instructions. I would prefer you not get in my way. In all honesty, I could probably handle this on my own, but it's always smart to have an extra set of hands."

I grit my teeth to keep from saying something snarky in response. Obviously, he's going to lead. He's the vet; what else would he be doing, knitting?

"Yes, sir." Okay, still snarky, but I couldn't help it. I did stop myself from saluting.

Ben's head whips around to look at me, his eyebrows

raised as if he can't believe what I said. There's something else in his eyes that I can't read. A gleam I can't place.

I raise my own eyebrow back at him in defiance. He's not going to get away with bossing me around like that. He can be respectful about it, or I'll give him sass.

I think Nat would be proud.

10

BEN

Huffing out a tired breath, I pull my glasses off my face and chuck them onto my desk. Running my hands through my hair, I stand, stretching out the tightness in my back. My brain feels like mush after three hours of staring at my computer screen, trying to make sense of Dad's notes. Completing the end-of-month paperwork should not be this complicated. None of his files are organized in any way that makes sense. He has his budget spreadsheets in the same folder as his employee information, for Christ's sake.

I've been trying to fix the mess he left me for the past two days straight. The German shepherd's birth a couple of days ago put me way behind, so now, I'm having to stay late to get all of this shit done before the end of the month.

I guess the good news is it's kept my mind off the shit with Rebecca. I haven't had a moment to stew about how she hasn't tried to contact me since I left her apartment. I should be grateful not to have to deal with her, but it stings a bit that, after three years, she doesn't seem to be affected by our breakup.

To be fair, I'm not sure how affected I am about it either. Shouldn't I be sad? Shouldn't there be more emotion in me than anger? And in all honesty, I think I'm madder at myself than I am her. I spent three years with someone who apparently cared very little about me. and I never fucking noticed. *Idiot.*

A noise outside my office makes me freeze. I've been the only one here since we closed, so whoever is here likely isn't supposed to be.

I open the door of my office, stepping into the hallway. The noise grows as I walk toward the back of the clinic. I'm fully prepared to scare the shit out of whoever is here. This seriously isn't what I needed tonight. I still have shit to do. I don't have time to be scaring some assclown thinking they can steal drugs from an animal clinic.

When I walk around the corner, I see shit all over the floor and the cabinets wide open. "What the fuck is going on here?"

Packages go flying in the air as the person startles.

"Jesus Christ!" Sara peeks around the frame of the closet door. "Was that absolutely necessary?"

"What are you doing here?"

"What does it look like I'm doing?"

"Stealing."

"Oh, sure. I can't live without IV tubes, Ace bandages, or syringes." She rolls her eyes so hard I think they may fall out of her head. Her attitude only further pisses me off. Why does she have to be so mouthy?

"It's eight-thirty. Why are you even here right now?"

"Because you mentioned this closet was a mess, and while I've known it was a mess for years, I never looked too closely, choosing to ignore it instead. When I finally did, I couldn't let it go. So, here I am, because you pointed out the chaos, and I seem to have a pathological need to fix it."

Her rant is punctuated by the swing of her arms, highlighting her tight tank and gym shorts. I wonder if she actually works out or if she just wears the clothes. That's what Rebecca did.

That thought pisses me off. I'm supposed to be getting caught up on work, not thinking about my ex.

"Can't you do this some other time? You're distracting."

"Why are you such an asshole? Seriously. I'm not even asking that as an insult. I genuinely want to know why you think it's okay to take your anger out on people who are just doing the job you wanted done. I'm not even getting paid for this, and yet, I'm still doing it because I thought it would ease some of your annoyance." She takes a breath before starting back into her diatribe. "You know what? I don't need this. You can clean this shit up while I go home and snuggle my dogs, who are very sad I'm not home right now."

She turns to grab her stuff, and before I can think better of it, I stop her. "Wait."

Sara freezes.

"You're right. I'm sorry I've been taking my anger out on everyone." I run my hands through my hair. "Things are just shitty right now." With my admission, some of the tension drains from my shoulders.

"That doesn't give you a pass to be a dick," she points out.

"No, it doesn't." I lean down to grab some of the supplies on the floor. Sara comes back to the closet and starts cleaning up.

"Do you want to talk about it? Or just tell me what the worst thing is right now?"

"Everything is the worst, but for tonight, my biggest annoyance is my dad's organization tactics."

"It seems we're both struggling with that." Sara chuckles. After looking at this closet, she's definitely right.

"He didn't have a system for anything, did he?"

"Not really. He was too busy taking care of the animals."

In one statement, Sara summed up my dad completely. All he cared about were the animals that came through his door. None of the business stuff mattered to him. He never saw the importance of taking the time to organize because he could be helping an animal instead.

Once we get the loose items picked up from the floor, Sara finishes taking stock of everything in the cabinet.

"This is making me realize the rest of the clinic needs to be organized, too." She sighs.

"Let's eat this elephant one bite at a time. We'll organize the closet, then do the rest some other time."

As we work, I'm surprised when Sara keeps up a steady stream of chatter. None of it is of any substance, but when our previous conversations have all been hostile, it's nice not to have any of the residual anger in our words.

"Hold on, you're actually saying you prefer the cereal part of Lucky Charms instead of the marshmallows?" Sara's incredulity makes me laugh.

"Yes, that's what I'm saying. Those marshmallows feel like I'm shoving a cavity into my tooth while I eat them."

"I knew you were strange, but that takes the cake. If I could get the box of only marshmallows here, I would have it in my pantry all the time."

"The next time I'm in Greensboro, I'll pick you up a box." I don't even think about the offer before I make it. For some reason, I have a very strong urge to drive to the city right now and find a box for her.

"Really?" Sara's eyes are wide, as if she can't believe I'd do something like that. Given my behavior, the disbelief is warranted.

"Sure." I shrug, not wanting it to be a big deal.

We finish organizing the closet in relative silence, only talking when we're deciding where things should go. It's comfortable, though. The tension that's been a constant presence since I started at the clinic seems to have abated. It's nice.

When we're almost done, Sara writes a note on the door

explaining where everything is and why. I never would have thought of doing something like that. I hate who I've become now. This constant buzz of anger isn't me. It's not who I want to be.

"Did you really come in tonight because I mentioned the storage was a mess?"

Sara sighs as if she can't believe she did it, either. "Apparently, yeah. It was bothering me that this closet was so disorganized. It's been this way since before I started. We just never did anything about it, knowing Dr. Charles would've struggled with the change."

It shouldn't surprise me how well she knows my father. She's worked with him for a long time, so it makes sense. But for some reason, the fact that she knows something so inherent about him makes me respect her a lot more than I would have previously. He really would have struggled with changing where all the supplies were kept, and instead of complaining about it, she just adapted.

Not many people would live that selflessly.

"Well, you may not believe me, but I am grateful you took the time to do it."

Sara shrugs her shoulders like it's no big deal as we put the final supplies back in their buckets. When we walk back out of the closet, I realize it's been an hour since we started this project.

"Do you think everyone would hate me more if I don't get payroll approved tonight and they have to wait an extra day for their paychecks?"

"More than likely, yeah." Sara smirks at me.

"You're enjoying the idea of me suffering, aren't you?"

"Definitely." This time, she grins.

"Evil woman."

"What can I say? A little payback for covering the clinic in your angry cloud all week is deserved."

She's right, of course, but I don't let her know that. Instead, I glare at her. "Leave me be to suffer alone, then."

"Yes, sir." She salutes, then hightails it out of the clinic.

God, the mouth on her. That's the second time she's said that to me, and I hate how much I like it. I catch myself staring at Sara's ass as she walks away. I again wonder if she works out. Going by how toned her legs are, I'm inclined to think she does.

I shake my head to disrupt my thoughts. I have no business thinking about a woman like that. It's not even been a week since I ended things with Rebecca. I shouldn't be imagining Sara naked, saying 'yes, sir' as she drops to her knees.

Fuck.

With a growl, I force myself to walk back into my office and do my job, all the while ignoring how tight my slacks are.

11

SARA

I can feel eyes on me. Judging, weighted eyes that see so much more than I want him to. I flick my gaze over my phone, coming in contact with dark chocolate eyes staring at me.

"It was just a quick search. It's not like I'm stalking him or something."

I swear Koda's eyebrow raises as if to say, *'sure you weren't.'*

I look back to my phone at the picture of Benjamin I have pulled up. It's several years old. When he was in college, if I had to guess. His arms are wrapped around two other guys, and they're all grinning at the camera, faces sunburned from whatever trip they're on. He looks like one of those douchebag frat bros, but I don't believe that description fits him well.

Quickly closing out of the social media app, I sit up on my couch. Koda is still judging me from the floor, calling me out on my lies. I just spent half an hour stalking all of Ben's social media pages for reasons I'm still not quite sure I understand. At first, it was to see if he had them at all. Then, when I found he did, I fell down the rabbit hole of looking at all his posts and pictures.

He was in a fraternity, went on spring break trips, got a dog, and not a single photo on there was of a woman. There were pictures with groups, and he was tagged in some photos from other girls, but he never posted a photo with a single woman. How is that possible?

He's a gorgeous specimen of a man. How could he have gone that long without a single photo? His posts started diminishing after college and then stopped altogether a few years ago.

And I've officially turned into a stalker.

It's a beautiful Saturday morning, and I'm sitting on my couch, creeping on my not-so-grumpy-anymore boss. I shouldn't be letting this guy into my head. Especially after how disruptive he's been already. Giving him any more space is only going to create more chaos in my life. Which I don't need.

"Why didn't I listen to you, Koda?"

He harrumphs, which I take to mean he has no clue and that he's brilliant and should always be listened to.

"How about a visit to the park?" I grin. Both Koda and Luna jump up from their beds, scrambling toward me with so much excitement I'm worried they're going to hurt themselves.

With a laugh at their crazy antics, I change out of my ratty T-shirt and sweats into only a slightly nicer T-shirt and shorts. With the beginning of June finally here, it's sunny and warm every day now.

I get the dogs loaded up in the car and head to the park. We could technically walk there, but Luna struggles with the sensory overload she experiences on walks: all the smells, the strangers walking by, the sounds. Everything is heightened for her since she lost her eyesight. When we're at the park, the enclosed dog area is a known comfort zone for her since we go there so often.

After finding a parking space, I get the dogs on their

leashes and walk them to the dog area. There are only a couple of other dogs here right now since it's still mid-morning. In the afternoons, it usually picks up, which can be hard for Luna to navigate.

Letting the dogs off the leash once we're inside the fence, the two of them take off running. It took Luna a while to get comfortable here, but now that she's had time to smell, and learn where the boundary is, she flies around this space without a care in the world. Koda keeps pretty close no matter what, but she loves having the freedom to run.

"Fancy meeting you here." Ben steps next to me, a golden retriever sprinting by us to chase a tennis ball.

"Benjamin." Am I still salty about his behavior? Yes. Have I eased up on being sassy? No. It's become our thing, even though he's less of a dick now.

He grins at my greeting. "Which one is yours?"

"The black lab is Koda, and Luna is the husky mix." The two dogs in question start wrestling across the grass, trying to nip each other. "Is the golden yours?" I ask because it's what I'm supposed to do. I already know the answer. I saw the photos of her during my stalking.

"Yeah, that's my Sadie."

The way he says that hits me straight in the heart. He loves her like she's a person, the way I love my zoo. They're my family.

We stand by the fence, watching the dogs play together, joining the other two in the area. They have a blast wrestling and playing fetch. Koda and Luna are going to be exhausted when we get home. They don't typically get this much exercise despite the regular runs I go on with Koda. To be fair, running sucks, so I only go a few miles unless I'm training for something.

Interestingly, Sadie has been helping Koda keep Luna from straying too far. I've never seen another dog help her out like that. They usually just let Koda keep her on track, waiting until they're ready to keep playing.

I've been forcing myself to keep my eyes focused solely on the dogs. Otherwise, I'd be staring at Ben until it got weird. The sun has been glinting off his blond hair and making his blue eyes shine. He seems lighter today than I've seen him. I hope that means he's settling into his new life a little better now than he was. I don't want to ask. It's not my place, and I don't want to ruin the moment.

Instead, we talk about our dogs and the joys of being a dog parent. I tell him about Koda and Luna and how they came to be with me. It's all very surface level; no groundbreaking information has been learned about either of us, but something in the air has shifted. We stand closer to each other, our smiles come more freely, and our teasing isn't laced with anger.

Things just feel easier. I don't know how much I trust it yet since a tiger doesn't change its stripes. All I can hope is he's finally realizing this place isn't as bad as he thought it would be.

Luna starts to get tired and trots up to me, Koda staying right next to her. Both of their tongues are hanging out the sides of their mouths. Reaching into the bag I brought, I grab out the water bowl and place it on the ground to give them a drink. When they're done, I leash them up, saying a quick goodbye to Ben and Sadie.

It takes about thirty seconds after we get home for the two of them to crash, leaving the house incredibly quiet. Walking over to the kitchen island, I flip through the mail I grabbed before we came inside. There's an unaddressed envelope in the stack, so I quickly tear it open.

I had a great time today. You always make me laugh. —G

My brows furrow at the note. This is the second note I've

gotten from someone named G, and I have no idea who they could be from. The first one said, *I can't wait to be together,* which made me think it was for someone else since I'm not dating anyone. They're never addressed or have a return label. It's as if someone is writing a note to their lover.

It's starting to make me uneasy. You'd think that the person who's sending these would have figured out they're going to the wrong person by now. And if they're actually intended for me... A shiver moves through me at the thought.

I have no idea who could be sending me these things or why they would be sending them in the first place. It's not like I have a guy in my life right now. I haven't even hooked up with anyone in the last year. Going through the whole song and dance hasn't appealed to me recently. And no one has piqued my interest enough to make me want to.

Benjamin has piqued your interest.

No. Nope. Not thinking about that.

I look down at the note in my hand. The two sentences are a mess of scratchy, handwritten letters, barely legible. None of this makes any sense to me, so I decide to throw it away like I did the other note. Maybe if I keep getting them, I'll take them to Cooper since he's the police chief in town.

Until then, I'll try to put the whole thing out of my head.

While the dogs are napping, I head into my gym in the second bedroom to work out. Even though I'm not currently training for anything, I still like to keep up my routines. It makes it easier to train when I do decide to sign up for a tough mudder or a triathlon.

As my muscles burn, all the stress from the note slides away. This is why I love working out. It gives me something to focus on instead of allowing my brain to keep spinning in circles, looking for answers I'll probably never find.

I wonder what Ben does for exercise. Lord knows that man does *something* to get his muscles. He's the size of a giant. At five-five, I barely come to his shoulder; add in the wide chest and thickly muscled arms, and he's a mountain. It's probably more than my high-intensity workouts. What I wouldn't give to watch him lift weights.

I have got to stop thinking about my boss like that. It's never going to happen. Nor *should* it ever happen. It would end in disaster like every other relationship I've ever had. Then I'd be working in the clinic for an ex-boyfriend, trying not to stab myself in the eyeball with a syringe.

Okay…a touch dramatic, but the point is still valid. I should absolutely *not* date my boss.

Ever.

BEN

The loud hum of power tools is music to my ears. I am finally getting out of Mom and Dad's house and into my own. I bought the first one that came even close to meeting my wish list, then promptly enlisted Levi Jackson's construction company to make it livable.

And yes, the record-scratching, wait-a-goddamn-minute feeling is coursing through me as I stand here. I'm buying a fucking house in Sonoma. I'm officially taking over the clinic. And my life looks nothing like I expected or wanted it to.

"I thought my house was a mess, but you've got me beat, man," Levi says as we walk around the property. With his navy blue baseball cap, dirty jeans, and tool belt slung around his hips, he looks like the epitome of a general contractor. I hope he lives up to the hype I've heard because it's going to take a miracle to get this house in shape.

"God, I know. I don't know what I was thinking when I bought it. Mainly, get out of Mom and Dad's house, whatever it takes." I grimace. Making life-altering choices solely based on needing to get out from under your parents is probably immature, but I'm losing my mind living with them again.

Levi laughs, his hazel eyes lighting up with humor. "A little too close for comfort?"

"I love them, but dude, I'm a grown-ass man. Having my mother smother me every day is about to kill me."

"I would never be able to move back in with my mom, so I can't imagine. We'll get you fixed up in a few months, and you'll be free as a bird."

"If only that were true," I mumble. Free as a bird would mean I'm not having to settle for small-town life in the middle of nowhere. Although, I am grateful to be free of Rebecca.

It's been a few weeks since we had our confrontation, and I'm still pretty angry about the whole thing. Despite the talk I had with Sara, I haven't been very good at keeping my temper reined in. I am working on it since the techs didn't do anything to deserve my ire. I even had lunch brought in a couple of times when I knew I was enemy number one. It mostly led to raised eyebrows from Sara, unimpressed stares from Susan, and indifference from Michelle. So, I won't be winning any boss of the year awards just yet, but I'm trying.

When I walked into my apartment in Greensboro after confronting Rebecca, I realized how little the place felt like home. Especially compared to how Mom's house feels to me now. The apartment was cold and unfeeling, almost sterile in a way I never noticed before. I didn't spend much time there, choosing to work extra hours instead of sitting around at home, so it's not a big surprise I never noticed.

The emptiness made me start cataloging why I was pissed about having to come home, which led me to realize my job and Rebecca were the only two reasons I had. Without Rebecca to consider, I had to wonder if I was pushing away the idea of taking over for Dad because that's what I've always done. There's never been a time in my life when I thought Sonoma was the place I wanted to live—until I came back and figured out that it holds a lot more appeal than my cold, dead apartment in the city.

Even though the anger is still simmering, my mindset has changed pretty drastically when it comes to running Dad's clinic. It's not going to be as exciting as the animal hospital in Greensboro. The days of interesting surgeries are over, so I'll have to get used to slightly more monotonous days. But finally making Dad proud of me will be worth the boredom. If I'm being honest with myself, I've come to enjoy the business side of things. It's challenged my mind more than I ever expected.

All of that to say, I've been a stubborn asshole over this whole situation. It's time to release the stranglehold I have on what I thought my life would be like and start accepting what it *will* be.

The first step is getting out of Mom and Dad's house. Having a little separation between us will do my mood a lot of good.

"Let's take a look at some of the design stuff," Levi says, gesturing over to his truck. He pulls out a couple of design samples as well as books with tons of options for flooring, tile, and anything else you could need in your home. If I'm honest, every option looks identical to each other.

Levi quickly picks up on the fact that I have zero design skills and helps me pick out the best choices. Everything he picks looks good to me, so I give him full rein. Then I won't have to worry about it.

"If you're looking for something to do, our group still gets together regularly to hang out. We'd love to have you join us sometime," Levi offers as he packs away his stuff.

"You and your brother still hanging out with Todd Montgomery?"

"Of course. We've all partnered up at this point, but we still have a good time. Natalie Carlisle and Tucker James are actually together now, if you didn't know. You were in the same class as Tucker, right?"

"I was a year ahead of him, but I know who you're talking about. It would be great to hang out with people my age again. Mom's friends are nice, but...you know..." My eyes widen at the thought of spending another dinner with my mom's friends.

Mom pried the reason I went to Greensboro out of me when I was at my moodiest, and now, she's made it her mission to set me up with someone else. I can't imagine dating someone right now. Rebecca's betrayal did a number on me. I'm glad it happened, though. She wasn't the person I believed her to be, so I'm happy I didn't end up marrying her, tying myself to a miserable life.

"I definitely know." Levi laughs. "We'll take care of you, man."

"God bless you."

We wrap up the final items on Levi's list before he heads to another project, and I go to the gym. Finding a place to work out was the first order of business when I decided to officially move back home. I was surprised to find a gym that catered to my favorite type of exercise. Boxing. I fell in love with the sport in college, but when I started working at the animal hospital, I didn't have time to keep training. I barely had time to run while I worked there, and I only made time because I needed the stress relief.

Walking into The Warehouse, I'm immediately hit with the smell of rubber mats and sweat. Since it's late afternoon on a Saturday, there are quite a few people here. The sound of punches hitting mats and weights clanking to the ground follows me into the locker room.

This place is set up to handle both weightlifters and fighters, so I can get both in one place. I train with the owner, Dax Pierce, a couple of days a week to help keep my form.

He's a bit of an enigma. All I know about him is he moved here a few years ago and was in the military.

Once I'm changed, I start warming up, going through my lifting circuit and pushing my body to the limits. Getting back into the gym has been one of those unforeseen benefits of my move back to Sonoma. With Dax's intense workouts, I've gotten jacked over the last few weeks.

"Fix your form, princess!" Dax yells across the room. He started calling me princess when I wore a headband to keep my hair out of my face while we trained. I asked him what else I was supposed to do, and he responded with, '*Grow it out like a man*,' then tightened his man bun.

I re-rack the bar I was bench-pressing, then flip him off without saying anything. His echoing laugh makes me grin. I have one more set to go, and then I'm going back to Mom and Dad's. Levi said they could have my house ready to go in two months, which sounded a bit crazy to me. There's a shit-ton of work that needs to happen, so I figured it would take longer. I guess since most of the house is gutted already, they can start installing new stuff instead of taking the time to remove all the old stuff.

Finally done working out, I grab my duffle bag and head back to my car. I'll shower when I get home, then play with Sadie for a while. I think she's enjoying getting to spend more time with me. She used to come to the animal hospital with me, but she'd still end up sleeping in my office most of the day. Now she has free rein over the house while I'm at the clinic and gets more attention since I come home at a decent hour.

She greets me with huge tail wags as I walk through Mom and Dad's door. There's nothing better than getting all the love from your best friend when you get home.

"How's construction going?" Mom asks from the living room.

"Great! Levi said they'll be done in a couple of months."

"I don't understand why you felt the need to buy that trash heap of a house, Benjamin."

For this exact reason.

I hold myself back from saying that thought out loud. "I felt like it was the next logical step in establishing myself here," I respond instead.

Mom just harrumphs since she's also given me shit about doing more to be a part of the town. I hold my laugh in as I head upstairs to shower.

When I come back down an hour later, I hear my parents' murmured voices in the kitchen. Naturally, I listen in, wondering what they're talking about.

"You need to talk to him about what's going on, Charles," Mom says in that tone that offers no argument.

"I know, Sybil, I just keep seeing the expression on his face when he said he thought I was disappointed in him. I can't get it out of my head. I figured if I just stayed quiet, he'd be able to make his own decisions without my interference," Dad responds. So that's why he's been so reserved these past few weeks. I guess calling him out on his feelings made him take a step back for a bit.

Deciding to put them out of their misery, I clear my throat, striding into the room as if I hadn't heard them talking about me. "Hey, guys." I open the fridge door to grab a water bottle before turning back to the two of them. They're both standing there with wide eyes, afraid I heard what they were talking about.

"What's going on?" I ask, continuing my charade of ignorance. Mom is the first one to snap out of the awkwardness.

"Your dad has something he needs to talk to you about."

Dad's head comically whips toward Mom. I can tell he wants to tell her off, but knows he'd never get very far if he did. He sighs, resigned to have the conversation instead of continuing to fight with her. "Yeah, I'd like to talk with ya, son. Shall we go to my office?"

"Sure, Dad." I bite my cheek to keep from laughing at the two of them until we start walking to Dad's office. The humor of the moment dissipates as my stomach begins knotting. I had no desire to have this conversation when I first started at the clinic. I'm still not sure I'm ready to have it now.

I could start by acknowledging how much of a stubborn asshole I've been about taking over. It would at least explain where my head has been these past couple of weeks. I'm just not sure it would make any difference. Dad's never seen me as anything other than a fuckup. Finally being okay with running the clinic is probably not going to make a huge difference.

We sit down in the chairs in front of his desk, just like we used to do when I was growing up. The silence is deafening, and I'm not sure if I should start or if he wants to.

"Well, you want to tell me how your trip to Greensboro went? You've been pretty cagey about the whole thing."

"Sure, we can rip the Band-Aid off right now. Uh, I found out Rebecca was cheating on me and went to confront her, then went to my sad apartment and felt shitty about being an asshole all week at the clinic, and then I came home and bought a house. It was an interesting trip."

"Jesus, son. Your mom just said you guys broke up. I didn't know about the rest of it."

I look at my dad, who looks a little uncomfortable, and a laugh bursts out of my chest at the absurdity of this whole situation. He joins in, making the tension between us ease. His hand reaches out, squeezing my forearm in a surprisingly comforting embrace.

"I'm sorry it didn't work out between you two. I never fully understood Rebecca, but losing someone special to you is still tough."

"Dad, she stopped being special to me several months ago; I just didn't notice until now."

"Well, she wasn't the best... Ya know, I'm just going to stop there. No sense in disparaging her."

I smile at Dad. He's always been a glass-half-full kind of guy, so if he wasn't a huge fan of her, I dodged a huge bullet.

"Look, son. I wanted to talk to you about what you said in my office on your first day at the clinic. I probably should've had this conversation a long time ago, but you know how much I hate conflict."

I stay silent as he gets his thoughts together.

"I'm sorry you feel like I'm disappointed in you. I've never once been disappointed in you. Have there been times I didn't completely agree with your decisions? Sure. Were there times I wanted to wring your annoying teenage neck? Absolutely. None of that means I'm disappointed in you. I couldn't be prouder of the man you've become."

I'm stunned. I have no words to even explain what it means to me to hear that from him.

After a few seconds of stunned silence, Dad asks, "Can I ask why you thought I was disappointed in you?"

"Forgetting about my sullen teen years, I guess it started when I went to school at Cornell instead of your alma mater. Then, when I got the job at the animal hospital instead of coming to work at the clinic, it felt like I'd solidified your disappointment in me."

"Well shit, son. I'm sorry. I never intended to make you feel that way. I guess I was just worried you weren't making choices that would ultimately make you happy. You always seemed so stressed at your job. Like you were clamoring for some unreachable goal. Every time I saw you, it seemed like another piece of the boy I remembered was gone. It was hard to watch you disappear and not say anything."

I sit with Dad's words for a minute, thinking over all of our interactions. I wonder if I projected that disappointment onto my dad because I was going against every idea he ever brought up for the sole reason of being too stubborn to think about any other option.

"You know, Dad, I don't think I was truly happy in Greensboro. I was striving for this lofty ideal of a fancy career, a beautiful wife, and the perfect family. I thought I'd never be able to achieve that standard in a Podunk town like Sonoma. I couldn't see how full your life was until mine blew up, and I was forced to recognize how miserable I truly was."

"I always wondered if the life you were living was really what you wanted. Maybe that's why you thought I was disappointed."

"Maybe. If I'm honest, though, I'm still not sure that clinic work is for me. I got used to the excitement of surgery making each day different. I don't know if I can stand the monotony of the clinic schedule."

Dad's laugh pulls a smile from my lips. This conversation was exactly what we needed. The weight of his disappointment is finally off my shoulders, no longer clouding every choice I've ever made.

"So, make it not boring. Son, when I opened the clinic, I was in my late forties with a surly teenager who turned the silent treatment into a sport. I didn't have time for fancy digs and cool programs. Why can't you make the clinic be what you need? As long as the town is still able to have their animals cared for, why can't you make the clinic your own?"

"I guess I never thought you'd be okay with that."

"I mean, I don't want you to stop serving our patients, but there are tons of programs you could start. Like a monthly adoption program to encourage people to rescue, or hell, you could do puppy yoga. I don't care. Whatever is going to spark your interest and will keep you happy. That's what I care about."

"I'll think about it. Thanks for this, Dad. It's good to know I'm not a complete screw-up in your eyes."

Dad leans into me, wrapping his arms around my shoulders. "I couldn't be prouder of you," he whispers.

When he releases me, I clear my throat of emotion.

"Want to go have a beer?" I ask.

"You'll have to sneak it out to me on the porch so your mother doesn't see."

I laugh. "You got it."

13

SARA

The buzz of the busy restaurant rings in my ears as I wait for my food. La Mensa is packed for a Tuesday evening. It shouldn't surprise me. This place has the best Italian food I've ever had. Not only is every single meal phenomenal, but their breadsticks are to die for. I usually get an entire order just for myself.

The past few weeks have been…interesting. Ben has been suspiciously less hostile than when he first started at the clinic. He still needs to work on his tableside manner—he tends to get annoyed very easily. However, he usually starts the day in a better mood, even when Michelle and I wear funky scrubs.

If the gossiping hens can be trusted, it sounds like Ben has officially decided to stay. Levi started working on his house sometime last week, which is a pretty big commitment in my book. You don't buy a house unless you're planning on staying for the long term. I'm hopeful it also means we won't have to worry about finding a new person to run the clinic. It would be tough to go through another monumental change when we're almost settled after the first one.

It's not like I'll ever ask Ben for confirmation, though.

He's still colder than a block of ice despite being hotter than blue blazes. I don't think anyone is capable of melting that icy exterior of his, no matter how many closets you organize together.

I wonder if he's a mushy marshmallow under all that steel. I could see him being a huge softy based on how he interacts with the animals at the clinic. He may not be great with the owners, but he's especially gentle with the animals. It's the only reason I haven't popped him in the nose for being an asshole.

"Hi, I'm here to pick up a to-go order for Ben."

My head whips up from my phone at the sound of his voice. Why is he always around when my thoughts stray to him? It would be great if, just once, I'm not blushing while he's around. It makes me feel like a schoolgirl with a crush on the football star. And it brings back those dormant memories of him looking at me like a bug when I was fourteen. I'd prefer not to reenact those particular moments.

I am enjoying the view right now, though. He's got on a fitted green shirt with gray running shorts. His back muscles look as if he's about to bust out the seams of his shirt. Have his muscles gotten…bigger? Is that possible? Is it weird that I'm even noticing? Now that I think about it, his button-down shirts have been fitting a little more snugly. Did he start working out? That's the last thing I need. More muscles on an already gorgeous package.

I shake my head as he turns around, forcing my eyes back down to my phone. I should *not* be ogling my boss. For a multitude of reasons.

The bench shifts as he sits next to me, but I keep my eyes on my phone, making it seem like I'm lost in the social media site I'm scrolling.

"How are you, Sara?"

God, the way he says my name. And why does he smell

good? Like a smoky campfire in the middle of fall. I want to shove my nose into his neck.

Stop it!

"I'm good. How are you?"

"Just fine."

Silence ensues. I have no idea what I'm supposed to say at this point. Usually, our conversations involve a lot more snark, followed by grins when we know we're being sassy. It's been kind of fun, actually, but these pleasantries are weird, even if we've been building a truce. The only time we're nice to each other is when we're at the dog park, letting the dogs play together. It's hard to be sassy while watching the three of them wrestle.

"Sara, your order's ready."

Thank fuck. I stand to pay for my food, then grab the plastic bag when I'm done. "See ya tomorrow," I say to Ben. He catches my gaze, freezing me in my spot. Those blue eyes hold so many emotions, I feel as if I'm swimming in them. His nod pulls me from the moment, and I step out the door. That was weird. I don't even know how to interpret the look he gave me. It was as if he wanted to say a million things but wasn't able to get any of them out. What could he have wanted to say?

That he wants to see you naked as much as you do him.

I roll my eyes at my stupid thoughts. That would be the worst idea ever.

As I unlock my car, hands are suddenly wrapped around me. One is barred across my chest, pinning my arms to my sides; the other wraps around my mouth, keeping me from screaming out. I struggle against the person restraining me, kicking my feet into their shins. My heart is pumping hard as my fight-or-flight response floods through my system.

I grew up wrestling with my brothers. I figured I was pretty good at getting out of holds, but this is something bigger. Something more. It's as if my feet are feathers for all the damage my kicks are doing to the person holding me. They're huge against my back, my small frame dwarfed by this guy. He's at least twice the size of me. I don't stand a chance.

We move across the parking lot, my breathing rapidly increasing as I continue to fight against the hold without any success.

I'm going to be kidnapped.

Tears stream down my face as fear crashes through my system. I can't break his hold. No matter how hard I try. I don't know what to do. If I stop fighting, he's going to win, but nothing I'm doing is working. I can't let him take me. But the fight I started with is diminishing with every step he takes across the parking lot.

"Hey!" someone yells.

"Please help me!" I scream, but with the man's hand across my mouth, only muffled sounds escape. I can't breathe. There's not enough air coming into my lungs, and I'm going to pass out soon. Then this asshole will be able to do whatever he wants with me. I won't be able to fight against him if I'm unconscious.

The kidnapper darts across the parking lot toward a car parked in the back, covered in shadows. If he gets me in that car, it'll be over for me. I start fighting as hard as can, bucking against his hold on me. I go nowhere, completely ensnared in the beefy arms of my attacker.

"Shhhh. Don't be scared," he whispers in my ear. "You're safe with me now. I'm going to keep you forever."

Bile rises in my throat. This can't be happening to me. This sick freak is going to get away with this, and there's not a goddamn thing I can do to fight him off. He's too big. Too strong.

Then he grunts, his hold loosening on me. I buck my body in an attempt to make him drop me further. It works, allowing me to fall to the ground. Another grunt comes from the man before arms grab me, pulling me away from him. I fight against them, still afraid he's going to take me. The hands on my arms let go immediately. My gaze flies around me, trying to take in the next threat.

When it lands on Ben, I freeze. He's glaring at a dark figure racing across the parking lot, disappearing into the surrounding trees behind La Mensa, no longer visible in the evening light.

What the fuck just happened to me?

"Are you okay?"

I look back at Ben, unsure of how to answer that question.

Am I okay? I take stock of how I feel. My chest and arms are sore from the tight hold the attacker had on me, my lungs are burning from not bringing in a full breath, and my mouth feels cut from my teeth grinding into my lips. Does any of that qualify as being okay? I'm not direly injured so...

"Um, yeah. I think so. He didn't hit me or anything. My arms will probably be a little sore." My gaze keeps scanning the parking lot, unable to focus on any one thing. My heart is racing as if I'm still in the throes of the attack while my chest heaves. Catching my breath feels like a monumental task. I've never been so scared in my life.

I was almost kidnapped.

Someone tried to take me from the parking lot of my favorite restaurant, and I couldn't stop them. Is there something I should be doing right now? All I can focus on is trying to get my breathing back to normal. This is too much.

I go to brush my hair out of my face, but my hands are shaking too badly. Dropping them back to my side, I clench my fists to try and stop the tremor. It feels as if every emotion inside me is going to spill out onto the pavement, leaving me broken in a million pieces, scattered across the ground.

I have to start shoring up my defenses, focus on anything but the swirling chaos threatening to break loose.

"I don't even…that was…" Ben runs his shaking hands through his hair.

My thoughts swirl, moving so fast I can't seem to land on one at a time. What time is it? It feels like days have passed since I walked out of La Mensa. My food is splashed across the pavement. I guess I won't be having dinner tonight. It's hot outside. The summer evening air feels thicker than usual. I wonder if it's going to rain.

"We need to call the police." Ben starts to pat his pockets, then pulls out his cell phone. Panic begins to move through me at the thought of talking to anyone about what happened. I can't even wrap my head around the fact that it happened at all, let alone try to explain it to someone else.

The sound of brakes squealing startles both of us. My head jerks up, interrupting the barrage of thoughts running through my head.

"Archie!" someone screams, and Ben and I both react to the commotion.

We run toward the street, coming upon a car sitting sideways in the road. The driver is out of the car, frantic with worry. "I'm so sorry! He came out of nowhere! I tried to stop in time but couldn't."

Ben races to the dog lying on the road, having apparently been hit by the car. "Call Michelle, get her to come to the clinic."

"Why? I can assist you. I've done it for your dad."

Ben tells the driver to get him something stable to put the dog on so we can move him.

"Sara, you were almost kidnapped just now. You're not coming with me. You need to go to the police, not aid in surgery."

"I don't give a fuck what happened to me. I'm fine. This dog won't be if we don't help right now. I can do this."

"It's not that you can't, it's that you shouldn't."

"You're not going to tell me what to do. I'm here. I'm helping."

"Sara…"

Those denim blue eyes are overflowing with worry. I almost cave. Taking a deep breath, I work to calm my racing heart, allowing the adrenaline of the moment to focus my attention on what needs to happen next.

"Ben, I need this." My voice is all but a whisper as I keep his gaze.

He looks at me for a moment longer before nodding his head in agreement.

"We need to get him stabilized. Find out what the damage is before we get him to the clinic." Ben takes over the scene, making sure we keep everything as controlled as possible. When we locate the biggest concerns, his back and hips, we load him up into the bed of the owner's truck, working quickly to get him back to the clinic.

When we pull up to the clinic, Ben and the dog's owner get him out of the truck while I rush into our surgery room to prepare for any eventuality. He was only hit on his back end, which is good, but you never know if there will be any type of internal damage we'll need to repair.

I get the X-ray machine set up right before they come in with the dog. He's a sweet boxer with brownish-red fur. He's come into the clinic a couple of times for checkups.

"I'm sorry, Dan, but you're going to need to wait out in the lobby. We need all the space we can get in here," Ben says in a surprisingly gentle way.

Dan's throat bobs as he stares at his pup on our table. I lay a hand on his arm, gently directing him out of the room. Once he's gone, I turn toward Ben. With blue gloves on, he administers a sedative to keep Archie still. Then we get to work, attempting to heal this poor little pup.

14

BEN

The pass-through door creaks as I walk out to the lobby of the clinic. "Hey, Dan."

The man startles, shooting out of his chair. "How's Archie?"

"He'll be just fine. He's got a cracked pelvis and a shattered back leg. I ended up having to set it with screws so it heals properly. All in all, he's very lucky. He'll just need a lot of rest and attention."

"Thank you so much." Dan sighs. He wraps me in his arms for a hug while I awkwardly pat his shoulder.

I pull away, unsure of what to do now. Clearing my throat, I finish the update. "I want to keep him here for the next few days to make sure he's healing okay. We'll all trade shifts to keep him company overnight so he won't be lonely. After that, we'll see how he's doing, and if all looks good, he can go home."

"I don't know what to say, Dr. Crawford. Thank you isn't enough."

"Just doing my job."

Dan hesitates before finally asking the question I know is coming. "How much is all of this going to cost? My daughter was just diagnosed with diabetes, and between the insulin shots and medical bills, we're strapped."

"Let's not worry about it tonight." I pat Dan's shoulder. "We'll get with Susan when it's time to pick up Archie and figure something out then. We'll take care of him no matter what."

Dan nods his head.

"Why don't you head home and get some rest. We've got it covered here."

When the door to the clinic closes, I take the first deep breath I've managed in the last three hours, releasing the tension that had been building in my shoulders. As I walk back to the surgical room, I pull my scrub cap off and run my fingers through my hair. What a fucking night. I can't quite process everything that's happened. First with Sara, then with Archie. It's all entirely too much to deal with for one person. I can't imagine how Sara is feeling right now.

I look over at her while she puts away all the newly cleaned surgical instruments. She was incredible during surgery, anticipating every need before I even voiced it. She would've made an extraordinary vet. Makes me wonder about her story. I know she's a few years younger than me, but I don't remember her from school. I also didn't care much about making friends since I was only here for a year before I went to college.

Sara comes over to me when everything is put away. The shadows under her eyes tell me exactly how drained she is from everything that's happened. I want to pull her into my arms and comfort her, make sure she knows she's not alone, but I know that would be weird. We don't have that kind of relationship, even if I've spent these past couple of weeks thinking about her in ways I should not be—as both her boss and someone she's not super fond of.

"Everything okay?" I ask, attempting to wade into discussing the events of tonight.

"I got all the supplies sanitized and put away."

That didn't exactly answer my question, but I can understand why she wouldn't be able to talk about how she's feeling just yet. "Thanks for doing that. Mom and Dad brought my car over while we were in surgery. Can I take you somewhere?" I had texted my parents on the way to the clinic, letting them know about the accident. Mom had responded a little bit ago saying my car was out front.

"I guess you can drive me home. I don't have any other option since my car is still at La Mensa." Sara's voice hitches.

"Happy to be your last resort," I tease, attempting to distract her thoughts. I get a small curve in her lips as our part-time tech comes into the clinic to take over monitoring Archie. I do a quick rundown of the surgery, then usher Sara out the door.

I wish I had the magic words to make all this better for her. I can't imagine what's going through her head right now. I mean, she was seconds away from being kidnapped. How are you supposed to react to a situation like that? I haven't quite wrapped my head around being the one who intervened before the bastard could get away with her.

I had just walked out of La Mensa with my food, and I remember looking across the rows of cars and seeing a flailing body being carried across the parking lot. My gut told me something was off about that scene, so I dropped my food on the ground and took off across the pavement. I didn't know who, but someone was fighting against a monster of a man, and every instinct told me I needed to do something to stop him from getting away.

When I got close, I just reacted. My right arm threw the punch before I even had time to think. I hadn't yet figured out that Sara was the one being kidnapped before I was throwing a second punch. It allowed her to fall to the ground, which is when I finally recognized who it was.

When I went to pull her behind me, she understandably

freaked out, and I guess the attacker took advantage of the moment to run off before I could stop him. I wanted to chase the asshole, but I was worried Sara was hurt. She had her arms wrapped so tightly across her middle that I thought maybe she'd been stabbed or something.

And as pissed as I was that he got away, I'm glad I managed to save Sara. What if I hadn't been fast enough to stop the guy from taking her? What would have happened if he'd gotten her into the car? I shut those thoughts down before they can continue spiraling.

"We should go to the police station," I say quietly once we're in my car.

Sara starts shaking her head. "There's no reason. I'm fine now. I don't want to make a fuss."

"It needs to be reported, Sara."

"I can't right now. I'm exhausted. I'll go after I've had some rest."

"Sara—"

"No. If you won't take me home, I'll just walk." Sara starts to open her door, but I stop her with a hand on her arm.

"Wait, I'll take you home. I'm sorry for pressuring you." As much as I disagree with her choices, I don't want her to be alone. There's something telling me she needs someone to be there for her tonight, and pushing her past her limit isn't going to help my efforts.

Sara sits back in the seat, pressing her lips together as she stares out the window. The drive to her house is quiet, only interrupted when she gives me directions to her house.

I pull into the driveway of Sara's little cottage, and I suddenly have a very big urge to see inside. I want to know everything about this woman. I've never met someone so strong, so capable of handling her shit like a warrior. I want to know what made her be this way. If something happened in her life to make her this strong or if it's just an inherent trait she was born with.

Deciding to push my luck, I get out of the car, following Sara up the sidewalk to the front door. She unlocks the door, leaving it open for me to come in, as well. I guess that's the green light to know she's okay with me coming inside.

As I step over the threshold, I watch a hoard of animals swarm Sara's legs. Koda and Luna are first, their tails wagging fiercely while a three-legged black cat joins the mix, weaving between Sara's feet.

Sara gives each animal a small greeting, then turns to the tanks on the side of the room, saying hello to a lizard and a hamster I didn't notice when I walked in.

Koda keeps looking back and forth between me and Sara as if he's trying to figure out what's going on. I can understand his confusion. I've never come over before, so I'm sure he's worried about why I'm here. He nudges Sara's hand again, understanding that something isn't quite right.

"I'm okay, Koda," she says quietly. Turning to me, she raises her eyebrows. "You want a drink? I need a drink."

"Sure." When I speak, Koda nudges Luna, and they both come toward me, almost warily. Koda is giving me the once-over, and I know if I mess up this greeting, I won't be welcomed back by Koda. Despite having hung out at the dog park, we've never formally met. I'm in his territory now. It deserves a whole different kind of greeting.

While Sara is in the kitchen, I squat down in front of the dogs, holding my hand out palm up, allowing them to come to me if they're interested. Koda gives me a sniff, then nudges Luna, almost as if telling her I'm okay. She nuzzles her head into my hand after giving it a thorough sniff. I laugh as she keeps nosing me, enjoying the pets I'm doling out. Koda decides to get in on the action, nosing my other hand until I have to sit down so I don't fall over.

"You should feel special. Koda doesn't tend to like men. He was in a fighting ring, which is how he lost his ear. He doesn't even like my brothers much, but he knows they're family, so he tolerates them. Luna usually takes direction from Koda, but is a lot friendlier."

I stand from the floor and walk toward Sara, who's holding out a glass with amber liquid in it. "Thanks."

"I should be the one thanking you." Her voice goes quiet. I can almost see the images flashing behind her eyes. I wish I could take the whole nightmare from her.

"I'm just glad I got there in time."

"I dropped my breadsticks." Her eyes meet mine as tears well in them. "I really wanted breadsticks tonight."

And then she breaks.

I drop my glass on the end table next to her couch and scoop her up into my arms. With one arm wrapped around her knees and the other around her back, I sit down on the couch, placing her in my lap. Her knees are tucked into her chest, while her arms are wrapped around my shoulders as she clings to me. Her sobs echo across the room as all the night's events finally hit her.

I gently rub her back as her tears drip onto my shirt. I feel so helpless right now. There's not a goddamn thing I can do to make this better for her except make sure she knows she's not alone. She won't ever be alone when she needs to break down. I'll make sure of it.

As her tears slow and her sobs turn into shuddering breaths, I squeeze her tighter so that she knows she's still safe here in my arms. We don't say anything; even when her tears have dried up, we just sit with each other. Then Sara's breathing slows, evening out until I know she's asleep.

Without even thinking, I press my lips to her head. I don't know why I felt the urge to do it. I know next to nothing about this woman, but having her in my lap feels so incredibly right; it's as if she was always supposed to be here. Even with the emotional toll tonight took, I've never wanted to stay in one place more than I do right now.

I stand with Sara in my arms, carrying her to the first

door I come to. When I look down, Koda is standing next to the third closed door. I walk toward it, opening it with the hand under Sara's knees. This one must be Sara's room based on the half-open drawers of her dresser and the clothes scattered on the floor.

"Thanks, buddy," I say to Koda before walking into Sara's room and placing her down on the bed. I move the comforter back, then take off Sara's shoes and socks. After covering her with the blanket, I step back into the living room.

I don't feel comfortable leaving her alone tonight. Plus, she doesn't have her car here. I don't want her to be stranded if something happens.

"What are the odds this is a guest bedroom?" I ask Koda, who's looking at me like he's not sure what I'm going to do next. I'm not sure what I'm going to do next either, but something is telling me not to leave her alone.

When I open the door to the second bedroom, I sigh. All that's in here is gym equipment, and while I'm happy to know another tidbit about Sara, it means I'm in for a night on the couch.

After checking the closet for an extra pillow, I sneak back into Sara's room to take one from her bed. She looks peaceful as she sleeps, and I hope it stays that way. I guess that can be my reason for staying. To be here if she has a nightmare instead of the ludicrous one in my head saying I just want to be close to her.

I make up my bed on the couch, settling in for a long night. The black cat jumps onto my stomach, curling herself into a ball while Luna and Koda nose my arm. I give them all pets before finding a comfortable position to sleep in. I have no idea what the morning will bring or if Sara is going to be pissed I'm still here, but I can't leave her. I'll happily take the consequences of my actions, knowing I will be here if she needs me.

15

UNKNOWN

N^{O!} *This is wrong!*

She was supposed to be mine. I had her beautiful body in my arms, willingly coming with me. She smelled so good. Like sunshine and happiness. I'd never been so close to her before. I couldn't ever risk it. And the minute I finally had her, some guy ruined it. I was so close to having her forever.

My fist flies through the air, punching into the bark of the tree next to me.

Everything is ruined now. The plan was supposed to start with her by my side. Now, I have to find a new way to get to her. She's going to be on edge now that she knows how much I want her. Maybe I can use that. Prove to her that my love is real. That it's everything she'll ever need.

I stare through the back windows of her house, wishing I could be the one to take care of her tonight.

Except someone else is with her. The man who ruined everything. Why is he there? She doesn't even like him. She loves me! She showed me when she accepted all the gifts I've left for her.

No! No! No!

She's crying. Why is she crying? And he's touching her! This is too much.

I should be drying her tears, making her feel better. I'm the one who loves her. Not him.

This is all wrong!

16

SARA

My eyes peel open like pieces of Velcro. Fuck, that's uncomfortable. I roll over in my bed, scrubbing my hands over my face to clear the sleep away. Why does my head hurt? And why am I still wearing regular clothes?

Flashes of the night before come barreling into my brain. Almost getting kidnapped, Archie's surgery, losing my shit on Ben.

Yikes.

Did I really sob my heart out on Ben's lap? My crusty eyes and throbbing head would say that's exactly what happened. I don't think I've ever been this embarrassed. What am I going to do at work today? I don't think I'm prepared to interact with a man who's seen me at my very lowest point and pretend like it didn't happen.

God, this sucks.

Okay. Time to buck up and get this over with.

I jump out of bed, making Koda lift his head from the floor next to me. He never sleeps in my room. He prefers to be out in the living room so he can keep an eye on things. I guess with my crying jag, he was probably worried about me.

I give him some love to thank him for protecting me, then walk out of my room to go to the bathroom.

"You're up," a man's voice says from the kitchen, startling me so badly I make Koda flinch.

"Fuck!" I whirl around to find out who's in my house, only to see Ben leaning against my counter. He looks adorably sleep-ruffled. His hair is sticking out everywhere, his eyes still have the haze of sleep in them, and holy shit, he's shirtless. My eyes roam across his muscular shoulders, the small smattering of blond chest hair, and his abs.

Sweet mother of God.

He clears his throat, pulling me out of the haze of lust that took over my body. When my eyes make it back to his face, a satisfied smirk tilts the corner of his mouth.

"What are you doing here?" I ask in an attempt at distraction.

"After last night, I didn't feel comfortable leaving you here by yourself, so I slept on the couch. You also don't have your car. Figured I could give you a ride to the clinic."

"Right." I sigh. There's a lot of shit I'm going to have to deal with soon. "I'm going to shower and get ready. Then we can go pick up my car, since it's still early."

"Sounds good. I made coffee but wasn't sure how you'd like it."

"Black is fine."

"I'll have it ready when you're done."

I stare into those denim blue eyes, unsure of how to convey my feelings right now. He's seen me at my worst, and he's still standing there.

I'll add it to the list of shit I'm not prepared to tackle just yet.

I turn to walk into the bathroom, hoping a shower will ease the weight sitting on my shoulders. I carefully avoid the mirror. I feel awful, so it's a guarantee I look just as bad. If Ben was able to handle my snot wiped across his shirt, he should be able to handle my crusty eyes, bedhead, and dark circles.

The hot water feels incredible, better than I thought it would feel, and I stay in there longer than I probably should have. If we end up late to work today, I can blame it on the fact that *my boss spent the night at my house.*

Wrapping myself in a robe, I walk back out into the living room. I'm going to need at least three cups of coffee if I want to make it through this day. Ben is now sitting on my couch, still shirtless, watching the news. His gaze flicks over to me as I walk around the sofa. Now *he's* the one staring. Which admittedly makes me feel better about my own ogling.

He swallows hard before shaking his head and then hands me the mug sitting on the coffee table. I sit down on the couch, enjoying the companionable silence between us as we both sip our coffees.

I feel oddly comfortable with Ben. If we'd been sitting on this couch last week, there would have been so much tension in the air I doubt either one of us could have withstood it.

Now, I feel as if I know Ben on a much deeper level than ever before. Sharing a traumatic experience with someone will do that, I guess. I look over at him; the dark circles under his eyes make me wonder how much last night affected him. He intervened in a kidnapping. That's not a small thing. It takes an especially strong person to have the guts to jump into the middle of something like that.

"Thank you."

He looks at me, his brows furrowed.

"I don't remember the finer details of last night, so, in case I didn't say it before, thank you for saving me."

His expression softens. "I'm just glad I made it there in time. I keep wondering what would've happened had I been just a few minutes later. Or if I hadn't been able to stop him..." He shakes his head. Worry lines his face, and it's as if

I can see his brain spinning a million miles a minute with all of the potential scenarios.

"Hey." I place my hand on his arm, squeezing gently. "None of those things happened. You saved me, took care of me. There aren't enough words to tell you how much I appreciate everything you've done."

He wraps his arm around my shoulders and pulls me into his chest. I wrap my free hand around his waist, soaking in the comfort of his arms. I have no idea where we go from here, but what I do know is I've never felt safer in someone's arms than I do right now.

"We should probably get going," I say after several minutes of snuggling on the couch. I'm suddenly very aware of the fact that I'm only in a robe, cuddled up against a very sexy, naked chest.

"Yeah, I need to go home and get some clothes before work."

"Let me go change. Then we can get going."

Ben presses his lips to the top of my head, making me close my eyes at the gesture. I force myself to pull away from him to go get dressed.

I'm going to need some time to work through all the things that have happened in the last twenty-four hours. None of which I can focus on at the moment, so I'm just going to go through my normal routine and hope I don't fall apart before I'm ready.

* * *

BEN PULLS into the parking lot of La Mensa. My car is one of only a few still in the lot at this time of day. Images of being dragged across the asphalt overwhelm me as Ben parks his car. My heart starts to thrum in my chest as I imagine getting out of the car. Being out in the open. Vulnerable.

My gaze frantically searches the parking lot for any

potential threat. The morning sun is shining bright, illuminating all the places that were once in shadow. It doesn't seem to matter to my brain. It's still preparing to find someone waiting to attack.

"Sara."

It sounds like Ben's voice is moving down a tunnel, a mile away from me. I can't focus on anything. It's all too much.

"Sara, look at me. Turn toward my voice."

My head whips to Ben, desperation running rampant through my body. I can't breathe, the panic overwhelming me to the point of paralysis.

"Breathe. In through your nose, out through your mouth." I watch Ben breathe, wishing I could do it, too.

"Right here, Sara." He pushes his hand into my chest, the pressure forcing my lungs to expand. "Let it out." He exhales loudly, and I mimic the sound. We keep breathing together, never taking our eyes off each other. Those blue eyes are filled with so much conviction, it makes me want to do whatever it takes to keep him looking at me like that.

"Great job, Sara. Keep breathing."

As the panic begins to recede, logical reasoning begins to creep in along with embarrassment. My eyes drop to the console between us. I can't believe I just freaked out in front of him again.

A finger lands under my chin, forcing my head back up to meet Ben's eyes.

"You are a fighter. You came out on the other side of a traumatic experience stronger than you've ever been. You may not *feel* strong right now, but you are the strongest person I've ever met."

"I used to feel strong," I whisper. "Confident. Now..." I don't even feel like the same person I was before last night. "I need to feel strong again. I need to do something."

"What if I trained you to fight?"

"Like self-defense?"

"Sure. I think Dax, the owner of the gym I go to, could help, too. How about we get him to show you some moves?"

"That might work."

"It's worth a shot at least."

I nod my head, glad to have something to focus on instead of the lingering panic. The classes could give me a sense of preparedness. A sense of strength that if it happened again, I'd be ready instead of completely helpless.

"How about I just drop you off at the clinic, and we can get your car another time?"

"I think that would be best for today."

It's going to take time to heal from this, but I'm determined to be okay. Even if I have to use La Mensa's breadsticks as motivation to move forward.

17

BEN

The noise at La Mensa is much louder than a few days ago as I stand in the lobby, waiting for my take-out order. With the start of the weekend, everyone seems to have wanted to eat out rather than stay home.

I knew I didn't want to sit at home with my parents tonight, so I thought I'd grab some dinner and see where the night takes me.

This has been an interesting week, to say the least. Sara has been acting as if nothing happened to her at all, which I can understand. Dwelling on something traumatic would probably lead to madness. I just hate how haunted her eyes look now. There's a shadow in them that wasn't there before. It makes the protector in me want to slay the dragon she's fighting in her mind, even though I have no right to.

I may have saved her, but that doesn't mean I'm anything more to her than a Good Samaritan, who was in the right place at the right time. Something in my chest constricts at the thought of being nothing to Sara. I don't want to just be a guy who happened to help her one time. I'm not exactly sure what I want to be, but I know I want to be more.

That's why I'm at La Mensa. Although, I'm not sure if this is the best choice for dinner.

Oh, god, this could seriously backfire.

What if she has a panic attack?

Running my hand through my hair, I contemplate canceling the order.

"Ben, your order is ready." The hostess interrupts my thoughts, holding up the white takeout bag.

Well, too late now. I stand to pay for my food, then walk back out to my car. My gaze flicks toward the back of the parking lot, where I saw Sara being taken. My heart starts beating fast just at the reminder of what could've happened. I'm so glad I got to her in time.

Shaking off the residual anxiety, I get into my car to head to Sara's house. Sadie peeks her head between the front seats to give me a sniff.

"I hope this works, Sades. What if she cries? Or punches me in the face for thinking this was a good idea?" *Or both.*

"I'm such an idiot. I shouldn't have done this."

Sadie's nose presses into my neck, so I give her some pats on the head. Her comfort is exactly what I need to calm my nerves.

Pulling into Sara's driveway, I take a deep breath. "Wish me luck, Sades. Hopefully, I'll be back in a minute to get you."

I get out of the car with the take-out bag in my hand and walk up the sidewalk to Sara's front door. With a tap on the wood, barking ensues as well as Sara's voice saying, "I don't know any more than you do, so give me a minute." I hope she's talking to Koda and not someone else.

The door opens to the dogs surrounding Sara's legs, which are completely bare. My gaze drags up her incredibly toned legs to find her in running shorts and a sports bra.

She has abs.

Holy hell.

Her shiny brown hair is up in a messy bun, and her cheeks are flushed like she just finished working out.

I clear my throat when she raises an eyebrow at me, a small smirk quirking up the corner of her mouth.

"I brought breadsticks," I blurt out. *Smooth... Real smooth.*

I hold up the take-out bag in my hand to show her they're from La Mensa. All the tension in Sara's body drains, and she smiles a beautifully vulnerable smile.

I've never met someone so open with her emotions. With one glance, you know exactly what Sara is feeling based on her expression. Over the past month, she's only ever looked at me with annoyance. Which, to be fair, is deserved.

"Breadsticks sound amazing." She nods her head to invite me inside.

"Uh, before I come inside, I brought Sadie."

Sara's eyebrows wing up in surprise.

"I felt guilty about leaving her at Mom and Dad's, so I took the chance of bringing her."

"Well, go get her." Sara laughs. "But give me the bread-sticks first."

Chuckling, I hand the bag over before turning back to my car.

"We're in, Sades," I say as I give her the command to get out. We walk back up to the still-open door, Sadie sticking close to my side. Koda and Luna come trotting over to us, and the dogs all give each other hello sniffs. Tails are wagging all around, so after saying my hellos, I step around them to help Sara dish up the food in the kitchen.

She's still in her workout gear, and I get an even better glimpse at all her silky skin. I never knew toned muscle was a turn-on for me, but I'm having a seriously difficult time keeping my body in check right now. I want to run my hands down her shoulders to the small flare at her hips.

Focus.

"I'm glad our dogs get along. Sadie's never had much of a

chance to make friends before," I say, forcing my gaze to them instead of on Sara's ass. She turns, laughing at the three of them wrestling with each other.

"She's incredible with Luna. I've never seen another dog help guide her before." Sara sets down the plates and starts dishing out pasta.

"Really?" In all the times they've played, I never noticed. Watching them now, Sadie noses Luna back to the center of the living room so she doesn't hit the coffee table.

"Most dogs stay back, letting Koda pull her back into the fray."

Hearing that makes me feel like a proud dog parent. Like I did something right in raising Sadie, which I recognize is ridiculous. They aren't kids. You don't teach your dog to share their toys. But I'm still proud to call her mine.

We plate up our food, piling them high with pasta and breadsticks. Sara has three on her plate, which makes me glad I got two orders.

We sit on the couch, the dogs finally settling down on the floor.

"Oh, my god," Sara moans around a bite of bread. I can't hold back my laughter as she shoves the rest of it into her mouth.

She glances at me, her jaw working around the large quantity of food. "Don't you dare judge me," she garbles, her mouth full of food.

I hold my hands up in surrender, digging into my food. It really is good enough to warrant Sara's savage behavior.

"I wasn't sure when I'd get La Mensa's breadsticks again," she says quietly, twirling some pasta around her fork.

"You'll get there. It may take some time, but one day, it won't be as hard. Until then, I'll bring you as many bread-sticks as you want."

"Thanks, Ben." Her hazel-eyed stare pierces through my

chest. Her vulnerability calls to something inside me that longs to have someone to take care of, to cherish.

"Anytime." I look back at the muted TV, unsure of what to do with these foreign feelings. "Have you heard anything from the police? Do they know who tried to hurt you?"

My question is met with silence, and I glance over at Sara, her fork picking at the noodles on her plate. "You didn't talk to them, did you?"

She shakes her head, a stubborn set to her jaw. "It's not a big deal. Nothing happened, so there's no reason to get anyone else involved." She shrugs her shoulders. "I saw your mom at the grocery store yesterday." The quick change in subjects tells me I won't get any further with my questions.

"What did she say? She's been grilling me nonstop since I asked her and Dad to pick up your car." After Sara's panic attack in the parking lot, I asked them to bring it to the clinic so Sara wouldn't have to go back to La Mensa until she was ready.

"Oh, nothing much. Just that she was glad her son was finally getting out on the town and that he needed to find himself a good woman to keep him in line. I agreed with her. Told her you might be ready to start looking for that special girl." She grins at me.

"Evil, evil woman." I glare at Sara. "She's going to double down on her matchmaking now."

Sara's laugh lights up her eyes, making the shadows disappear for a moment.

"Do you know how many dinners I've been to in the last month that were setups for a date? It's ridiculous. I can find my own woman, thank you very much." It's gotten to the point where I've just stopped accepting any dinner invitation Mom gives me. I don't trust her anymore. "Even if I were looking to date, I don't think I know how anymore," I say quietly.

"Why?"

I should've known Sara wouldn't have let that comment go. Sighing, I tell her all about my ex. Despite coming to terms with the whole ordeal, I'm still a little wary about dating. How do you dive headfirst into the dating pool after being deceived by the one person you thought you'd be with forever?

"Well, she sounds like a bitch," Sara says vehemently. "I don't like saying that sort of stuff about other women because it's hard enough out there without us fighting with each other, but who does something like that when your partner needs you to be supportive?"

"Yeah, looking back now, I can see all the red flags I should've noticed."

"You were a bit busy making sure your dad didn't die, Ben. Looking for red flags in a relationship that should've been stable wasn't a priority at that point. Nor should it have been."

Watching Sara get worked up on my behalf has the knot of tension that always shows up when I talk about Rebecca loosening just the slightest bit. I have a feeling Sara would never consider behaving the way Rebecca did. It makes a smile grow on my face.

When Sara notices me smiling, she pauses her diatribe about how a good fiancée would have done whatever they could to help. "What?"

"Nothing, just enjoying how heated you got for something that happened to someone you don't even really like." I grin at her.

"I don't...*not* like you. You can just be an asshole sometimes."

"Ouch! Fair, but ouch."

Sara's belly laugh is loud and so full of joy I can only laugh along with her. It hits me how comfortable I am sitting next to someone I barely know anything about. Being an unfriendly *asshole* at work hasn't led to many get-to-know-you conversations at work.

Except, it feels like I've known Sara for years. There's a connection between us now that keeps pulling me closer to her. I have no idea if I'm ready to get closer to a woman again or if Sara even wants me to. I guess we can just see where our friendship goes first. Then, if it seems like she might want more, we can explore that together.

18

SARA

The smell of rubber mats burns my nose as I try to take in my surroundings. Men are scattered around the room, standing next to various gym equipment, casting me interested glances. I would venture to guess not many women work out here. I know the gym is tailored toward heavy lifting and fighting. At least, that's what Ben told me when he picked me up for my first lesson tonight.

"There's Dax," Ben says, pointing to a man with a thick beard, fully tattooed arms, and brown hair tied in a knot at the back of his head. Based on his size alone, I think I'll get my money's worth in training. Nerves keep skittering down my spine every time I remember why I'm doing this.

I need to feel strong. Prepared. Just in case something else happens. Not that I think it will. I know what happened to me was a fluke. Nothing like what happened to Quinn when she was kidnapped. That was for revenge. They were out to get Quinn from the very beginning. Not because Quinn happened to be an easy target.

I won't be an easy target anymore. I'll make sure of it.

Dax slaps the shoulder of the guy he was talking to, then walks toward us. "Hey, man." Dax does a bro hug with Ben, their hands clasped at their chests while they slap each other's backs. The show makes me want to roll my eyes. Although, I'm thoroughly enjoying the arm porn that's happening in front of me. Ben's biceps are popping hard in his cut-off T-shirt. Dax's muscles aren't horrible to look at either.

"Dax, this is Sara. Sara, this is Dax Pierce."

I hold my hand out to Dax, who takes it in his very large, calloused one. "Nice to meet you."

"Glad you're here," he says to me. His dark eyes, along with his very muscled, tattooed vibe, give me both a sense of comfort and worry. There's no way I'll ever be able to take on a guy like him, but I'm glad he's the one who's going to teach me.

"You were in the Navy?" I ask, referencing one of the tattoos in the sleeve running down his arm. It's a bald eagle wrapped in an American flag, holding an anchor in its claw.

Dax looks at the tattoo as if he's only now remembering he has it. "Uh, yeah, I was a SEAL for a few years." He clears his throat, then gestures toward the mats. I guess that means we're done with the get-to-know-you portion of the night. "I'd like to get an idea of where you stand physically, so let's start with some conditioning to warm up, then we'll go from there. You and Ben are going to be doing the same things since this is technically his training time, but I'll modify where we need to for you."

"Sounds good." I nod.

Dax leads Ben and me to a set of treadmills to start on cardio, then we hit the mats for pushups, sit-ups, and crunches. I keep up well enough as we go through each exercise, which gives my pride a boost. Ben's just as winded as I am, so I don't feel as if I'm falling behind him. My competitiveness would never allow that.

"You're in pretty great shape. That will be helpful for you

when we start working in the ring," Dax says as we take a quick water break.

"Good. I'm comfortable out here, but *that* scares the shit out of me," I say, pointing to the three fighting rings sitting in the middle of the warehouse.

"It won't for long."

When we're finished with warm-ups, Dax leads me into the ring. Ben hangs out on the floor, having given up his normal training time so I could give this a try.

"Okay, what sports have you played?"

"Mostly soccer growing up. I still play some with my brothers."

"So, you've got decent coordination in your feet, but you're not going to be as quick with your hands," Dax muses. "I'd like to do a combination of mixed martial arts and jiu-jitsu. The MMA will help with your punches and kicks, giving you the skills to fight if needed. The jiu-jitsu will help if you get into a position where hand to hand isn't an option."

I nod, unable to fully get my words out through my nerves. Then Dax starts walking me through the moves. The minute I start using my body as a weapon, a sense of empowerment washes over me. It's as if every insecurity I felt before walking into the gym has melted away with the first punch I threw. Every movement feels as natural as breathing, and I pick the moves up quickly enough that Dax has me start a few more complex combinations.

"Harder. If you keep punching as if it doesn't matter, you'll fail the moment it does."

A growl tears through my chest as I push through my exhaustion to make each punch land with a pop. I push and push until my body physically can't move anymore.

"That's it. One more, Sara. Prove to me this asshole won't be able to touch you again," Dax murmurs so only I can hear. I dig down deep into my gut for one last burst of energy. The echo of my would-be kidnapper's arms around my body pushes me to throw the combo harder than ever before. The snap of my punch against the blocker rings across the warehouse.

It's only then, as I pant in the middle of the ring, that I realize the crowd of weightlifters have surrounded the outside edge, watching me train with Dax.

"Train her up a bit more, Dax, and you could have a prizefighter on your hands," someone says from the crowd. I search the unfamiliar faces until my gaze lands on the blue eyes I've come to count on. Pride is glowing in them as well as a heat I recognize in myself. I'm not sure what we're doing, or if this is anything more than friendship, but I do know that without his strength, I wouldn't have been able to stand up tall this week.

"You've got a talent for this," Dax says to me as I unwrap my taped hands.

"Thanks. Something clicked, I guess. I also have four brothers, so fighting is in my nature." I grin at him.

"You have four brothers?" Ben asks, stepping up next to me. He's standing close, his arm brushing against mine. I have to tamp down the need to wrap my arm around his waist.

"Yeah, I sit smack dab in the middle. Adam and Matthew are the ones who got me started in sports. Playing against them made me a much better athlete."

"Your brothers are Adam and Matthew Ellis?" Dax and Ben say almost simultaneously.

"Yeah, why?"

"No wonder you've got such an innate talent," Dax says, awe in his voice.

"I should've put it together before now. How did I not realize they're your brothers?" Ben muses. I'm not sure who to respond to or if either of them is even talking to me, so I just stand there.

"Sara! I didn't know you trained here." Tucker James

strides across the floor, a smile lighting up his face. He picks me up in a bear hug that makes me laugh. He used to be so reserved before Natalie. Now, he's become like another brother to me, and he treats me like a sibling, too.

"I just started." I glance over to find Ben frowning at me. I can't tell if he's upset or confused. I quickly do introductions just in case he doesn't know who this is. "Tucker, have you met Ben Crawford? He took over the animal clinic for his dad."

"Ben Crawford. It's been a long time, man." Tucker sticks his hand out to greet Ben.

"Yeah, it has."

"It's good to see you again. You settling in okay?"

"I'm getting there. Levi is fixing up a house for me, so once that's done, I'll feel a little more settled."

"We need to get together. I'm sure the guys would like to see you again."

"Sure, I'd love that."

After exchanging phone numbers, the two of them chat for a while longer, catching up on what's been going on in their lives. It's nice to see Ben making friends here.

He told me last night that he's still struggling with having to move back to Sonoma. I can only imagine what it would be like going from Greensboro to our small-town community. It would be a difficult transition for anyone. Add in the fact that Ben wasn't super happy with taking over the clinic, and you've got a recipe for disaster.

"Well, I gotta get home. It was good to see you guys. I'll see you at family dinner next week, Sara."

"Bye, Tucker." He quickly pats me on the shoulder, then leaves the gym.

"Shall we go?" I ask Ben, turning to grab my gym bag from the floor.

He stares at me for a moment, then nods his head. "Sure."

We drive back to my house in silence. I'm lost in my

thoughts about how the training went today. I need to get on Dax's schedule to start doing that regularly. I've never felt so strong or capable. To have that training at the ready anytime I need it will relieve a lot of the worry I've been holding on to.

"Want to come in for a bit?" I ask when he pulls into my driveway. I'm not quite ready for him to leave yet.

"Have you told your friends what happened?"

I freeze, my hand on the door handle, poised to let me escape this moment.

"I haven't had time. Everyone has been dealing with Hope's mobster ex coming to town; I didn't feel it was necessary to add to their stress. Besides, nothing happened, so what would be the point?" The words feel like they're true, but the tone of my voice doesn't quite hold the strength I need to make them true.

In all honesty, I've barely acknowledged the incident happened at all. Thinking about having to say it out loud to my friends…there's no way.

"You need to tell them. Cooper needs to know someone is trying to abduct people in his town."

"I'm sure we'd have heard about someone else being abducted by now, if that were the case."

"That doesn't change anything, Sara. Do you think your life means less than someone else's? That your attempted kidnapping is somehow less important because they weren't successful?"

"I don't know!" I yell, unable to stop my emotions from overflowing. I sit back in the seat of Ben's car, feeling all my anger at this situation drain out as quickly as it came. "I don't think it's less important. I just… Trying to explain what happened to me…how weak I was… I can't, Ben. And having people hovering over me is only going to make me feel even smaller."

He reaches over the console to grab my hand, squeezing

my fingers in his. "You aren't weak." When I look away from him, unable to take his words to heart, he uses his other hand to force my gaze back to his. The intensity in his eyes brings tears to my own. I hate how emotional I've become over this whole situation.

Ben's hand slides across my jaw, his thumb stroking my cheek. "You're the bravest woman I've ever met. I feel incredibly lucky that you've allowed me to be a part of this journey, but I'm not the only one who could help support you. It's not weak to need help. Acknowledging you can't do it alone is the strongest thing you could ever do."

"I know," I whisper. "I'm just not ready."

He looks at me for a moment longer before nodding his head. We stay staring at each other far longer than would be normal, taking each other in. I'm so grateful for this man and how much he's done for me. He didn't have to do any of this. He didn't have to save me; he didn't have to stay with me while I cried, and he didn't have to help me find a trainer. Yet he did all of that and more.

Before I can think too much about it, my lips crash against his, trying to convey how much he's come to mean to me over the last week. I don't even know how that's possible in such a short time, but it's happened all the same.

For a moment, Ben is frozen, unmoving against my lips. Then, snapping out of his surprise, he wraps his hand around my head and fully takes over the kiss. It's deep, full of longing and passion. I'm completely swept up in him. The twining of our tongues, the pulling on my scalp where he has a hold of my hair.

It's everything I've ever wanted in a first kiss.

Slowly, we pull apart with gentle kisses to calm the building inferno. "Holy shit," Ben breathes. His forehead pressed against mine.

"Yeah. I didn't exactly see that coming. I was just trying to say thank you."

Ben's laugh is loud in the confines of the car. As usual, it makes me laugh along with him. "You're something special, Sara. I hope you know that."

"Thanks," I whisper, overwhelmed by the turn of the evening's events.

"I'm going to walk you to your door, and then I'm going to leave because if I go inside with you right now, I can't guarantee I'm going to be a gentleman."

As much as my body doesn't want him to be a gentleman right now, my brain needs some space to figure itself out before things move too far, too fast. Leaning on him for support is one thing, using him to forget what happened is a whole other.

"Okay." I grin at him, then open the door to get out of the car. The summer air feels cool against my fevered skin, although I think that has more to do with the kiss than the air actually being cold.

Ben grabs my hand and leads me up to my front door. He wraps his arm around my waist, pulling me closer to his body. "I need one more to get me home." He leans in, kissing me far too quickly before pulling away with a groan. "Addicting. What am I going to do with you?"

"Keep coming back for more."

"You're damn right I will." He leans in to give me one more peck before walking back down the sidewalk and to his car. He stands next to the driver's side door, watching me unlock my house and step inside before he gets in and drives away.

I press my fingers to my lips, unsure of how to process exactly what happened tonight. A lot of good things have come into my life recently. I can't allow the one negative thing to ruin any chance I have at making this life exactly what I want.

19

BEN

As I pull into the parking lot of the clinic, a grin stretches across my face. Sara's car is already here, which means I'll see her when I walk inside.

What am I, a middle school boy?

I'm giddy to see a woman. God, I feel ridiculous. All we did was kiss. It's not like I've seen her naked.

I sure as hell would like to, though.

Fuck. Okay, time to focus on doing my job.

I walk into the clinic, nodding at Susan, who's sitting behind the front desk, pulling up files. Scanning the back rooms, I don't see Sara, so I head into my office to put my things away. I smell her perfume before I see her, the scent of oranges reminding me of summertime. She peeks around the corner of my doorway, a hesitant look on her face.

I stand from my chair and step around my desk, ready to embrace her, when I spot Michelle watching from behind Sara. "Did you need something?" I ask, sliding my hands into the pockets of my slacks to keep from grabbing her. I'm unsure of the right move to make, so vague feels the safest.

Apparently, that was wrong because Sara frowns. I look

behind her again to find Michelle gone, so I grab her arm and pull her into my office, closing the door behind her.

"Is everything okay?" Sara frowns.

I run my hand through my hair. "No. I have no idea how to navigate this. Is this even a *this*? Am I making a bigger deal out of nothing?" I clamp my mouth shut in an attempt to stop the word vomit. I don't know what's happening to me.

Sara finds it hilarious, though, because she starts giggling.

"Stop, it's not funny." I point my finger at her.

"Yes, sir." She bites her lip to keep from laughing while my body immediately reacts to her words.

My eyebrow raises, and I step into her space, forcing her to lean against my desk. My hands land next to her hips, bracing my weight against the edge. "Feeling particularly sassy today, are we?" Our faces are only a few inches from each other.

Her throat bobs as she swallows, her hazel eyes heating as she takes in my stance. My short-sleeved button-down shirt is stretched across my shoulders, and my tight slacks don't give me much room as my cock swells. "If we were anywhere else, I would show you what your sass will get you."

"Tell me instead."

Fuck me. I was not prepared for this to happen this morning. I lean into Sara's ear, pitching my voice low. "I'd bend you over this desk, push those scrub pants to your ankles, and slap your ass until it was pink with my hand-print." I pause, waiting to see how Sara takes my certain level of dominant preferences.

Her chest is heaving, and the blush blooming across her chest tells me she's into it more than I could have ever hoped for. "Then I'd fuck you so hard you'd feel me for the rest of the day. To remind you of the consequences of your sassy behavior."

I lean back from her, using every ounce of control I have not to act upon my words.

"Jesus," she whispers. "I didn't... I don't... Fuck." Sara's eyes meet mine, and I laugh.

"I didn't mean to get into that so quickly, but there you have it." I know my proclivities aren't for everyone. It actually takes a certain kind of woman to be willing to be dominated. To give up total control of your body is an incredible gift and requires a level of trust you have to build with each other. Rebecca was never really into the domination, which was fine. I never want someone to do something they aren't comfortable doing.

"So, you're a dominant?"

"Sexually, yes. Outside of the bedroom, not so much."

"Okay."

I frown at her. "That's it?"

"Well, I don't really know what all of that entails, but I figure it's something we can talk about in more detail. I liked whatever happened a few minutes ago, so I'm not opposed."

"Okay," I say slowly, a little surprised at how this morning has gone.

"We should probably get back out there." Sara straightens, stepping closer to me. "We should also keep this on the down-low at the clinic until we know for sure what we're doing."

"Probably a good idea."

Sara grins, then walks out of my office like I didn't just drop a sexual bomb into the already uncertain relationship we've started. I give myself a moment to calm down before I walk out to the front desk.

"Hey, Susan, can you make sure everyone is in the break room at lunch? I want to talk about some things."

"Sure. Would you like me to order food for everyone?" She raises her eyebrow at me as if she's waiting for me to say the right answer.

"Um...yes?"

With an approving nod, she responds, "I'll get some sandwiches ordered from the café."

"Great." Glad to have passed the test, I head back to my office to work on some paperwork until the techs need me for a consult. When I first took over for Dad, I didn't think I'd have the attention span to handle the amount of paperwork required to keep the company going. Turns out, I enjoy it. There's a certain level of satisfaction in being in control of the clinic. Every decision I make will impact the well-being of the company, good or bad. It's been an interesting conclusion.

When lunch comes around, I find Susan, Michelle, and Sara in the break room, dishing up their sandwiches. Sara hands me mine already plated, fighting a blush rising in her cheeks. I love how big of an effect I have on her. It gives my ego a solid boost, not that it needs it. She has the same effect on me, too, which makes keeping this secret difficult.

After everyone is settled at the table, I start telling them about my idea. "I wanted to talk with you guys about something for the clinic. After we did the emergency surgery for Archie, Dan confided in me that he was worried about paying for the surgery. It made me wonder how many other people are not getting their animals the best care because they also can't afford the costs. So, I'd like to start a fund for those people."

"How would it work?" Sara asks, excitement shining in her eyes. I knew out of everyone, she'd be the most interested in my plan.

"I was thinking it could cover the bigger expenses like surgery or vaccines, maybe even medications. We'll need to come up with an application process. Most people in town won't try to take advantage, but there will be a few, so we'll want to do our due diligence. We'll also need to host regular fundraisers to keep the funds coming in, so I'll need some help to plan those."

"I can help with the application process," Susan offers. She'd be the perfect person to handle it.

"We could partner with the local shelter for a fundraiser," Michelle suggests.

"Oh, that's a great idea. We could do an adoption thing with them so they could get something from it, too." Sara grins at Michelle. Suddenly, the two of them are going back and forth with ideas, and I can barely keep up with them.

"This is great. Would you two write down all those ideas? I missed a lot of what you said." I laugh.

After a nod from Sara and Michelle, we finish our lunch, keeping up a decent amount of chatter as we eat. For the first time since I took over, it feels like they no longer see me as the asshole boss. There's a tentative truce between us now, and I hope I don't screw it up.

A little while later, Sara pops her head around the corner of my office. "Ready in exam room one."

I follow her into the room for another wellness visit. A Great Dane is sitting on the floor next to his owner, peering at me as if he doesn't quite trust me. I hold out a treat to the dog. "Hello, Duke. I see here you're never too sure about being at the vet. I can understand. We tend to do some uncomfortable things. You think we could be friends?"

He continues to stare at me for a moment before coming over to take the treat I held. "That's great, buddy." I turn to Sara. "Everything ready?"

"Yep, on the counter." She's looking at me expectantly, as if I'm supposed to do something else, but I have no idea what that is, so I just nod at her and administer Duke's vaccines. When everything is wrapped up, I say goodbye to Duke's owner, then leave the room only to find Michelle wrangling a hissing cat in the back. I help her get the rather persnickety animal into one of our overnight kennels with minimal scratches between the two of us. Muffin is here to get spayed and is not happy about it in the slightest.

When Sara walks into the back, she whacks me on the arm. "What was that?"

"What was what?"

"You were an asshole in that exam room."

"I was not," I scoff. "That Great Dane was putty in my hands."

"I'm not talking about the dog. I'm talking about the human. You didn't even say hello to them!"

"I did, too!" Although, now that I think about it, Sara might be right.

She raises one eyebrow at me, then looks at Michelle.

"You are pretty bad with the owners, boss man," she adds.

I go over all of my interactions with animal owners since I started. They might have a point. "Well, what am I supposed to say to them? I'm there to take care of their pet, not them."

"You could start with pleasantries. A *'Hey, how are you doing?'* is a good place to start," Sara says.

"I never really had to worry about that kind of stuff at the animal hospital. Our focus was the animal."

"Welcome to small-town living." Michelle snorts.

Sara laughs at her quip, but I just sigh.

"I'll try to do better."

"That would be appreciated by most everyone around here." Sara elbows me. "You'll figure it out."

I nod, then turn to go back to my office. My surly attitude has nothing to do with Sara pointing out my lack of pleasantries and everything to do with feeling like I'm failing at something else. I thought I had it all figured out when, in reality, I know nothing.

At least Sara felt comfortable enough to tell me I was messing up. I probably should've said thank you for letting me know. I don't want her to think I'm pissed at her.

It'll be a good reason to bring her dinner tonight. And maybe we can talk more about what happened earlier today.

SARA

The noise level in the house is at an ear-splitting level. It always is when we have family dinner at Mom and Dad's. With my four brothers acting like buffoons, Natalie's spitfire personality, along with her fiancé, Tucker, who tends to get roped into whatever the boys are doing, there's never a dull moment around here.

I love these people. I love how loud and loving they are, even how they act like middle school boys. Which they're currently excelling at right now as Nolan and Matthew wrestle on the floor.

"If you break my table again, neither one of you will get dessert!" Mom yells from the kitchen. Nolan and Matthew freeze. An unspoken communication happens between them before they let go, move the coffee table to the side of the room, then proceed to continue wrestling with the extra space. Carter is standing off to the side, his arms crossed as he watches to make sure neither one gets in any cheap shots.

Natalie and Tucker are snuggling on the loveseat, completely ignoring the madness happening in front of them. If Matthew wins, Nolan will start a video game tournament and force Tucker to play. It's the only way Nolan stands a chance to beat Tucker at anything, and even then, Tucker wins nine times out of ten.

"You okay over here?" Adam, my oldest and most serious brother, asks and sits down next to me on the couch.

"Yeah." I smile at him, content to be surrounded by my family.

"You're quieter than usual."

"It's kind of hard to get a word in with those two yahoos."

"Fair, except you'd normally be refereeing the two yahoos to make sure they didn't hurt each other." Adam's stare makes me want to squirm. He has an uncanny ability to know exactly what to say—or not say—that makes people open up. Especially me. Out of all my brothers, I'm closest to Adam. He's the one I've always gone to when I had a problem I needed help solving. He's the one I'd seek out when I had a bad day or just needed a steady presence when I felt like my world was tilting. And after all this time, I think he knows things aren't quite right in my world. He's seen me at my worst enough times that it's probably instinct by now.

He'd be right, too. I just can't bring myself to talk about it. Every time I try, my heart races, and my throat closes on the words that so desperately need to come out. Logically, I know if I tell people, it'll make me feel better. But I also know these people will start smothering me with their need to protect me, and if I let that happen, I might just break in two.

So, I keep my mouth shut and keep the words locked inside my heart, hoping that eventually, they'll just go away. "Just not feeling myself today, I guess."

Adam's gaze is scrutinizing, reading everything I'm not saying. Instead of pushing, he wraps his arm around my shoulder and squeezes me. "When you're ready," he whispers. The sting of tears behind my eyes makes me clench my teeth to keep them from flowing. That's the last thing I need right now.

"Tap out!" Matthew shouts, thankfully pulling my attention back to the mayhem on the floor.

The frustrated growl from Nolan precedes his hand slapping the floor. Mathew stands with a whoop while Nolan pouts. The whole interaction is the distraction I needed to make me forget the heaviness of the moment.

"How's it going with Ben?" Natalie asks. My cheeks immediately start burning at the mention of his name. Her question was innocent since all she knows is he's been a jerk of a boss since he got here. I haven't told her anything about us as it would lead to questions about how we became friends in the first place.

I'm not even sure what I would tell her. Since our moment in his office earlier this week, we haven't had time to talk about it. Hilariously, his mom has been cockblocking him in the evenings while she renovates his dad's office. He's been having to move around all their furniture because his mom can't decide how she wants things arranged. There have been several text messages sent containing only curse words. Then he FaceTimes me with his adorably grumpy face, threatening punishments when I laugh.

"Who's Ben?" Matthew demands.

"Her new boss. He's been an asshole to the whole clinic. Has it gotten any better?"

"Um, yes. He's been much better the last few weeks. He included us in his plans to start a fund for people who can't afford to pay for visits."

"That doesn't sound assholish," Nolan points out.

"I think he just had a hard time adjusting to the change in circumstances. He never planned to take over his dad's clinic in the first place."

Natalie squints her eyes at me, a calculating expression taking over her face. I don't have time to figure out what it's about before Adam interrupts. "Wait, is your new boss Ben Crawford? Didn't we go to high school with him?"

"Yeah, I think you did."

Being the most popular guys, they had a lot of friends. I'm surprised they remember Ben at all. I was lucky to have already established friendships before high school because the number of girls who thought they could get to my brothers by being friends with me was astounding. Without Natalie, Lucy, and Megan, I wouldn't have had any real friends.

"I remember him. He was the guy we went out to Bendan Point to…" Matthew trails off. Everyone knows Bendan Point is where teenagers go to either get high, have sex, or jump the cliffs into the lake. A lot of times, it's all three.

"To what?" Natalie grins.

"Nothing. The point is we know who he is." The steel in Adam's voice offers no room for argument.

"But he's better now? He's not giving you any more trouble?" Carter, the quietest of all of us, asks.

"No, things have calmed down a bit."

"How have your training sessions been going?" Tucker asks, and I cringe. Jesus, what is with my family outing all my secrets without knowing they're outing my secrets?

"They've been fine."

"What training?" Adam asks.

"And why didn't you tell us about it?" Matthew's words have a hint of hurt behind them, which makes my gust twist. He and I have always bonded over our athleticism. He's the one who helped me train for the triathlon I did a few years ago. The one who gives me workout routines to keep my strength up. If I was going to start doing any type of training, I should've done it with him.

"I started learning self-defense. I'd always wanted to try my hand at it, so I went to Dax Pierce's gym and asked him to train me."

"She's pretty good. I saw her train the other day." Tucker adds. All I'm hoping for is a distraction. I know they're going to ask more questions I can't answer right now, and I don't want to lie to them any more than I already am. It's killing me to keep what happened from them, but the alternative would be worse.

"Dinner's ready, kids!" Mom shouts from the kitchen. I let out a deep breath, thankful for Mom's distraction.

"You and I are going to talk, missy," Natalie hisses in my ear. Being my best friend, I'm not surprised she picked up on all my distress. Unlike Adam, she'll have no qualms about forcing me to talk. I just have to figure out what to say before she corners me.

Dinner is as loud as it always is, with everyone talking over one another. All my parents can do is grin at each other across the long table, since neither one of them can keep up with their kids.

Their relationship has always seemed so unattainable to me for some reason. As if they have this perfect marriage you could only ever dream of copying in your own life. I think I've been perpetually single because I know it will take a very specific person to give me all the things I want in a relationship. It's why I just date around if I feel like it instead of putting pressure on myself to find the right one right now. I don't want to settle for just any random guy who comes along. I want the man who is going to worship me while I worship him.

My mom would be pissed at me if she knew I thought her marriage was perfect. She's always been open with me and my siblings about how hard it can be to maintain a solid relationship. It doesn't only apply to marriage either. Communication was drilled into us siblings, too, which is why I think we're all so close. We don't typically fight with each other or have petty arguments over dumb things.

It makes lying to them so much more difficult. One day soon, I'll have the courage to tell them.

Just not today.

21

BEN

She's magnificent. Fucking heart-stopping. I've never seen someone move with as much grace and precision as Sara does. My workouts fall by the wayside every time she's here to train with Dax. A quick look around the room tells me I'm not the only one affected by her. More than half the guys working out can't take their eyes off her either.

A little flare of jealousy burns in my stomach at seeing the looks on their faces. I have no idea what to do about it because Sara isn't technically mine. Not yet. I have no claim to her, no leg to stand on to justify my possessive feelings. She could go off with any one of these guys, and I wouldn't be able to say boo about it since I haven't told her what I want.

I could have.

We've talked on the phone almost every night this week while Mom's been the cockblocker extraordinaire. I've just been too much of a chickenshit to tell her how I feel. I'd like to say it's because I'm not ready to try again so soon after Rebecca's betrayal, but it wouldn't be the truth. For the very first time in my life, I've met someone I can be my whole self with. Someone who has already seen me at my worst and still wants to hang out with me.

I know how rare that is.

I know she's special. It's why I'm scared out of my mind to jump into this. What if I hurt her? What if the person I am now isn't who she truly wants? Being the successful vet at one of the top clinics in Greensboro was the person I thought I needed to be. The one who had it all. The beautiful fiancée, the slick downtown apartment, the successful career. I ticked every box that society measures as success.

And it was all fake.

Everything was built on the lies I told myself in order to reach a level of success I thought would finally make me happy. I did love my job, but it was also a crutch. Another way to prove I was good enough. When all the lies were stripped away, I was finally able to see exactly how miserable I was in that life.

Now, as I watch Sara get so close to kicking Dax's ass, I know this is the life I've truly wanted.

And I'm scared shitless I'm going to mess it up.

When Dax and Sara take a breather, Sara's eyes meet mine across the room. She grins at me, a beautiful flush creeping up her neck. Then she winks at me before turning back to listen to whatever Dax is telling her.

This is so happening. Even if it ends in destruction, I couldn't stay away from her if my life depended on it.

I walk toward the ring, my eyes glued to the play of muscles in Sara's legs. "Got enough gas left to show me your moves?" I ask, leaning my arms against the ropes.

"You sure you want to chance it? Wouldn't want to ruin your bad-boy reputation," Sara taunts.

A laugh bursts from my chest. I know she's fully capable of taking me down. She's only been taking lessons for a little over a week, and she's almost able to take down Dax.

"Careful man, she's lethal."

Sara grins at Dax's praise.

I jump into the ring and throw on some gear. "Show me what you got, Shortcake."

With a glare, she squares up with me. Out of the corner of my eye, I see a crowd forming around the ring. Everyone here knows I'm a fighter. I'm decent at it, too, so they know this will be a good show. My attention solely on the woman in front of me, I make the first move, jabbing at Sara's ribs. She blocks, countering it with a jab to my solar plexus. Round and round we go, trading jabs, each of us putting more effort into our hits.

I'm having a hard time focusing on the fight, completely distracted by my opponent. The flush in her cheeks, the wisps of hair falling from her messy bun framing her face, the way her chest heaves when trying to catch her breath. All I keep seeing is her exactly like she is, surrounded by white sheets, her hands tied to the headboard.

Sara takes advantage of my distraction, grabbing my arm, wrapping her leg around mine, and taking me straight down to the mat with a thump. My breath puffs out of my lungs with the impact as the crowd cheers her on. All I can see is Sara's gleaming hazel eyes hovering over my head as she gloats. It takes every ounce of control I possess not to wrap my hand around her neck and pull her body down onto mine. If there wasn't a crowd, I would've done it.

"I win." She laughs, making me grin back at her. She holds a hand out to help me up as the crowd whistles their approval before breaking up.

"Don't think this game is over yet, Shortcake," I say low in her ear so only she can hear. "We're only just getting started."

The shiver that moves up her spine tells me she knows exactly what I'm talking about while the heat in her golden eyes says she is ready for whatever comes next. I shift away from her, giving myself some room to breathe before I strip her down in the middle of the gym.

"We need to work on your form, princess," Dax taunts.

"I'm only as good as my teacher, right?" I throw back at him. I haven't trained with him since Sara took my spot, so I'm rusty. Sara's also just good enough to take down a six-foot-five man. Pride be damned, she's 100 percent better than me.

With a quick punch to my arm that makes my fingers tingle, Dax jumps out of the ring.

Sara and I follow behind, grabbing our stuff from the floor. "You really are a natural. I'd happily get my butt kicked by you any time."

Sara looks up at me as if she doesn't quite believe my words. I get it. I'm a mountain of a man with asshole tendencies. You'd never guess I'd be cool with getting beat by a girl. However, this girl deserves every accolade.

"Thanks. It feels good to know I have the skills now." She says it so quietly I almost don't catch her words. The impact of them is still the same. With how good of a fighter she is, it's hard to remember the reason she's learning all of this in the first place.

"Want to come over?" Her eyes are wide, vulnerability seeping out of them. I'm just not sure if it's because of the attack or because of what might happen when I come over.

"Yes."

"I'll meet you at my house, then."

All I can do is nod my head. I'm not sure what she wants from me tonight. I thought I knew a few minutes ago when we were in the ring, but after mentioning the attack, I'm not sure what she has in mind. It doesn't matter either way. As long as I get to spend more time with her, then I'm good.

Although, if I'm honest, I would really like to have sex with her tonight. It's been close to torture this week, having her so close and not being able to do a single thing about it.

It only takes us a few minutes to get to her house before we're walking up the sidewalk and inside. Koda and Luna greet us with wagging tails, following Sara closely as she walks into the kitchen.

"Do you want a drink?" She's drumming her fingers on the counter, not quite making eye contact.

"Sara, look at me," I say, stepping into her space. When her eyes meet mine, it feels as if my whole world tilts back to normal. Like it's finally right-side-up, all because I have her full attention on me. "Tell me why you're nervous."

"I haven't done this in a while."

"Haven't done what?"

A flush creeps over her cheeks. "Invited a guy home with me." She raises her eyebrows, suggesting she means for sex.

"Good," I say before I can stop the word from coming out. A small part of me is glad she hasn't been in a relationship with anyone recently despite how hypocritical it is. "I won't have to worry about any ex-boyfriends trying to come back into your life."

"What about your ex?"

"She was pretty content with me leaving, so I doubt she'll be back at all."

Sara just nods her head. I can tell she's still unsure of what to do next, so instead of letting her continue to stew, I boost her up onto the counter. My hands land on her hips as I step between her legs. With the added height, she's only a few inches shorter than me now, allowing us to take each other in.

"So, here's the deal. My preference is to take over right now. Tell you exactly what to do, when to do it, and fully expect you to follow instructions. The only decision you have to make is whether you want in." I pause, letting her soak in my words. My hands roam down the side of her legs then back up the top of her thighs. "On the flip side, if you don't listen, I'll punish you, which can look any number of ways. A spanking, delaying gratification, whatever works at the moment. All that requires a lot of trust, so we'll take things slow. One experience at a—"

"Yes."

"What?"

"I want that. All of it. I need to let go, and I need you to take control so I can. I'm tired of constantly worrying about doing the right thing. Praying that I'm making the right choices. I need you."

Her words have the spit drying in my mouth. Blood drains straight into my cock so fast, I'm light-headed. There's one more important piece she needs to know before I let my baser instincts take over. "You have full control. If you say stop, it does. Do you understand?"

"Yes."

"Take off your shirt."

22

SARA

"Take off your shirt."

The words pin me to the counter almost as steadily as Ben's hands. Something in my brain took over when he started laying out all of his preferences, and I said yes. I wanted to say yes. I still want to say yes, but that doesn't mean I'm capable of turning off my brain immediately, no matter how amazing it sounds.

Ben runs his hands up my sides and underneath the hem of my tank top. "Stop thinking," he whispers in my ear. The brush of his lips against the outer shell of my ear makes a shiver run down my spine. The feeling of his calloused hands against my skin makes me want more, and I finally follow Ben's instruction to take off my shirt.

"Good girl."

Jesus, that should not be as hot as it is.

"Wait."

Ben's hands immediately freeze on me.

"I'm sweaty. I smell horrible. Taking off my shirt, I just got an awful whiff of myself."

A laugh bursts from Ben at my statement, and I realize he was probably worried I didn't want to keep going.

"I don't mind a little bit of sweat, Sara." His hands start to roam again, his thumbs gently brushing over my nipples through my sports bra. They immediately tighten, begging for more. "We're both sweaty and a little smelly. It's a part of being human. We can shower later."

I open my mouth to protest, but Ben bites down on my bottom lip, effectively ending whatever rebuttal I was about to say. My hands lift into his hair as his mouth descends over mine, pulling me into the most drugging kiss I've ever experienced. His tongue twines with mine, exploring every inch of my mouth, while his hands begin kneading my breasts.

Needing him closer, I grab my sports bra and awkwardly yank it off my body. Those were not made to take off sexily.

Ben didn't seem to notice because his hands immediately cup my breasts, squeezing and playing with them like he knows exactly how I want to be touched. I fist the hem of Ben's cutoff T-shirt and lift it over his head. I'm momentarily struck dumb at the sight of his chest. I've seen it before, but not this close and not in this context. It's just a wall of muscle. Each ab is perfectly outlined, leading down to what I can assume is... Holy shit. "You have a penis ravine." My hands fist into the waistband of his shorts, yanking them down so I can see it clearly.

Ben laughs, but I think it's more out of confusion than anything. "What?"

The minute Ben's shorts are around his ankles, my hands land on his hips to trace the V-lines leading to a fucking *impressive* erection. He groans at my touch, his muscles flexing his hips forward.

He grabs my hands, pulling them away from him. "This is not going how I expected it to go," he grumbles, making me laugh.

"Sorry. I got a little distracted by the ravines."

Shaking his head, Ben steps out of his shorts, taking his socks with him. Fully naked and not a bit uncomfortable about it, he steps up to the counter, wraps his hands around my ass, and lifts me into his arms. Reacting to the sudden movement, I wrap my arms and legs around him to hold myself steady.

"What are we doing?"

Instead of answering me, Ben continues walking to my bedroom. I glance at the dogs, who are laying in their beds, not giving one care that some guy is manhandling their mom. Apparently, they trust Ben as much as I do.

Once we're in my room, Ben lays me down on the bed before scanning the space like he's looking for something. When he finds it, he comes back to the bed, a dark look in his eye that makes me squirm. He looks so dominating and strong, it takes everything in me not to beg him to fuck me right this minute. No amount of pleading would get me what I want.

"I'm going to get you out of your head and into the moment. Do you trust me?"

"Yes." My answer doesn't even require thought. I trust this man more than I trust most of the people in my life.

His lips tip up in the corners at my answer. "Good. Close your eyes."

I do as I'm told before feeling something silky being laid across my eyes. Ben wraps it around my head, tying it by my temple.

"Is that okay?" His words whisper across my neck, sending goose bumps down my arms.

"Yes," I breathe. Ben's lips coast down my chest, ringing my breast in a soft caress. I lift my hands to direct his head where I want it, but before I can get to him, Ben grabs my hands, lifting them above my head.

"I can tie your hands to your headboard, Sara, or you can keep them still. Your choice."

The idea of having my hands tied sends a shiver of desire down my spine. God, this is more than I've ever experienced in my whole life, and we haven't even done anything yet. Instead of answering Ben, I wrap my fingers around the iron rails of my headboard.

"Good girl."

Fuck, I love that.

Ben's tongue traces the bottom curve of my breast. I have a fleeting thought that I wish they were bigger, but then he pulls my nipple deep into his mouth, shutting off every thought I had before. His teeth pull on the bud, making my hips flex. Jesus, that feels good.

His hand starts manipulating my other nipple, stirring a long-dormant inferno in my core. Is it possible to orgasm just from nipple play? It's never happened before, but I'm ridiculously close right now.

"Ben," I moan, needing more from him.

His hands slide down my rib cage to the waistband of my shorts, pulling them off in one smooth move, leaving me fully bared to him.

With Ben at the foot of the bed, not touching me, I feel as if I'm putting on a show for him, even though I'm just laying here.

His hands run down the tops of my feet, slowly roaming up my shins to right above my knees. I gasp when he pushes on my inner thighs, opening me up to him.

"Fuck, you're beautiful." Ben's hands slide further up my thighs, his thumbs rubbing at the juncture where my leg meets my hip. I whimper at how close he is to my pussy. I need him to touch me more than I need my next breath.

"Ben, please."

Suddenly, his tongue runs up the length of me, eliciting a long, keening moan that seems to come from somewhere deep within me. Without being able to see him, every touch and slide of his skin against mine feels like electricity is snapping across my body.

Ben chuckles against my center while keeping up the

slow exploration with his mouth. He hitches my legs over his shoulders, opening me wider to his tongue. As he builds up speed, my hips start to rock against him in an attempt to get more. I feel as if I'm on the edge of a mountain, wanting to leap off the side but too afraid of the impact when I land.

When he slides two fingers inside me, I don't have a choice. My thighs start to tremble around his head while my hands ache around the bars of my headboard. Every muscle in my body tightens as my orgasm barrels through me so hard I'm not sure I'm going to survive.

Ben doesn't slow his fingers or his tongue, fucking me into either a second orgasm or making the first one continue. I can't tell through my delirium.

"I can't…" I pant. "Fuck."

"I'm pretty sure I just proved you wrong. You absolutely can fuck," Ben says, his hands running across my thighs that are still wrapped around his shoulders.

"You did all the work."

"And it was fucking phenomenal."

Ben starts kissing up my stomach, his hands sliding up my sides until he reaches my arms. He gently pulls my hands from around the bars of my headboard, rubbing the life back into them. When he's done, he slides the material covering my eyes off my face. I blink the darkness away to find Ben's denim blue eyes taking me in, a small smirk pulling at the corner of his mouth.

I pull him down to kiss me, my taste still on his lips. As our tongues twine, my hips flex into his, his cock rubbing against my slit. We both groan at the slide of him through my wetness; the pressure on my still-sensitive clit is almost more than I can bear.

"I need more, Ben," I whisper against his lips. "Please give me more."

"Shit. I don't have a condom."

"I'm clean. And I have an IUD, so I'm protected," I tell him hesitantly. "I have some in the bathroom if you're not comfortable with that, though. I'd completely understand."

"I'm clean, too. I got tested after I found out about… Anyway, I'm clean." Ben spears me with a look so full of longing it takes my breath away.

Reaching down, I take his cock and guide it to my entrance. He drives his hips forward, entering me in one quick thrust that makes us both groan out loud.

"Fuck, you feel good." Ben groans as he starts to pull out, only to drive back in again, going deeper than before. He sets a punishing rhythm of hard drives, hitting a spot I've only ever been able to reach with a vibrator. It sets my body into a frenzy of sensations, the pressure mounting higher than the first time.

My hands dig into Ben's shoulders, his back muscles flexing under my grasp. He leans onto one elbow to grab my breast, pinching my nipple in between his thumb and forefinger.

"Yes, yes, yes. God, don't stop." The words are desperate, pleading as my body reaches the peak of pleasure.

"Never," Ben growls into my neck.

His teeth clamp down on the space where my neck meets my shoulder, and I detonate. Every inner muscle clenches around Ben's cock, letting me feel each ridge as he pumps into me.

"Oh, fuck." Ben's body tenses up, his shaft swelling inside me as he comes. It sends tremors through my body, triggering another small orgasm.

As Ben's hips slow, both of our chests are heaving, trying to catch our breaths. My entire body feels as if I ran a triathlon and then did a tough mudder after that, except way more satisfied.

How is this man real?

Ben wraps his arms around my body, then rolls onto his

back, taking me with him. The sudden switch has a squeak popping out of my mouth.

"That was quite the move." I settle my hands on Ben's chest, laying my head down on top of them.

"I sucked if that move is the one that made the biggest impression," Ben grumbles, his chest rumbling under me.

"Well, if I complimented you any more on your sexual prowess, I don't think your ego would fit in my tiny house."

A laugh flies out of him, which makes me lift my head. His eyes are shining in the lamplight as he looks at me. I set my chin on my hand to keep staring at him. His blond hair is a mess on his head, his crooked nose gives the indication it was broken at some point, and his full lips are tipped up in a smile.

I think I could stare at him for a long time and never grow tired of it.

"You okay?" he asks, his hands running across my back in soothing circles. It makes me want to purr.

"I'm perfect."

"Good."

"You're a good man, Benjamin Crawford."

He looks at me as if trying to gauge my sincerity. "You make me better."

"Only because I'm not afraid to kick you in the ass when you need it," I joke.

"Exactly," Ben says, but he's not smiling. "I can be an asshole, even when I don't want to be, and without you telling me to fix it, I would've kept letting my anger fester until it was all I could see. You make me better."

Overwhelmed and unsure of what to say back, I lean forward to kiss him. I've always wanted to find the one I can be my full and honest self with. Someone who will see me for who I am, not who they think I should be. Ben makes me feel that way.

I just hope I can be that person for him, too.

UNKNOWN

She's finally home.

As her car pulls into the driveway, I release a breath I didn't know I was holding. She's normally home most of the day on Saturdays. Where could she have gone that would keep her from me? I can't imagine why she'd need to do anything today. She grocery shopped yesterday and took the dogs to the park this morning. There was no reason for her to leave again.

She gets out of her car, walking up the sidewalk. I love when she wears tank tops. They show off all her creamy white skin. So soft, I want to run my hands across it, my mouth. So beautiful.

Wait.

What's he doing here? Why is he parking in her driveway?

I thought they only worked together. He's not supposed to still be hanging around her. She showed me she loved me. Every time she read my notes, she smiled. I watched her accept each gift I've given her, knowing I was the one to send them.

I walk around the house to see through the back kitchen window she always leaves open. The lights are dim, but I can see everything as plain as day.

When muscle man boosts her onto the counter, I have to bite

down on my fist to keep from yelling. No one is allowed to touch her but me!

How could she do this to me?

We were going to be together soon. Now, she's let another man touch her how I want to touch her. He's getting to see all her silky skin that was only for me.

Her shirt clears her head, showing me every inch of her beautiful body. My cock starts to grow at the sight of her. She's so beautiful. I've never seen this much of her.

A growl rips through my throat as she grabs hold of his pants.

No.

I close my eyes. This wasn't how it was supposed to go. I squeeze my shaft, trying to rid myself of the pressure.

The plan has changed.

She's ruined everything, and now I'm going to have to tell her exactly what happens when she doesn't do what she's told.

SARA

A knock on the door precedes a chorus of barking as the dogs race to see who arrived at their house. Even Minnie strolls into the living room from her hideaway in the gym to find out. The dogs are probably hoping it's Sadie. Those three have become such good friends over the last month.

Instead of a handsome man with his adorable pup, I open the door to Natalie, who has about six bags in her hands. Which, admittedly, is just as good for everyone involved.

"Hi, my sweet babies. How are you?" Natalie coos, squatting down to say hello. "Yes, of course, Auntie Nat brought you treats. She always brings you treats." Digging down into one of her bags, Natalie pulls out two peanut butter-flavored bones and a plush mouse toy. She hands each treat to their respective animal with a kiss on each of their heads.

"What about me?" I fake whine, giving her a hug when she stands up again.

"Don't you worry. I didn't forget about you." She opens one of her canvas bags, revealing a mountain of junk food, then rifles through another one to pull out a bottle of wine.

I fist pump the air. "I love you!"

"I know." Natalie walks through the living room into the kitchen to set her bags on the island. The dogs, having taken off with their treats the minute they were given, are lazing in their beds. They know they won't get anything else from Natalie.

I grab down the wine glasses, sliding them across the counter so Natalie can fill them.

"So, Tucker and I have news."

"What?"

"Noah is officially ours!" she squeals. "With the mess that went down with Hope and her bastard of an ex, we didn't want to say anything, but he's all moved in now."

"Oh, my god!" I wrap my arms around Natalie's shoulders, giving her a firm squeeze. "I'm so excited for you guys. How excited is Noah?"

"Ecstatic. He's picked out all the decorations for his room and has settled in really well. I'm not sure I'm prepared to handle all the downsides of being an official parent. He's always so well-behaved since we only get him on weekends. It's going to be hard when he starts pushing his boundaries."

"You're going to do just great. He loves you, and as long as he knows you're coming from a place of love and not meanness, you'll be just fine."

"Thanks." Her smile is wobbly as she takes a fortifying drink of wine.

There's a short silence as we both take another drink.

"I slept with Ben!" I blurt out. I don't think I realized how hard it's been to hold on to that little nugget of information.

Natalie chokes on her wine, her eyes bugging out at me. "What?"

I cringe. "I had sex with Ben."

"Holy shit. Way to bury the lead!"

"I also have to tell you something else, but you have to swear not to tell anyone."

She squints her eyes. "Does this have something to do with why you were weird at family dinner the other night?"

All I do is nod.

Natalie thinks over my ask before waving at me to continue.

"I..." This is just as hard as I thought it would be. "A couple of weeks ago, I was attacked. Someone tried to kidnap me in the parking lot of La Mensa. Ben saved me from whoever it was, and we've been hanging out ever since, and now, we're sleeping together, and it's the best sex of my life." The words tumble from me like a dam being opened after years of doing its job.

"Well, fuck." Natalie blows out a breath. She picks up her wine glass, knocking back the rest of its contents before filling it again. She walks into the living room and plops down on the couch without so much as a word. I follow behind her with my wine glass dangling from my fingers.

"Okay, let's start with the bad stuff, then end with the good. You were attacked?"

"Yeah, I'm not 100 percent on the details, they're still a little fuzzy, but I was walking to my car when some asshole grabbed me and tried to get me in his car. Ben came out of nowhere to stop the whole thing, saving my life in the process."

"Why didn't you tell us? Cooper needs to know what happened."

"For starters, I was freaking the fuck out, then Ben and I got caught up in emergency surgery that same night. I didn't have too much time to think about it when it happened. When I woke up the next day, I couldn't wrap my head around the attack, so I just sort of pretended like it didn't happen until I could process the whole thing. It feels a little pointless to tell Cooper now."

Natalie's glare says exactly what she thinks about that last part. If our roles were reversed, I'd probably feel the same way. The logical part of me knows I should've told Cooper the night it happened, but the emotional part of me wasn't ready to voice how weak I was. How I let some asshole take me with barely any fight. And if I'm honest, I still don't want to make a big deal of it. There's nothing Cooper can do to find this guy; making a big show of telling everyone feels silly.

"Right, well, I don't think it's pointless, but I'm not going to push you to do things you're not ready to do. Just know, I don't agree with your choices. Is this why you've been taking self-defense classes?"

"Yeah, I started them to feel prepared in case I was ever attacked again, but now, it's become something I enjoy doing. A lot. I feel strong, capable. Like a major badass."

Natalie grins. Of all people, she's the one who would understand wanting to be a badass. She's always been head-strong and in charge of her life. She's independent, almost to a fault, and barely lets Tucker have an opinion about what she does. But she was also assaulted and then subsequently had her house set on fire with her trapped inside. She almost died that night and still battles the scars both inside and outside. She's a survivor. Someone I look to when things get hard. It's why I didn't want to bother anyone with what happened to me. Between what happened to Hope and even to Nat and Quinn, my issues weren't nearly as important.

"Okay, now tell me about the best sex of your life."

Heat rushes into my cheeks. I didn't mean to tell her that part, but when the word vomit started, there was no stopping what came out.

It's true, though. Ben is the best sex I've ever had. The dominating thing was hot. Seriously hot. There's also a deeper level of connection between us that wasn't there before. Which feels weird to say since we haven't been seeing each other very long.

"He took care of me, Nat. After the attack, he let me be a

part of the surgery, knowing I needed the distraction. Then he held me when I broke down after we got home. And then he stayed and spent the night on the couch. I didn't even ask him to. Ever since then, we've been getting closer."

"Wow."

"I was surprised, too. He can still be moody, but he's no longer an asshole. Sometimes it can be a little hot."

"I so understand how hot the broody thing can be." Nat's eyebrow raise makes me laugh. Tucker is the epitome of the dark, bad boy vibe.

"Nat…"

Her face goes serious when she hears my tone.

"He has the penis ravines."

Natalie groans. "God, those V-lines are so hot. I don't blame you for jumping on that faster than a tick on a dog." She leans in to clink her glass against mine. "Proud of you."

I bust out laughing, happy to have this time with my best friend. Getting the truth off my chest helped me feel lighter than I have in weeks, which is not a surprise. Still doesn't make it any easier to talk about, though.

"You better not tell my brothers anything."

"Cross my heart. Even though I think you need to tell them."

"Adam asked what was going on at dinner." I grimace.

"He's always had an inside track on your emotions."

"I'll tell them soon. I promise."

"Good. Now tell me more about these penis ravines."

Giggling, I tell her about how seriously sexy Ben was the other night. I never realized the dominance thing would work for me. I guess I've always found the idea of it interesting but hadn't found a guy I trusted enough to experiment with it. I trusted Ben the minute he held me while I cried. It was like he unlocked something inside me that's been long dormant, waiting for someone like him to come around.

We haven't talked about what it is we're doing with each

other. I'm certain we're more than a friends-with-benefits situation, but what does that mean in the long run? Are we in a relationship? Dating? Are those the same thing?

I don't know. What I do know is I love the orgasms this man can dole out, so if I'm getting those, I'll be okay for a while.

25

BEN

The steam hangs heavy in the small bathroom as I step out of the shower. The room was not designed for someone of my size. If I stretched my arms out, I could almost touch the walls at the same time. Makes me wish my house was done. I've been stopping by periodically to see the progress, and it already looks twenty times better than it did, despite the mess.

Wiping the steam from the mirror, I shave my face and brush my teeth. When I'm done in the bathroom, I head to my bedroom to get dressed and slip on my favorite grey slacks and a short-sleeved button-down shirt.

Tonight, I'm finally taking Sara out on a date. Even though we've been hanging out for a few weeks now, I have yet to actually take her out. The start of our relationship was a little unconventional, and tonight, I want to make sure she knows I'm in this and ready to make her mine. This isn't some summer hook-up or rebound from Rebecca. She's the real deal to me. Someone I could see myself building a future with instead of checking off a box like a to-do list.

I know that's what Rebecca was to me. She was filling a role I thought I needed to have in order to be successful. She was independent, had her own money, and came from a good family. Those were all the requirements I thought I needed. What we had wasn't truly a partnership; it was more of a business deal.

Sara could be a real partner to me. Someone I can trust to be my true self with instead of feeling like I have to put on this façade of strength. I also want her to feel comfortable relying on me. To know that I will always be there for her anytime she needs me.

I hope I can prove it to her tonight. She decided she wanted to try to eat at La Mensa. She hasn't been back since she had a panic attack when we tried to pick up her car. I told her she doesn't need to push herself too hard, that what she went through was intense, and it doesn't make her weak if she's not ready.

By the set of her jaw and her raised eyebrow, I knew she was dead set on having dinner there, so I just kissed her until she melted into me and told her how much I admired her strength.

I head downstairs to get ready to leave, finding Mom piddling around in the kitchen. She and Dad already had dinner, so I know she's only hanging out to weasel details from me about what I'm doing tonight. She thinks she's sneaky, but I know her game.

"You going out?"

"Mm-hmm. I'm taking Sadie with me. Probably won't be back tonight." I bend over to give Sadie some love. She's become buddies with Koda and Luna, which is great for me since I don't have to feel guilty about leaving her with my mom and dad all the time. Plus, I miss her when I'm gone all night.

"Who are you going out with?"

"A friend."

"A lady friend?" The hopefulness in Mom's voice makes me laugh.

"Yes, Mom. I'm going out with Sara Ellis." It's probably not a good idea to give her more information than necessary, but I'm hoping if she knows who I'm dating, she'll stop trying to set me up with her friends' daughters.

"Oh, I love her. Bring her over for dinner. How about Sunday night? That'll be perfect. Your dad can grill up steaks. It'll be a special occasion."

Well, shit. If I don't bring Sara, Dad's going to be pissed at me for messing with his chance to get red meat, which Mom knows will bother me since Dad and I are finally getting along again.

I glare at her, shaking my head. "You're something else."

Mom's grin is triumphant as I kiss her cheek to say good-bye. "Tell Sara I say hello."

I roll my eyes. Scheming, manipulative woman. But what would I do without her?

* * *

SARA SQUEEZES my hand as we pull into the parking lot of La Mensa. The summer sunshine is still going strong, brightening what would've been the dark corners of the lot. I park my car and wait for Sara to tell me she's ready. I didn't make a reservation, so we'll probably have to wait on a table for a while, but I didn't want to make her feel guilty if she decided she wasn't ready to go inside.

I glance at Sara to make sure she's not having a panic attack and find she's staring at the corner of the lot where the car was parked.

"Hey." I wait as her eyes slowly meet mine; fear is mixed with so much strength, it takes my breath away. "You can do this. You're strong, capable, and have the skills to kick ass."

She stares at me, seeming to gather all her courage to overcome the rising panic I see in her eyes. Then she nods her head and opens her door. I jump out of the car to meet her on the other side, and we walk towards the building. The minute we step through the doors, Sara takes a deep breath, her shoulders relaxing while a small, triumphant smile lines her face.

"I'm proud of you," I whisper into her temple as we walk up to the hostess stand. Sara squeezes my hand, letting me know she heard me. "Table for two, please," I ask the tiny high school girl behind the podium. She tells us it will only be about fifteen minutes, which I think is the universe's way of rewarding Sara's bravery.

And true to her word, fifteen minutes pass when we're able to get a table. As soon as we sit down, I put in an order for breadsticks, and Sara and I both order glasses of wine.

The minute those baskets of breadsticks land on the table, Sara is well on her way to being back to normal, which naturally makes me laugh. A good breadstick can go a long way to making you feel better. And if this is all it takes for me to keep her happy, I'll happily go broke buying them for her.

"How much longer until your house is done?" Sara asks around a bite of bread. Her eating habits crack me up. She told me it's because she grew up with four brothers who were like a hoard of hungry crocodiles when it came to food. I think she just couldn't care less what people think. Either way, I love it.

"About a month. I just hope Mom doesn't come up with more ideas for redecorating. Oh, hey, speaking of my mom, she shanghaied me into forcing you to come over for dinner on Sunday, if you're available." I cringe. "Please be available. She told my dad he could grill steaks since it'll be a 'special occasion'. He'll be so mad at me if I don't make sure you're there."

Sara laughs, apparently finding my pain hilarious. "Sure, I can be there."

"Thank you." I squeeze her hand across the table. "And just know, I would've gotten you out of it if I could."

"I don't mind. You know I like your parents. It'll be fun." She shrugs her shoulders, a happy smile on her face.

"You know, it actually might be kind of fun. I've never brought a girl home before."

"What about Rebecca?"

I shake my head. "She wasn't a small-town kind of girl, so my parents always came to Greensboro. Or I came home alone."

"Weird. You didn't bring any girls home when you were in high school?"

"Nope, I didn't date much in school. I was too mad at the world."

"You know, I had the biggest crush on you back then." Pink tints her cheeks at her confession.

"Really?"

"Yeah, I even tried flirting with you once, and you looked at me like I had three heads." Her laugh is filled with embarrassment.

"Wow, you've had to deal with way more of my asshole tendencies than I thought. Sorry about that."

"Eh, water under the bridge at this point, although, when they come back, don't expect me to just lie down and take it."

"*When* they come back?" I ask incredulously. Her smart mouth makes me want to take her home and spank her. Or give her something else to do with it instead.

"Yeah. Those sorts of things don't just go away, ya know. But I'm prepared now and will dole out my sass appropriately."

"What if I spanked the sass out of you?"

A shiver moves through her. "Not possible. But you sure as hell can try."

"Fuck. Okay, new topic before I scandalize the entire town with the raging hard-on I have in my pants right now."

Sara's eyes glint with something mischievous, but she

nods her head. I hope that look means she's planning something for later. "Do you ever miss Greensboro?"

Unprepared for her question, I have to take a moment to formulate my answer. "In some ways, yes, I do. I miss the frenetic energy of the city, although I'm getting used to the slower pace of Sonoma far quicker than I expected." I pause, thinking back on my life there. "You know, I mostly miss going to this little bakery around the corner from my apartment. They were dog-friendly, so on the Sundays I woke up early enough, I'd take Sadie with me to get breakfast. They had these famous dog biscuits she loved, and we'd sit on their patio, eating our treats. It was always a great start to the day."

If I'm honest, those moments were the only time I felt content. Everything was always about striving to reach the next goal. Working as hard as possible to meet these unachievable standards because I thought that's what would make me a good vet, a good son. But being in Sonoma, being forced to slow down and take inventory of what I want, I know I wasn't happy in Greensboro.

"I bet Sadie loved that."

"She absolutely did. People-watching was always her favorite. That's about it, though. My life there was hectic. Constantly moving from one thing to the next. It's been an adjustment coming back to the slow pace of Sonoma, but it's also been nice."

"You talked before about finding someone else to run the clinic in your place. Are you still thinking about it?"

Ah, Sara's questions don't feel so out of the blue anymore. "I'm sticking around, Sara. For good. When I first took over, I stubbornly thought I could find someone else to run the clinic and it would be fine, but in all actuality, I would never have been able to let go of the reins. It was always going to be mine; I just needed a little push to see it that way."

Her smile beams across the room, making me feel ten feet

tall. It's nice to know she wanted me to stay. That she was worried I wasn't going to stick around.

When our food arrives, our conversation switches to something lighter, but her comments stay in the back of my mind as we eat. Does she not know how much she's come to mean to me over the past few weeks? Even before the attack, I noticed her. How much she cared for the clinic, her willingness to put her own needs aside when someone else needs something. She's unlike anyone I've ever known.

We finish eating, pack up the leftover food into containers, and head back out to the car. With the food bag in one hand, I wrap my arm around Sara's shoulders, leading her across the parking lot. I can feel the tension in her shoulders as we get close, her breaths coming quicker than before. I open the car door, helping her into the seat before jogging around the back to get in on the driver's side.

Instead of trying to distract her, I just drive us out of the parking lot. I know being safe at home will be better than any distraction I can come up with.

I pull into her driveway, ready to head inside, when Sara stops me with a hand to my forearm.

"Thank you. For dinner, for fucking phenomenal sex,"—she laughs—"but most importantly, for being someone I can lean on. You're a special guy, Benjamin Crawford, and I'm one lucky woman to have you."

"I am the lucky one here. You're everything a guy could ever hope for in a partner, Sara. I'm grateful you're letting me be a part of your life when I know you don't really need me around. You're plenty capable of living a beautiful life without me. And you do, for the record. Have me, that is. I'm yours wholeheartedly until you tell me you don't want me anymore. Which hopefully doesn't happen. Ever."

Sara grins, then leans in to press her lips against mine.

Naturally, the kiss turns indecent, our tongues dueling

for dominance while my hands fist in her hair to remind her who is in control around here.

I groan, pulling away from her before things get too out of hand. "Get inside. I want you naked and lying on your bed by the time I get the dogs settled in for the night."

With a whimper, Sara races into the house, me following closely behind her.

This woman is something else.

SARA

"I was able to get ahold of Margie at the animal shelter, and she's in for August."

Ben scribbles down my update on his legal pad, looking adorably scowly. "Fantastic. What about food?" he asks, keeping his eyes on the page. We're in the middle of an impromptu planning meeting for our first fundraiser, and Ben has gone into intense planning mode. He's been obsessive about the details, and if I didn't understand why he's been so serious about it, it would probably piss me off.

This fundraiser is his first attempt at doing something different from how his dad ran the clinic. I think he's worried people are either going to scoff at his efforts or laugh at them. What he doesn't realize is when one of our own is trying to make our town better, the entire community is going to show up to support it. Getting this city boy to understand that, though, has been a feat of epic proportions. I guess he can just be surprised when everyone shows up instead of believing they won't.

"The café is ready to provide an assortment of baked goods—cookies, mini cupcakes, that sort of stuff."

Ben checks a few more things off his list before looking

up at me. "This is coming together nicely. Thank you for all your hard work."

I grin at Ben. Before we got together, I highly doubt he would have even acknowledged the amount of work I did. Not because he wasn't thankful, but because he wouldn't have noticed. "No biggie. This is a great thing you're doing, Ben. I know a lot of people in town will benefit from it."

A small, self-conscious smile pulls at the corner of his lips. God, he could not be any cuter. I lean over his desk to give him a swift kiss. As soon as his lips meet mine, my body calms while simultaneously tightening in anticipation of what's to come. It seems being at work does nothing to tamp down my libido.

Ben groans against my mouth, my short peck turning into more as if we're teenagers unable to help ourselves. This is what he does to me—what he's done since he first stepped into the clinic.

I pull back despite Ben's fist in my hair. "Just because the door is shut does not mean we should be getting busy in your office. Save that for when the clinic is closed."

"But it sure would be fun to see how quiet you can be." Ben's grin is filthy, and I have to glare at him to hide how much I truly want to find out the answer.

Standing straight, I leave him with a final thought. "How about tonight you see how loud you can *make* me scream instead?"

Ben's jaw drops as I leave his office, giving me almost as much satisfaction as his dick does.

Walking out to the front, I check in with Susan to see if any of our appointments have changed and catch her up on the plan for the fundraiser. She's helping to organize everything, but I think she's secretly impressed with Ben's ability to plan. She's also been letting him do things that Dr. Charles was never allowed to do because nobody trusted him to keep the details straight. The man was brilliant with an animal, but he could not keep this clinic organized to save his life.

The front door chimes preceding the entry of someone I don't think I'd ever expect to walk into our clinic. Although, that's probably judgmental and unfair. She has sleek black hair, flawless makeup, a designer dress, and kick-ass heels. She's the embodiment of class. Someone I would expect to see in a magazine.

"Can I help you?" Susan asks, her normally haughty tone even icier than usual. I glance at her, wondering why she's being so standoffish with the woman.

Runway Barbie lifts her sunglasses to the top of her head, a cold indifference in her expression. "I need to speak with Benjamin. Where's his office?"

I no longer want to be this woman's friend. Or want to know where she got her shoes. Based on my limited knowledge, I'd wager this is Rebecca, and it takes every ounce of control I have not to scowl at her.

"I'll see if he's available," I reply, my tone neutral. She takes me in, assessing everything about me, and within seconds, dismisses me entirely with a nod.

Interesting.

I head back to Ben's office, finding him staring at his computer screen with a frown. "You have a visitor waiting in the lobby."

Ben's eyes meet mine, his frown deepening. "Who is it?"

"We weren't formally introduced, but I believe it's Rebecca."

His eyebrows wing up in surprise, as well as something else I can't read. He stands, throwing his glasses onto his desk before walking out of his office. I follow closely behind him, not entirely sure what's about to happen.

"Rebecca. What are you doing here?" Ben asks, his tone indifferent.

"I need to speak with you. Can we go to your office? I'd

prefer not to have an audience." Rebecca's eyes roam around the room, and I finally notice Susan and Michelle are sitting at the desk, pretending to be busy working.

"Sure." Ben opens the pass-through door, gesturing for Rebecca to come back. I stand next to Susan and Michelle, slightly dumbfounded that he would be so calm around her. After everything she did, I can't imagine he'd want to have a conversation with her, let alone be in the same room with her for any amount of time.

When his office door closes behind them, all I can do is stare at it. What's going on? Did she come all this way to try and get back together with him? Will he say yes? What does that mean for me?

Whatever. I don't have time to analyze the potential end of my relationship right now.

"Was she an actual bitch, or am I being judgy?" Michelle asks after a beat of silence.

"I don't think you're too off base," I respond, turning to find Michelle and Susan staring at me. Susan's eyebrow is raised as if to say, *'Are you going to do anything about that?'*, while Michelle is looking at me as if she finds this whole situation entertaining. From her perspective, it probably is.

After our date, there was no more hiding what was going on between us. The whole town started gossiping the minute we walked into La Mensa together. We weren't trying to hide anything; we just wanted to make sure this was what we wanted before letting the whole world know.

They definitely know now.

The front door chimes again for an actual patient this time, and Michelle and I get back to work. About an hour after she arrived, Rebecca leaves without a single word to anyone, her face impassive, giving no indication of what was said. Instead of sprinting into Ben's office to interrogate him, I continue doing my job.

If he wants to break up with me, then he can grow some balls and come to me first.

* * *

THE WEIGHT of Luna and Koda against me is bringing a measure of comfort I didn't know I needed. I'm lying on the couch, watching my favorite guilty pleasure movie, *Stardust.* I've been home from work for two hours and have received exactly one text from Ben, telling me he went to the gym and will come over later.

Did I pettily ignore that text message? Yes, I did. Do I feel guilty about ignoring the message? Also, yes.

I recognize my jealousies have taken over my brain, and I'm not in the right headspace to talk to him rationally. I'm also struggling with how much his ex showing up affected me. I've never been in a relationship where I cared this much.

My dating history comprises mostly of one-night stands and the occasional date with the same guy a few times. I was never sad if they ghosted me because I was more than likely going to ghost them first. Seeing them out with other women later never made me feel anything other than hopeful they found the right person for them.

With Ben, I care. A lot, apparently.

I think I'm struggling the most with how he didn't come and talk to me after she left. He just stayed in his office the rest of the day, only coming out when he was needed for a patient, then would go straight back to his office. He didn't even acknowledge me when he took her back to his office. It was as if his asshole personality took over, and he couldn't care less about anyone else.

Michelle kept trying to ask me questions I didn't know the answers to, which only further pissed me off. Was she moving to Sonoma? Were they getting back together? Did they ever even break up in the first place?

I knew the answer to the last one was yes, but it still put a little niggle of doubt in my brain that I couldn't overcome. It also didn't help that Michelle started speaking as if we'd already broken up, comforting me and telling me I didn't need him anyway when I had her in my life. I appreciated her trying to be there for me, but it only made everything worse.

I hate how much I've started second-guessing our entire relationship, as well as myself. I don't normally have negative thoughts about myself. I am who I am, and I won't change based on anyone else's opinion, but standing next to Runway Barbie, it's kind of hard not to compare.

Is that what Ben wants? A woman who is sleek and sophisticated, who ensures she's presenting her best self every day?

"Ugh!"

This is annoying. I don't do this. I don't overanalyze my life because something negative happened to me. Ben deserves the time to talk to me about what happened today, and I'll give it to him. Even if that means he breaks up with me. If he doesn't want to be with me anymore, I will be just fine.

Completely gutted, but fine.

A knock on the door makes Koda and Luna jump off me and race toward the door. I follow slowly behind, knowing it'll be Ben.

When I open the door, he's standing there with his hands braced on the frame, a dark look in his eye.

Suddenly, he surges forward, smashing his lips against mine as hunger and a little bit of anger pulse between us.

I get completely swept up in his kiss, forgetting about how mad I was only moments before.

"God, I should've come here sooner. I knew that, but I was being a stubborn asshole and thought I could handle it on my own," Ben growls against my lips. He kisses me for a moment longer before pulling me into a tight hug.

None of these actions were expected, and I sort of hate myself for that. I hate that I immediately believed he would break up with me because his bitch of an ex walked into the clinic as if she owned it.

Rubbing my hands up and down his back, I ask the question I should've asked a long time ago. "What happened?"

Ben lifts me into his arms and carries me to the couch, settling me on his lap before answering my question. "She told me she missed me and wants to reconcile—her words, not mine—and when I pressed her for more information, she told me her boy-toy dumped her soon after I broke up with her. Then she said her father was not happy that our engagement was broken off since it will look bad to the voters and was requiring her to fix it."

"So, she wants to get back together with you because she needs you, and you're an easy option…"

"Pretty much. Of course, I told her no, and her response was, *'I'm the best thing to happen to you, Ben. You'll come crawling back when you're tired of slumming,'*" he mimics in a high-pitched voice. "God, Sara, I was so pissed off, I could barely see straight. I knew if I interacted with anyone longer than the two minutes I was required, I would ruin every relationship we have with our patients.

"Then I went to the gym, hoping a strong workout would relieve some of the tension. I was determined to calm down before I talked to you when I should've just come to you first. The minute you were in my arms, my whole body relaxed. I'm sorry I'm such a stubborn asshole."

I can't help the chuckle that flows through me at his words. I should've known he would be angry about Rebecca's visit instead of contemplating getting back together with her. "You're not the only one to blame. I may or may not have let my jealousies cloud my judgment. I should've come to your office after she left instead of being mad and leaving without talking to you."

"I probably would've yelled at you if you had come into my office, which you wouldn't have deserved."

"But the difference is you wouldn't have been mad at me, and I could've helped you work it out instead of letting us both stew in our anger."

"I guess we know for next time."

I lean in to kiss his soft lips, telling him I'm sorry in the best way I know how. He holds my face in his hands, his actions saying the same thing.

This is what I've been looking for in every man I've dated. This mutual feeling of trust, where we're free to be ourselves because we know the other person will be a safe landing pad when we need it.

It's not going to be easy for me to drop my shields and start letting him in. I've held on to my independence for too long to let go completely.

But I'm willing to start trying.

SARA

"Ben, we have to go," I moan as his lips coast down my chest and wrap around my taut nipple.

"You should've thought about that before you walked in here naked." His lips whisper against my skin as he shows my other nipple the same treatment. He's kneeling in front of me, his hands coasting across my damp skin. We're supposed to be getting ready to go to Natalie and Tucker's to celebrate Noah's official adoption.

"I walked in here naked to get dressed, not for sex." My words end in another moan as Ben's tongue runs across my hips. He throws my leg over his shoulder, sucking my clit deep into his mouth.

"Oh, Jesus."

"Mmm." He hums against my pussy. "My name's Ben, Shortcake."

My fingers tangle in his hair, gripping hard as he pushes my body higher. His hands squeeze my hips, holding me up while his tongue swirls around my clit. Unable to help myself, I start riding his face, needing my orgasm more than I need anything else right now.

Ben groans against me, guiding my hips until I break

apart, my moan porn star worthy, and I couldn't give two shits. Fuck, he is good at that.

He brings me down slowly before gently setting my foot back on the floor and standing. Once my legs feel stable enough to hold me, I take in Ben's smug face, his mouth shining with my arousal. Feeling the need to bring him down a peg or two, I quickly drop to my knees, pulling his gym shorts down with me. Thank God he hadn't changed yet.

"Sara—"

I don't let him get another word out, wrapping my lips around his cock, and sucking him deep into my mouth.

"Oh, fuck."

I chuckle against him while flicking my tongue over the pulsing vein running along his shaft. Ben fists his hands in my hair, directing my movements while he starts to thrust into my mouth. I love when he is so overcome with pleasure, his control slips, and he forgets to be gentle with me. It gives me a certain sense of empowerment.

I reach up to grab his balls, making another groan fall from his chest. My eyes roll up to find him staring at me, heat blazing in those blue eyes. He thrusts a little harder, pushing deeper into my throat. It makes tears well in my eyes, so I close them, sucking just a bit harder so he knows I'm okay.

"Sara, I'm about to—" is all the warning I get before his cock pulses in my mouth, his orgasm shooting down my throat, forcing me to swallow. His thrusts slow until he pulls out of my mouth and lifts me to meet his lips. His kiss is ferocious and adoring at the same time.

"You're incredible, you know that?" he says against my mouth. I just shrug my shoulders, happy he's happy.

"We really should go, though." I remind him with a laugh.

"I equally want to hang out with your friends and tie you to this bed and spend hours worshiping you."

"Who says you can't do that when we get home?"

He groans. "Now I'm going to be imagining it all night. I swear you've turned me into a horny teenager."

"If it makes you feel any better, I feel the same way."

Ben slaps my ass. "Get dressed, please, before I really do tie you to the bed."

"Yes, sir."

"Fuck!" He storms out of my bedroom butt naked as I laugh.

After getting dressed and brushing my teeth, again, I find Ben waiting in the kitchen. Dressed in grey shorts and a fitted T-shirt, he looks back to his normal, in-control self. I'm fully prepared for a punishment tonight for my *'Yes, sir'* stunt, and I can't wait. It makes my core clench in anticipation.

"Ready?" I ask, giving our pups some love. Sadie spends most of her time here since Ben and I are together most evenings. She's blended into our pack seamlessly, and I love her like my own now.

After Ben says bye to the pups, too, we take his car to Natalie and Tucker's. This is the first time I'm bringing someone with me to hang out with my friends. It's a little weird, but it also feels like he's always been around. Most everyone already knows Ben, which has eased any lingering worry about how introductions would go. I'm pretty sure Ben is more excited than I am about hanging out with everyone. He's been talking nonstop about getting to hang out with people his own age instead of with his mom's friends.

Tonight, we're celebrating Noah, but we're also celebrating that Levi and Hope are still with us. This is the first time we're all getting together since Hope's ex attacked both her and Levi. They're on the mend now, but they've still got a way to go before they'll be back to normal.

Ben pulls onto Nat's street, finding a spot behind Cooper's truck. The noise level coming from the house makes me laugh. We've never been subtle, and I love that about our group.

I walk through the front door with Ben's hand gently wrapped around mine. As usual, the girls are all huddled on the couches and chairs while the guys stand by the dining room table.

"Hey, everyone!" I shout above the noise. It only gets louder as they come to say hello. Ben is re-introduced to everyone, and he laughs as the guys shove a beer in his hand and pull him into their circle.

"He looks even better without the broody cloud over his head," Natalie whisper-yells, making the girls laugh. Shaking my head at her, I squeeze onto the couch between Nat and Quinn. Megan and Lucy are on the loveseat, and Hope is in the recliner, a small smile curled at her lips. It's good to see her up and about after everything. She still has to wear a back brace, and her dislocated shoulder hasn't quite healed yet, but she seems to be in good spirits.

"Anyone else notice the orgasm glow surrounding Sara, or is it just me?" Nat teases.

I lightly punch her in the arm as she cackles. "I'm sorry. It's just so good to see you happy."

"I was happy before."

"You were content. Which was good, but this happiness is different." Quinn's smile is soft, and I know she's thinking about Cooper. I look around at my best friends to find their smiles are all the same. Each one knows the difference between being content by yourself and being happy with a partner who brings more to your life than anyone else ever could.

Ben has always been different from any other guy I've dated before. I noticed it the first time he let his shields drop when we organized the closet at the clinic. But seeing myself in the eyes of my friends, I understand the impact he's made on my life. He's become the steady presence I can rely on when it feels like my world is spinning too fast. All I need is one look from him to know that, no matter what's going on around me, he will be there, standing by my side.

I never realized how comforting that knowledge would be. Glancing across the room, I find Ben grinning at something Levi is saying. He looks happy with them. More relaxed than I've seen him in a while. After the shitshow with Rebecca, I'm glad he's not still stuck in his anger. Although, I thoroughly enjoyed him using my body to release his built-up tension.

As if he knows I'm thinking about him, Ben's gaze finds mine across the room. His blue eyes flash with unrestrained lust, and I have to fight the shiver trying to move through me.

"Whew, I can feel that tension all the way over here." Lucy's voice makes me tune back into the conversation. The girls are grinning at me, and a blush spreads through my cheeks. I'm not used to being the center of attention, so this whole situation is weird.

"Can I just say how happy it makes me not to be in the hot seat anymore?" Hope asks, making everyone laugh. I smile at her in thanks for turning the conversation away from me. I love how much she's opened up to us over the past few months.

"Oh, no. You still have dirty details to share, missy." Natalie wags her finger at her.

"Hold your ground, Hope. As soon as you give an inch, Nat will take a mile," Quinn teases. She'd know all about it, too. When she started dating Cooper, Nat was relentless about getting all the dirty details about their sex life. It was mostly to get Quinn to drop her walls with us, but we also were super curious. The guys are like brothers to us, so we had no idea if they lived up to the rumors of their sexual prowess.

"Please, you were dying to share; you just needed a little push." Nat grins at Quinn.

"Mommy, can you get me some more water?" Noah asks, walking up to Natalie. Her body completely melts when he calls her *mommy*, and it hits me square in the chest. I didn't know he'd already started calling her that, and it makes me so happy for her.

"Sure, love." She stands, leading Noah into the kitchen while the rest of us watch the two of them together.

It's weird to think our group dynamics are going to start changing. Everyone is paired up now, and kids are around the corner. Lucy's pregnant, and I wouldn't be surprised if Quinn and Cooper are trying. Megan and Todd are fostering Nathaniel now and are hoping to adopt him one day.

Our lives are moving forward, growing and changing in beautiful ways, and I'm so grateful to have friendships strong enough to withstand those changes. Our time spent together looks a lot different than it used to, but our deep-rooted connections only seem to grow when we are together.

It's a beautiful thing to be a part of.

BEN

The noise level in Natalie and Tucker's house is ear-splitting, with everyone talking over each other, laughing, drinking, and carrying on. It's fantastic. I've never been around a group of people who can go from ragging on each other one minute to being completely vulnerable the next. These people love hard, and with every interaction, I want nothing more than to be a part of their group.

I've never seen friends care more for each other than Sara's friends do, and I've only spent a couple of hours with them.

"I'm telling you, it's going to happen. We're taking home the trophy this year," Cooper says while Todd nods. The two of them run the town's police department and are currently in a battle with Tucker, the captain of the fire department, about who is or isn't going to win the co-ed softball league's trophy.

"There's no way. Charlie is on our team this year, and she kicks ass." Tucker shakes his head.

"Neither one of their teams is good," Levi whispers to me. "The high school team usually wins every year because all of the coaches make the team practice."

I grin at his admission. "But you still let them talk smack."

"Fuck yeah, I do. It's the only time they aren't tearing me a new one." He laughs. "Being the youngest sucks."

Levi glances into the living room to check on Hope. He's been doing that every few minutes since we got here. This time, he crutches over to her, his leg in a cast to his thigh. I don't know all the details about the attack on him and Hope, but it sounds like Hope's ex attacked Levi, then kidnapped Hope. The whole mess ended with both of them in the hospital for a few days, and they are only recently recovering from the whole ordeal. I'm surprised they're here at all today.

Although, if I were laid up like they are, getting out of the house would be a necessity.

"You settling in okay?" Cooper asks. "Levi said your house will be done in another month." His brown eyes are almost a honey color and looking at me more seriously than I expected.

"I am. Sara's made the transition a lot easier, if I'm honest."

"And you're sticking around for good?"

I smile at Cooper. "I'm in it for the long haul."

I'm glad Sara has people in her life who are looking out for her. I know her brothers are going to give me the third degree one day, but it's nice to see her friends have her back, too.

Cooper nods his head, a smile pulling at the corner of his lips. "Good deal. We're happy you're here. And with her. She deserves to have someone in her life that's going to put her first."

"I'd be an idiot not to."

"We're all idiots, but we try our damndest not to be." He laughs.

"Hey, guys." Sara walks up to us, holding out a beer for me. She has another one in her hand for herself.

"Hi." I wrap my arm around her shoulders. "Thanks for

this." Leaning in, I kiss her quickly before pulling away. She beams at me, her hazel eyes lighting up brighter than I've seen them in a while. I think this outing was good for both of us.

"Did you get food? Tucker made a ton of stuff."

"Yeah, I'm good. Anything exciting happening over there with the girls?"

"Mostly just them teasing me for bringing a guy around for the first time."

I quirk my eyebrow at her. "I'm the first?" The idea of being the only guy to make it into the inner circle makes me oddly happy.

"Shit, that ego of yours just grew three sizes. I don't think your head will fit through the door anymore."

I throw my head back, laughing at Sara's sass. It always comes when I'm not ready for it, and I can never control my reaction. It drives me crazy despite how much I love it.

"Do I need to keep that sassy mouth of yours busy again?"

"Maybe." She grins.

I lean in to kiss her, unable to help myself. "You're going to be the death of me. I swear."

We hang out at the party for a while, eating and celebrating being together. I haven't, for a moment, felt like an outsider without a clue as to what's going on. They've explained inside jokes and stories to me countless times, letting me be a part of every taunt they throw. I've even been on the receiving end of their teasing, which, oddly enough, makes me feel even more like a part of the group.

I'm grateful they've accepted me into the group because I have a feeling these people are going to come to mean a lot to me.

"You ready to go, Shortcake?" I ask Sara, wrapping my arm around her shoulders. It's starting to get late, and, in all honesty, I'm missing our pups.

"Yeah, I want to go home and see my babies." Sara smiles up at me, her hazel eyes happy.

"I was just thinking the same thing."

Our goodbyes take a solid half-hour to get through before we finally make it out the door. Holding Sara's hand on the drive home, I'm hit with a sudden burst of happiness. This is what life is supposed to be like. Spending time with people who add value to your life instead of people who only want to be seen with you. This is what I've been missing.

I pull into Sara's driveway and follow her inside. The dogs swarm, fluffy tails wagging, as we try to say hello to all of them. Once they've had their fill, they go off to wrestle each other, trying to work off their excitement.

I grab Sara around her waist before she can get too far. "You owe me for your little *'Yes, sir'* stunt earlier, Shortcake," I say into her ear. A shiver moves through Sara, making me grin. "Are you ready for your punishment?"

Sara nods and I let her go, watching her ass sway as she walks into her bedroom. My imagination has been running wild from the moment those words fell from her lips earlier. I haven't quite decided what I want to do to her yet. No matter what, it's going to be fucking phenomenal.

I walk into Sara's room to find her spread out on her bed, her beautiful ivory skin on display while her hands roam her body. My cock swells, wanting to get in on what I'm seeing immediately.

An idea begins to form in my head while a devious smile takes over my face. Sara's gaze finds mine, heat blazing in those golden hazel eyes. With her attention on me, I grab my belt buckle, the metal clanking as I undo the clasp. It whispers through my belt loops, making Sara squirm.

This is going to be good.

I stalk toward the bed, taking in my fill of her. She's magnificent and all mine.

Climbing onto the bed, I crawl over the top of her, grinning as her eyes blaze.

"You're overdressed for this party," Sara states, a little pout to her mouth.

"Since it's my party, I don't mind for now."

Her eyes narrow, but before she can ask the question in her eyes, I loop my belt into cuffs. I slip one over her hand, thread the belt through her headboard, then slip the leather around her other hand, binding her arms above her head.

Seeing her trussed up like this almost makes me lose the thin thread of control I have.

My hands slide across her soft skin, momentarily mesmerized by the feel. "Gorgeous."

I get off the bed, keeping my gaze locked on Sara while I take off my clothes. "Your punishment tonight is a little taste of your own medicine."

"What does that mean?" Sara breathes, her chest starting to heave. I run my fingers lightly across her legs, gliding up over her knee and toward her thighs.

"I want you to know how it feels to be turned on and unable to do anything about it. To be out of your mind with need."

"Fuck. This is going to suck."

"It'll end fantastically. That I can promise," I say, hovering over her. Sara grins, and I get to work. Starting at her jaw, I tease my way down her throat, alternating between soft kisses, licks, and bites. I nip at her collarbone, making Sara pull on her restraint, her whimpers spurring me on.

My hands glide across her skin, her muscles tense under my palm. "You smell fantastic. Like oranges," I whisper against the swell of her breast. Sucking the fleshy underside into my mouth pulls a keening moan from Sara that makes me want to explode with need.

"Ben," Sara pleads.

I pull her nipple deep into my mouth, lashing it with my

tongue, then biting it gently. It'll never be enough for me. No matter how many times I have her, it won't ever be enough to quench this desire flowing through me.

I move down Sara's body, needing to focus on driving her higher before I lose all semblance of my control. I circle her belly button with my nose, then my tongue. Sara's whimper of need has me grinning against her skin. "Not so nice, is it?"

She growls. "I really want to hate you right now, but I don't want you to stop."

Chuckling, I shake my head. "I'm not nearly finished with you." I nip at the soft skin on the inside of her thigh, making my way toward her pussy. Instead of continuing to tease her as I planned, I dive in, lapping at her arousal, growling when she squeezes my head with her legs.

"Ben!" she shouts, the headboard creaking as she pulls against the cuffs. I build her up before backing away, keeping her right on the edge of orgasm until she's desperate, her body shaking with need.

I slide two fingers inside her, flicking her clit with my tongue. This time, I don't back away when she reaches the peak. I slide in a third finger as she detonates around me, her whole body tensing with the strength of her orgasm.

I pull away from her body, grab ahold of her hips, and flip her over. A shocked gasp flies from Sara at the suddenness of the move. The cuffs force her arms to cross, keeping her chest flat on the mattress. With her ass in the air, I thrust my cock into her pussy, her walls still spasming from her orgasm. We both groan at the tight fit, despite my efforts to prepare her. Jesus, she's unlike anything I've ever felt before. It's addicting.

Sara pushes her hips back in an effort to get me to move. My hand crashes down on her ass cheek, a red print forming immediately.

"Fuck!" Sara shouts.

"You need me to move, Shortcake? You want to come on my cock?"

"Please," she begs.

"Greedy girl." I pull back before slamming into her, my hands squeezing her hips for leverage. Thrusting into her, I feel wild and untamed. She's a goddess who has taken full control of my life. I'll never want it to be any other way.

"Fuck, I'm so close. Your body is so goddamn perfect," I grate out.

"Don't stop. Please, don't stop."

I thrust harder as Sara's walls tighten around me. I can't hold on any longer, her orgasm pulling me with it so hard my vision swims. Groaning through each pulse of my cock, I thrust until my entire body feels spent.

Sara's knees give out, dropping her hips to the mattress, her body loose and languid. We're both breathing hard as we come down from the high.

I run my nose up the back of her neck and across her jaw until I finally make my way to Sara's mouth. I place a gentle kiss against her lips as they quirk up at the side.

Her hazel eyes flick open, shining with warmth and drawing me deeper into her orbit than I ever thought was possible. "I think I'm good with any type of punishment you want to give me from now on." She grins.

A laugh bursts from me, followed by a feeling so strong I almost blurt it out. I bite my tongue from saying the words I desperately want to say. Instead, I undo the belt around her wrists, the words sitting on the tip of my tongue. I'm just not sure if she's ready to hear them.

I rub her wrists, massaging any tension from her muscles and making sure I didn't hurt her at any point.

I thought I had this kind of love before. Turns out, I had nothing at all. Nothing like what I feel for Sara.

I just have to find the right time to tell her.

29

UNKNOWN

God, I've missed her.

It's been too long since I've gotten to see her this close. Too long I've had to stay away from her. I didn't want to, but it was necessary if the rest of the plan is to go perfectly.

And it seems, in my absence, she's only gotten closer to the animal man. Why has she pushed me away like this? Is she mad at me? Did I do something to make her turn to someone else?

I'll just have to remind her that I'm still here. That I love her, and no matter what she does, she's always going to be mine. Nobody else's.

The black dog stands on the edge of the front lawn, staring at me. No one else can see me; I'm too hidden. But he can. He's always seen me when I'm watching his mom. He's a good dog. Takes care of her when I can't. He doesn't like me, so even though it'll make Sara sad, he'll have to go when it's time for her to come home.

Sara gets into the car with the dogs and the animal man—one big, happy family. It's wrong. It should be me with her. Not him.

Without much thought, I head to the backyard, opening the gate and making my way to the back door.

I know I shouldn't. It could mess everything up, but I've gone too long without her. I need to feel close to her again.

Like I've done before, I pick the back door lock and step inside Sara's kitchen. If only we could stay in this house together. It would be perfect for the two of us. It's not part of the plan, though, so she'll have to live at my house with me.

I walk into Sara's bedroom, her clothes strewn haphazardly across the floor. We'll have to work on her messiness. I finger the sports bra sitting on her dresser, the material silky in my hands. The image of Sara taking it off at the end of a long day filters into my head. The top drawer houses all of Sara's underwear, and I let my hands roam across each silky, soft piece. What does she look like in these?

One day, I will find out. Until then, I need to let her know I'm back. That I've missed her, and she doesn't need to be with the animal man anymore.

I'm the one who will take care of her.

Forever.

30

SARA

Turning to look in the back seat, I find three dogs sacked out on top of each other. They played hard at the dog park today, having a ton of fun, wrestling and playing fetch. Luna is even getting braver with having both Koda and Sadie watching her back. It made my heart full to watch her come out of her shell a little more.

We've got dinner with Ben's parents tonight, and I'd love to have the rest of the afternoon to spend on the couch, snuggling with my dude. For as hard and prickly as he can be, the man is a world-class snuggler.

"I'm thinking either a Batman marathon until dinner or Captain America. I'll let you pick," I say to Ben as he pulls my car into the driveway.

"Batman because at least Christian Bale's face is covered for a good portion of the movie."

"Why does his face being covered make the movie better?"

"Because then I don't have to see you panting after him the whole time."

"But you look a little like Chris Evans, so it would be like

I'm panting after you." I wink at him before racing up the steps, anticipating the moment he reacts.

I'm grabbed around the waist and lifted into the air before I can make it to the door.

"How about I just make you pant right now?" Ben growls in my ear.

The dogs circle us, impatiently waiting for me to unlock the door.

I push my ass back into Ben's thickening erection, hoping to push him.

"That's how you want to play this, huh?" He bites my ear lobe, then steps away from me completely. "Open the door, Sara."

I stifle my protest while also wanting to melt at the heat in his tone. I flip the deadbolt, letting the dogs race ahead. I turn to Ben, waiting for the rest of my instructions. It's the most freeing experience to give up my control to him. To feel safe enough to know every move he makes will be for my benefit first.

"Go to the bedroom, take everything off except for your panties, and lie on the bed, face up."

I nod. "Yes, sir." For once, I don't mean it sarcastically. I turn to walk into my bedroom, my shirt clearing my head before I even make it through the threshold. I chuck it to the floor, then freeze. All the clothes I had lying on the floor are now in the laundry basket, my dresser drawers that are usually askew are neatly shut, and there's a note sitting on top of my bed.

"Ben, did you clean my room?" It's the only logical explanation. Entertaining anything else is preposterous.

"What?" His voice comes up behind me, his hands skimming down my sides. "Why aren't you following directions?" he asks into my neck.

"Ben, did you clean my room?"

I'm not sure if it's my tone of voice or something else, but he drops his hands from my body and steps up next to me. "No, it wasn't this clean before we left for the park, was it?"

He walks further into the room before he sees the note on my comforter.

"Wait, don't touch it."

Ben's arm freezes mid-air before retracting it back to his side. Pulling my T-shirt back over my head, I dig out some winter gloves from my closet.

Carefully, I open the folded piece of paper, my hands shaking as I read the words printed in the same handwriting as the others.

I'm sorry I've neglected you. I'm back now, and we'll be together soon. Wait for me. Love, G.

"Who the fuck is 'G'?" Ben asks, his voice hard and angry.

"I don't know. I've received a few other notes from this person, but never like this, never in my bedroom. Ben—" Chaos tears through my body as the implication of what happened floods my brain.

Someone broke into my house, cleaned my room, and left me a love note. The same person who has been leaving me notes and gifts over the past few months.

And if I had to guess...the same person who tried to abduct me.

Ben's eyes are hard. "We need to call Cooper. *Now.*"

* * *

Red and blue lights reflect off the side of my house, flashing brightly in the waning afternoon sunshine. The dogs are leashed and attached to the patio chair I'm sitting in, and I'm so zoned out, I don't even notice when Cooper comes to sit by me.

"You ready to tell me the whole story?" he asks, his elbows leaning against his knees while his serious gaze is trained on me. Despite the underlying anger, his golden eyes are shining with worry and affection. I know he's in police chief mode, but he's always going to be my friend first.

Ben's hand runs across my shoulders as he sits in the chair on the other side of me. His silent support is overwhelming, but so needed.

"I started getting gifts at the end of May. The first two were flowers: a single rose and a daisy. I honestly thought they were sent to me by accident, and I just moved on. Then I started getting notes. None of them were addressed to me, and they were all signed with the letter 'G'. They all said a variation of the same thing: I miss you; I love you; you're mine forever."

If I think back to when I got those notes, there was a part of me that knew they were for me. That someone had been watching me, stalking me. I just didn't want it to be real, so I pretended like they were for someone else. That it was a mistake.

"I'm guessing you don't have them anymore," Cooper says.

I shake my head. "I threw them away under the pretense that I couldn't give them to the person they were meant for without a name. I think, in all actuality, they scared me, and I didn't want the reminder of them sitting on my counter."

"Did anything else happen after the notes?"

I glance at Ben, his face serious as he nods his head. I can see how worried he is about me. This, on top of the attempted kidnapping, doesn't bode well for my safety.

"Someone tried to kidnap me."

"Excuse me?" Cooper stands and begins to pace. "What the fuck, Sara?"

I cringe. "I know. I should have told you. I should have called it in the night it happened. After Ben saved me, we heard shouts and found Dan Beckett's dog, Archie, had gotten hit by a car. We immediately went into surgery, so by the time my adrenaline had come down, I was too shell-shocked to think straight. Then I was too traumatized to tell anyone what happened."

"You saved her?" Cooper asks Ben.

"Yeah." He looks at me, eyes shining from the memory of that night. "I'd walked out of La Mensa and saw her fighting some guy in the back of the parking lot. I didn't think; I just reacted."

"Jesus." Cooper runs his hands across his face. "You know this is all connected, right? The notes, the abduction, the break-in tonight. It's all the same guy who won't take no for an answer." He sighs, then sits back down in the chair. "Any chance you got a look at him?"

I can only shake my head. My memories from that night are fuzzy at best, blank at worst.

"He was big, like bigger than me big, and was wearing overalls, but I don't remember what he looked like," Ben says, reaching out for my hand, squeezing it as if he needs to be reminded that I'm okay.

"Okay. I'll check with Tammy at La Mensa about cameras, but I doubt she set any up in the parking lot when she took over management."

"Thanks, Cooper."

"What can we do in the meantime? We need to protect her somehow," Ben asks.

"Could you stay with your parents in Westlake for a few days? Give my guys some time to run DNA on the note."

I turn up my nose. I really don't want to go to my parents' house, but I guess I will if I have to. "Probably. Too bad your house isn't done yet," I say to Ben.

His lips quirk up. "No kidding. We'll figure something out."

As Ben's hands massage my neck, easing the tension there, Cooper gets his guys rounded up and leaves my house. It took them about three hours to catalog everything they thought could be important, and while I appreciated the thoroughness, it made the creepy crawlies worse knowing they'd be going through my stuff. At least this time, I gave them permission to do it.

The image of someone pawing at my underwear and playing with my dirty clothes sends a shiver down my spine. Why is this happening to me?

"Do you want me to tell my parents to reschedule dinner tonight?"

I stand from my chair, letting the dogs off their leashes now that the police are gone. They sprint across the back-yard, goofing around, happy they no longer have to be tied down.

Sitting back down in my chair, I sigh as I try to decide how I feel about going to dinner. "No, I think it could be good for me to get out of the house, away from the idea of me having a"—I swallow—"stalker. Plus, your dad would be sad if he didn't get his steak tonight."

"Okay, why don't we pack a bag for you and the dogs, then we can fulfill one of my long-time fantasies. Having a hot girl in my bedroom." He grins at me, turning his face adorably boyish.

"Deal." I grin back.

* * *

"Benjamin Charles, you get that poor girl a refill right now," Ben's mom snaps. She turns back to me in the cream-colored patio chairs we're cozied up in and rolls her eyes. "I swear I raised him better than the heathen he's become. Now, tell me everything you've been up to. I haven't seen you since the Christmas party."

Sybil immediately knew something was up when we arrived at dinner. Our less than enthusiastic greetings probably gave us away. The woman should be training the military on interrogation tactics because Ben and I folded in a matter of seconds. We told her everything that had happened today, and she pulled me into a big hug and told me everything would be just fine.

Then she made Ben take my bags upstairs while she made a pitcher of sangria. We've been sitting on their back patio, soaking up the sunshine and drooling over the smell of grilled meat. It's exactly what I needed after what happened.

Since then, Sybil and I have talked about everything and nothing while the boys stood over the grill. They've been murmuring about something since we got here, and even though I have a guess that it's about me, I'm glad to see the two of them getting along again. Their rocky relationship has been mended all because of some solid communication.

"Ladies, please find your seats at the table. Dinner will be served momentarily," Dr. Charles says, plating up the steaks from the grill. Ben walks out with the side dishes as we all find a place to sit.

When we're settled, Ben's mom grabs my hand. "I am just so thankful you're here with us and with my baby boy. He needs some happiness and the occasional swift kick in the ass, and I know you're the perfect one to do it."

"Mom!"

A laugh bubbles up from my stomach before I'm able to shove it back down. I know Sybil meant her comments seriously, but the whole thing tickled me.

"You know, love, you're right. He does need the occasional kick in the ass," Dr. Charles agrees.

"Hey!" Ben's outraged shout brings more laughter around the table as well as a pat on his shoulder from his dad.

"It's kind of true, son. Us Crawford men tend to be a little dense sometimes. Those kicks are necessary." Dr. Charles winks at me.

As we eat dinner, the laughs continue, making me forget the chaos surrounding my life. I'm able to pretend, just for a moment, that everything is normal. That my life isn't being flipped upside down by some psycho.

But in the back of my mind, I know this is only the beginning of the chaos.

31

BEN

Today...sucked. There's no other way to describe walking into Sara's bedroom and finding out someone had gone through her things. Angry was an understatement for how I was feeling. I wanted to throw something or put my fist through a wall. Anything to expel the fury that was coursing through me.

Instead, I clenched my teeth for three hours straight. Sara needed me to hold it together, not rage through the house like a Neanderthal. I was so proud of how she handled the situation, especially after everything she's gone through the last couple of months.

Now, she's getting loved on by my mom, and I think it was exactly what she needed. If it was coming from her own mom, it probably would've been stifling. What's better is Mom knows exactly what she's doing, too. Mother-henning Sara after what happened today while making her think it's because I brought a suitable woman home.

She's pretty ingenious.

"How about dessert?" Mom asks the table.

"Steak *and* dessert? Sara, you're coming over more often." Dad winks at her, making her blush.

"You act as if I starve you," Mom huffs.

"Sara, have you ever had fish three days in a row, each one tasting exactly like the last, despite being named something different?"

The sigh from Mom is about as big as a gust of wind while Sara just shakes her head at my dad.

"I don't believe I have."

"Let's just say, this is a special treat, and I would like for it to continue. What did you make, darling?"

"Cheesecake, but I'm tempted to shove your face in it right now."

"It would still be the closest I've been to dessert in months, so I'll take it." Dad chuckles.

"Insufferable man." Mom gets up from the table, grabbing plates to make room. I help with the rest of the dishes and follow her inside.

"I just want him to be okay," she whispers as I set the dirty dishes next to the sink.

"And he loves you for it, Mom." I wrap my arm around her shoulders. I can't imagine what it would be like to see your partner on the brink of death. I'm scared for Sara's well-being as it is, so the idea of her being harmed is enough to make my heart pound.

"You could probably ease up on the fish, though." I give her one more squeeze before I let go to grab the dessert plates from the cabinet. She swats me on the arm as she laughs, nodding her head in agreement.

We work together to plate the cheesecake, an extra-large slice cut especially for Dad, which makes me grin.

"Hush, you," Mom says, taking her two plates out to the patio.

As dessert is eaten, we continue chatting about all the new things happening in town. I update them on the latest changes to the fundraiser, which Dad has been stoked about since I brought up the idea. He's been insistent on being part of all the plans, not because he wants to manage it, but because he's excited about the changes I'm making. His enthusiasm has helped me relax a little about the event.

The dogs run around the yard, a little more subdued than normal, as Luna scopes out the new space. Sadie has been showing her all her favorite places, which has been adorable.

Despite how nervous I was about bringing Sara over, it's been a great evening. Mom has been less embarrassing than I expected, probably because of the break-in, and I've enjoyed hanging out with my girl. It gives me glimpses of what our future could look like. Holidays and evening barbecues, lots of laughter, and constant teasing. It's everything I never knew I needed.

"Should we turn on a movie or something?" Mom asks. The sun is almost set now, and the patio lights, while nice, are attracting the bugs.

"That sounds lovely, darling," Dad says.

"You're just sucking up since I gave you dessert."

"You're damn right. I'm going to want leftovers tomorrow, so I have to butter you up tonight." Dad kisses Mom's cheek, and I watch her melt into him. I used to wonder if their bickering was dysfunctional, but as I got older, I realized it was the way they loved each other. Dad puts up a fight over whatever Mom is making him do, purely to make her feel good when she wins the battle. He also enjoys sending her into a tizzy because she's so easy to rile up. Then he gets to swoop in and love on her to make it all better.

Sara likes riling me just the same. We both get a pretty great reward out of her riling me up, though, so it's worth it for both of us.

I hold my hand out to help Sara out of her chair. She calls for the dogs to come inside as we follow my parents to the living room. I pull Sara down next to me on the couch while Mom and Dad pick a movie to watch.

Leaning in, I whisper in Sara's ear, "Think we could get away with some under-the-blanket fondling?"

"Doubtful. You tend to be a screamer."

My laugh causes Mom and Dad to look at us questioningly. I can't exactly tell them what Sara said, so I just shrug.

"We decided on that new Keanu Reeves movie where he punches a lot of people," Mom says, ignoring my outburst.

"Sounds great." I glance at Sara, who's biting her cheek to keep her giggle in.

Grabbing a blanket, I pull it across our laps and pull Sara into my chest. She settles in, her hand resting on my pec. I wish we were alone at her house, but this is surprisingly nice, too.

Mom starts the movie while Dad turns off the lamp, sending the living room into complete darkness.

It's not thirty minutes into the movie before I feel Sara's hand slide down my chest, landing at the waistband of my pants. My cock immediately reacts to how close she is, and I shift in my seat to make room. Sara's shoulder shakes as she holds in her laugh. It makes me want to spank her.

I was mostly kidding about fondling each other under the blanket, but if she wants to play, I'm so down. My hand moves from around her shoulder to her waist, my hand splaying across her hips. Our position is completely innocent, while our intentions are anything but.

Sara's hand pops the button of my shorts, then slowly lowers my zipper. Her hand is gently resting on top of my shorts, so close to my cock, it takes everything I have not to thrust my hips into her hand.

Her fingers slip into my boxers, coasting across my hardening shaft. I clench my fist into the material of her shorts. Our current position doesn't lend for any sort of retaliation since I can't reach her pussy right now.

As her fist wraps around my cock, I think of every possible way to tease her when I get her back to my bedroom. God, I'm going to spank her ass until it's covered in my handprints.

"Sorry to duck out early, Mom, but we've had a long day, so I think we're going to go to bed." Despite the blood pounding in my cock, I manage to keep my voice even. I grab Sara's hand, standing quickly and keeping my back to my parents so they can't see the evidence of what her hands are capable of.

"Good night," Sara singsongs. I will be adding that to the list of wrongs she'll be punished for. Why? Because she's enjoying this entirely too much.

"Night, dears," Mom responds, completely clueless. I hope.

When I finally get Sara into my bedroom, I throw her down on the bed with a quiet growl. "You're an evil, evil woman, Shortcake. And I will be retaliating for that little stunt."

"You're the one who suggested the fondling."

"I meant fondling you, not me." I rip the T-shirt off her body, along with every other scrap of clothing. My mouth wraps around her nipple, causing a gasp to escape her chest. Finally, the tables have turned.

"If you make any noise, I will stop. Understood?" I raise my eyebrow at Sara, waiting for her to understand the state she put me in.

"Yes, sir," she whispers, and fuck me, I almost explode right then.

"Good girl." I make quick work of my clothes, then climb back on top of her. Her smooth, silky skin feels like heaven against me, and I plan to explore every single inch of her tonight. I know we've got at least an hour and a half before the movie will be over and my parents come upstairs.

I start at Sara's collarbone, dipping my tongue into the hollow there. I nip and suck my way across her chest, taking my time in an attempt to get my fill of her taste, her scent.

"I'll never get enough of you. You know that, right?" My lips whisper against her nipple, and I glance up to see her staring at me, her hazel eyes half-lidded with lust.

She nods her head in response. "Same," she pants.

I make my way down her stomach, circling my tongue in her belly button as her hips lift, trying to move me along. Not going to happen tonight.

I run my tongue up the inside of her right thigh, stopping just short of her pussy, then do the same on the other side. A tiny whimper escapes Sara, and instead of stopping, I take pity on her and suck her clit into my mouth.

Her entire body tenses at the onslaught. Trying to hold her moans in will only heighten the whole experience, keeping her so in the moment, she won't remember what happened today or how scared she is about having a stalker. I want her so out of her mind she won't even be able to say her name when we're done.

I slide two fingers into her while I continue to flick her clit with my tongue. Her hands slide into my hair as she starts to ride my face, so caught up in the moment.

I build her up until I know she's right on the precipice of her orgasm. Then I press my thumb against her ass, and she full-on detonates. Thighs shaking, fists clenched in my hair, absolutely shattering around me.

Fuck, that's the best thing I've ever seen in my whole life.

Not able to hold myself back, I thrust my cock into her while she's still coming, her tight walls squeezing me so hard I almost come that second. I bite my lip, trying to hold on to the small amount of control I have on my body as I begin to move my hips.

I wrap my arms around Sara's shoulders, pulling her closer to me as we move together. This is raw, unfiltered, and so much more than I've ever had with anyone else. I don't think I'll ever be able to tell her how much she's come to mean to me, but I'm going to damn well try.

Suddenly, my orgasm is barreling forward before I can do anything to stop it. My entire body tenses as Sara keeps up with me, her pussy tightening around me like a vise, milking everything out of me until I'm coming so hard my vision goes black.

"Fuck, Sara," I groan, unable to hold back.

My body shutters with aftershocks as we both attempt to come down from that religious experience.

"What the fuck was that?" Sara whispers, making me laugh.

"I have no clue, but we're definitely going to need to do it again when I recover in three to four business days."

I roll off of Sara, pulling her onto my chest instead. She lays her cheek on her folded hands, completely relaxed, and looking more beautiful than I've ever seen her before. I run my hands through her chocolate-colored hair, the smooth strands running across my skin like silk.

"Sara." She slowly lifts her head, her sleepy eyes finding mine, and I can't hold back the words bubbling up in my chest. "I love you."

Surprise flashes in her eyes before they melt into a happiness I haven't seen there since before the attack.

I lean forward, pressing my lips against hers. "I didn't think I'd ever open myself up again, but for you, I want to. You have every part of me. And I swear I'll do whatever it takes to deserve your heart."

I wish I had more words for her. Better ways to tell her exactly how I feel, but I don't.

I only have my actions and my ever-expanding heart that's hers forever.

"I love you, too," she whispers, grinning down at me. "And I'll do whatever it takes to protect our love."

32

SARA

"How are you, slugger?" Adam asks as he unlaces his soccer cleats to put on his tennis shoes. The squeals of children's laughter surround us from the other fields while they play. Normally, their games would bring a smile to my face, but it's not quite cutting it tonight.

"Um…okay in some aspects. Shitty in others."

"You ready to talk about it yet?" He stands from the bleachers, watching Matthew, Nolan, and Carter kick around the ball after our regular sibling grudge match. It's the only way we're able to spend time with each other outside of family dinners since Matthew and Adam are always busy with Sidelines.

"I think I might be."

"Good, let's go get a drink at Donna's. I could demolish their wings right now."

We say goodbye to the boys before heading to the bar. It's still early, so it's not too crowded, and the music doesn't get loud until the sun goes down. I send a quick text to Ben, letting him know I'm telling Adam about the break-in and then put my phone away.

"Whenever you're ready," Adam says, his blue eyes serious

but full of love. It's the look of understanding and steady strength that makes the flood gates open, allowing everything to spill out.

I tell him everything that's happened since Ben got into town: how he was an asshole and then he saved my life, about the attack and the break-in, which led to me telling him that I have a stalker, and lastly, I tell him how much Ben has come to mean to me.

Adam doesn't say a word throughout my whole rambling story, although by his expressions, I know he's pissed at me for holding back.

When I finally run out of words, we've made it through two baskets of wings, two beers each, and enough under-the-breath cursing to last for a year.

Adam runs a hand over his face, taking his time to formulate a response.

"First of all, I'm relieved you're safe and that Cooper is finally looking into this. Secondly, I am beyond pissed at you for keeping it to yourself. I don't fully understand your reasoning for keeping it from all of us, but what's done is done. What are the next steps in finding this bastard?"

"Cooper ran prints from the break-in, but I guess he's not in the system or something because nothing came of it. At this point, I'm to be on guard and pay attention to my surroundings, as well as doing my best to never be alone."

"Hmph. I'm going to call Cooper and see what else can be done. That's not good enough."

I roll my eyes at Adam. I know he wants me safe, but the caveman behavior can be annoying.

"Now, on to Benjamin. I'm happy you've found someone capable of taking care of you without stomping on you. That's incredible, although he'll still need to be put through the brother test. I don't care if he was my friend first. It's been twenty years, and he's trying to get in my sister's pants."

"Not *trying*," I mumble under my breath. "He's coming to

family dinner on Sunday. You can do your alpha posturing then. Just know, he and Tucker are already gym bros, so Tuck will be on his side."

"Of course he will be." Adam rolls his eyes, then looks at me as if something occurred to him. "That's why you started self-defense classes, the attack, isn't it?"

I nod my head.

"Good. I'm proud, even though I'm mad at you." He glares at me as any good big brother would.

"Thanks. I'm sorry I didn't come to you sooner."

"You can make it up to me by beating the shit out of Nolan. It'll make him sad that his sister can knock him on his ass."

I grin at Adam, enjoying the idea of using my defense skills for something other than actual defense. We clean up our table, and Adam pays for our meal. As we walk out to the parking lot, I see someone talking on the phone by my car. If I'm not mistaken, I think Model Barbie is about to attack me.

"What is it with parking lots these days?"

"Huh?" Adam's gaze lands on Rebecca as we walk closer. She's wearing another flawless dress, this one tightly fitting with a deep V showing off her admittedly fantastic cleavage. Her heels look like they could be weapons while making her Amazonian tall.

"Rebecca." I raise my eyebrow at her in question.

Her face pinches as she hangs up her call without even a goodbye. "Well, if it isn't Ben's revenge side piece. You should know Ben is just getting back at me for our misunderstanding."

"Ha! Sure, you cheating on him was a misunderstanding." I laugh, my tone dryer than the desert.

"Which means you're temporary," she continues, ignoring my comment. "He told me we can get back together when he finds someone to take over. It shouldn't be much longer now, so enjoy him while you can. It's not like you have what it takes to hold his attention, anyway. I've seen the two of you together around town. It's pathetic. You might as well cut your losses now." It's then she notices Adam standing next to me. She eye-fucks him for a solid few seconds before speaking again. "It seems like you have already moved on. Lovely."

"Excuse me?" Adam starts.

I put a hand to his chest to stop him from going into protector mode. "Not that you deserve this information, but this is my brother, Adam. And I love that you think you have Ben all figured out, but you know nothing. This is his home now. You were the distraction until he found what made him happy. So, you can take your designer heels right on out of town because nobody wants you here."

Rebecca scoffs. "Ben wants me. I know it. He told me so himself. And when he comes crawling back to me, I'll get to tell you *I told you so*." Her smile is icier than a snow cone before she walks away without waiting for me to respond.

"What the fuck just happened?" Adam asks, staring at me with wide eyes.

"We just had a run-in with Ben's bitch of an ex."

"Jesus, he has poor taste in women."

"Hey!"

Adam grimaces. "Sorry, I didn't mean you. How could he not see the crazy in her when he started dating her?"

"I don't think he cared much when they got together. Or he just shoved his head into the sand. I plan to find out when I get home, though."

"Is it safe for you to be there? After the break-in?"

"I don't have another option. I can't just uproot my whole life. Ben's staying with me for the time being."

"Wait, so you guys moved in together?" Adam's outrage is almost palpable.

"You can't have it both ways, Adam. Ben is there to help protect me. It's either that or I'm alone." I glare at him.

A growl rumbles from Adam's chest, but he doesn't respond.

"I love you, caveman. Thank you for looking out for me. I'm going to go home and have words with my boyfriend."

Adam kisses me on the cheek. "Tell him to expect a kick in the ass for being an idiot."

* * *

I WALK INTO MY HOUSE, the dogs racing like lunatics from the kitchen to say hello. "Yes, hello. I missed you, too." I give pats out to everyone, even Minnie, then make my way into the kitchen.

The smells permeating the room make my mouth water despite the plate of wings I ate an hour ago. "What's cookin', good lookin'?" I ask, stepping around Ben to see what's on the stove.

"Stir fry." He plants a quick kiss on my lips before adding some sort of sauce to the pan of sautéed vegetables.

"Sounds good."

"How was your talk with Adam?"

"It was good. Nice to finally get everything off my chest. I know he'll call the others to tell them on his way home. He's always been good at diffusing that bomb for me."

"I'm glad you told him. Now you just need to tell your parents."

I roll my eyes. I hate that so many people need to know my business, but I also recognize that I'm being a petulant child about this. I'm just ready to move on from the whole thing, even though I know it's not possible.

"Soooo, you talked to Rebecca recently?"

Ben freezes, then pulls the pan off the burner before turning around to look at me. "Why in the fuck would I have talked to Rebecca?"

"I don't know." I shrug my shoulders. "She just seems to

have some ideas that I'm temporary, and when you find someone to take over the clinic, you'll come crawling back to her, begging for forgiveness." I raise my eyebrows at him, waiting to hear what he has to say about that.

There's a small part of me that's still a little worried he's going to do just that. That Sonoma is going to get too small for him, and he'll go running back to Greensboro the minute he can.

"Did she confront you? Fuck, she's such a bitch. I wouldn't put it past her. She was so mad when I told her no the day she came to the clinic."

A little of the steel that had been in my spine leaks out at his words. He immediately made her the bad guy, despite the way I asked him about her. "I think she's still mad. Adam and I ran into her when we left Donna's, and she started spouting all this nonsense about how I was nothing and she would end up the winner. All while eye-fucking Adam, which was strange to watch."

Ben's hands run down my arms. "I'm sorry you had to deal with that. I can talk to her and tell her to leave you alone. Being told no isn't something Rebecca is accustomed to, so I'm sure she's trying to do whatever it takes to win."

"No, if you talk to her, it'll only add fuel to the fire. Eventually, she'll go away."

"Are you sure?"

"Yeah."

"I love you, Sara. I'm in this with you. I know I suck at telling you how I feel, but just know, my old life doesn't even come close to making me feel the same way you do. I don't want to go back. Ever."

Ben's blue jean-colored eyes bore into mine, imploring me to believe him. And I do. I believe every word he's saying. Letting my insecurities and petty jealousies get in the way of my happiness is asinine. I deserve to have all the love Ben is giving me, and I'm going to do whatever it takes to give that same love back to him.

"I love you, too, Ben." I lean in to kiss him, hopefully conveying exactly how much he means to me. "Now, feed me this delicious-smelling food.

33

BEN

"They're loud."

"Okay." I glance over at Sara as she twists her fingers together.

"And they're going to interrogate you," she continues.

"I'm prepared for that."

"And Adam called you an idiot the other day after we had to endure Rebecca. I forgot to tell you." Sara has been running through the list of why me attending her family dinner is a bad idea since we left for her parents' house in Westlake.

"That's fair. I was an idiot for dating her."

It doesn't seem to matter what I say. Sara keeps coming up with things she thinks are going to make me run screaming. I think she's forgotten that I used to hang out with these guys, and while I know that doesn't give me a pass to date their sister, it does give me some insight into what's about to happen.

I remember how protective they were of her back then, and I know that hasn't changed as they've gotten older.

"Yeah, you were. And they're going to beat you up for it. They're probably going to challenge you to a boxing match, and then there will be bloodshed, and Mom will be pissed they got blood on her carpet again, and the whole day will be ruined. We should just go home."

I pull onto the Ellises' street, parking the car next to their mailbox. "Sara, what's going on right now? Why are you so freaked out?"

She swallows, then looks at me with wide eyes. "I've never brought a boy home before. Not even high school guys. My brothers always scared them away before I could even attempt to date anyone. You're the first. Probably the only. I just don't want you to run away."

"I'm honored to be the first one, and I hope to God I'm the only. Everything will be fine. I'm a tough guy; I can handle your brothers because we all want the same thing. You to be happy. Do I make you happy?"

"Yeah, really happy."

"Good, then let's go inside." I give her a swift kiss before I get out of the car and jog around to her side. Helping her out, we walk hand in hand to the front door. Sara walks right into the traditional house, the entryway opening immediately to the living room. The guys are gathered around the television, playing a video game, but they pause it when they hear us come into the room, moving toward the door.

"Hey, guys, you remember Ben Crawford, right?" Sara starts the introductions.

Adam's the first to shake my hand. "Good to see you, man. Thanks for what you did for Sara." He nods his head at me as I shake Matthew's, Carter's, and Nolan's hands.

Before they can say anything else, Mrs. Ellis elbows her way through the group to pull me into a hug. The tiny woman only stands at my chest, and a moment of sheer awe floods through me when I realize she birthed four men the size of tanks.

"I'm so glad you guys are here," she squeals, pushing Matthew and Nolan out of the way to pull me into the kitchen. I raise my eyebrows at Sara, unprepared for her mom to be my biggest concern.

"Tell me everything. How did you guys meet? How long have you been dating? Are you getting married? Sara, are you pregnant? God, that would be wonderful!"

"Mom! Jesus Christ, let the man breathe." Sara leans in to extract her mother from my arm as a laugh tumbles from my mouth.

"We've been dating for a couple of months. Hopefully, one day, Sara will marry me, and I don't think she's pregnant, but you'd have to check with her."

"I think I'm in love with him," Cindy stage-whispers to Sara.

Sara rolls her eyes while fighting a grin.

"You trying to steal *both* of my girls?" Sara's dad asks, giving me the once-over.

"Just one of them, sir, and only if she'll let me."

"That was a good answer. I like him. Want a beer?"

"What is wrong with my family?" Sara asks the room.

"Sure," I say, following Sara's dad to the fridge. He hands me a beer after popping off the top.

"Steve, by the way. It's good to meet you." He reaches out to shake my hand. "Look at the wolves circling. Don't let them get to ya. They're all bark and mostly no bite." He chuckles.

I grin at him, happy to have made an ally in Steve. Matthew and Nolan are whispering to themselves while Adam and Carter are sitting on the couch, pretending like they're not waiting for me to come back. "I should probably get in there before they get too worked up."

"That's a good idea, kid. I'll have another beer ready for ya when you're done."

Laughing, I walk back into the living room. Sara is distracted by her mom and Natalie, who must've come in when we were talking with Cindy.

"Hey, Tucker."

"Hey, man!" Tucker pulls me into a bro hug, which is a bit of a surprise. "Glad you're here."

"What do you want with Sara?" Matthew asks.

"You gonna dick her around?" Nolan says at the same time as Matthew.

"Jesus, guys." Carter sighs.

"Well, we need to know!" Nolan defends, and I just stand there and wait until all five men are standing around me, including Tucker, waiting for my answer.

"Look, guys, I love her. I'm here to stay for as long as she wants me around. You know your sister is a badass who can take care of herself, so she's in control here."

They all nod their heads, seemingly happy with my response.

"Did you really save her from being abducted?" Matthew asks quietly. The worried looks on all their faces melt the remaining tension in my shoulders.

"Yeah, but she can kick my ass now, so I think she'll be okay," I say in an attempt to lighten the mood. I can understand why they're worried about her. They've been her protectors since day one, which is also why I can understand why Sara didn't want to tell them what happened. Maybe if they see how capable she is now, they won't have to worry so much.

"Psh. Now you're blowing smoke up our asses," Nolan mocks.

"Hey, Shortcake," I holler into the dining room. Sara's head whips up, her face immediately worried I'm getting pummeled by her brothers. "Nolan doesn't believe you can kick my ass."

"Oh, shit," Tucker and Adam whisper.

Sara's jaw sets in a stubborn lock as she takes in Nolan. "Is that so?"

"Please just move my coffee table," Cindy huffs before

walking into the kitchen. Steve steps next to me as Sara stands up to Nolan.

"Let's see what you can do, *Shortcake.*" Nolan smirks.

Sara winks at me while grinning, and I couldn't be prouder of her. Matthew moves the table while Carter stands between them as referee.

"No junk shots, please. I'd prefer not to hear Nolan whine about his baby-maker." Carter sighs. "And go."

Within three minutes, Sara has Nolan pinned on the ground.

"Holy fuck," Matthew says, his slack-jawed look mirroring Carter's, Nolan's, and Adam's. Steve looks pleased as punch while Tucker and I are snickering behind our fists.

"Okay. I'll be honest, I wasn't prepared for that. Let's go again," Nolan says, suddenly way more serious than he started.

Sara also becomes more analytical, watching Nolan, anticipating his every move before he makes it. This next round takes about seven minutes, but she pins Nolan again. They're both panting and grinning at each other.

"My turn!" Matthew yells, shoving Nolan out of the way. Sara just laughs at the two of them.

Matthew and Sara grapple for a while, using mostly jiu jitsu holds. With Matthew's size and athletic ability, Sara struggles to get the upper hand for a minute, but she finally does, pinning him with an armbar.

I swear she's Wonder Woman, and I fall just a little more in love with her.

"Fuck, who is training you?" Matthew asks as they guzzle water.

"Dax Pierce at The Warehouse. He's amazing."

"Dax is good, but Sara has a natural talent for jiu jitsu, which makes her better," I tell the guys. Sara beams at my praise, and I move closer to her. Taking my chances with her brothers, I wrap my arms around her. She leans into me, pressing her lips against mine.

"We may tolerate you being with our sister, but public displays of affection will not be allowed," Nolan whines.

Sara flips him off, then kisses me again, making me laugh.

Natalie comes over to us, gushing about how she wants to learn self-defense so she can take down Tucker. If I'm not mistaken, there's a little glimmer of insecurity in her eyes when she talks about wanting to take classes. The only reason I recognize it is because I saw the same look in Sara's eyes when I first brought it up to her.

I don't know what happened, but the burn scars on Natalie's arms tell me there's more to her story than I originally understood.

I guess that can be said for everyone. We all have backstories. Some we can be proud of, others we don't really want the world to know about, and those stories affect how we present ourselves to the world. It's just further proof not to judge someone based on the version you're seeing at that moment.

"I've been talking with Dax about setting up a regular class for people to learn self-defense. He actually suggested I could help him teach it after I get trained up some more," Sara says, which is news to me. I didn't know she'd brought up the idea to Dax already. She'd be an amazing teacher, and I'm sure some people would prefer to have a woman instructor instead of the tattooed behemoth that is Dax.

"Really? That would be amazing. When you guys get it going, tell us so we can join," Natalie says.

"Dinner's ready, hoodlums!" Cindy calls from the kitchen.

We all pile into the dining room, cramming ourselves around the large wooden table. We don't fit all that well, but I've never seen someone as happy as Cindy is right now.

"Seriously, we're going to have to buy a new house if any more of us partner up," Nolan says.

"I would gladly buy another table if you brought someone home, Nolan." Cindy grins at him.

He rolls his eyes at her.

"He's the least likely of us to find a woman," Matthew starts. "Just look at him. Who'd want to be with that ugly mug?"

"Oh, fu—" Nolan's gaze flicks to his mom, whose eyebrow is raised in judgment, "—udge off."

The whole table erupts in laughter while Nolan pouts. The rest of dinner is spent loudly talking over each other until my ears are buzzing.

I finally understand what it would've been like to have siblings. It's insanity, and while it would've been nice to have a buddy growing up, I'm sort of glad I was an only child.

Sara's hand finds mine under the table, her soft fingers wrapping around my calloused palm. When I look into her eyes, I see my whole world reflecting back at me. I see everything I've always wanted right there, and I don't think I will ever be able to look away.

34

SARA

"Ben, it's like a billion degrees outside."

"I still want chicken noodle soup and a BLT. Can we meet at the café?" Ben's tinny voice comes through my Bluetooth speakers as I park my car in one of the few empty places on the street.

"Yes, but don't complain to me when you're too hot from the soup."

"I'll just take off my shirt."

"I'd prefer you save that for home."

Ben laughs. "Good. I'll see you in a bit, then."

"I love you."

"Love you more." He hangs up before I can respond, and I roll my eyes as I get out of the car. Crazy man.

I walk down the awning-covered sidewalks of Main Street, making a mental list of all the shit I need to get done today.

The first stop is Quinn's store, Paint and Paper. She manages the gallery while also creating jaw-dropping paintings herself. I need to find a birthday gift for Ben's mom, and I know she loves all things handmade. Then I have to pick up a few things for the fundraiser before grabbing lunch with Ben. Which wasn't on the agenda until now.

The door chimes as I walk through, my eyes adjusting to the shade of being inside. Quinn looks up from the reception desk with a smile that grows wider when she recognizes me.

"Hey, I didn't expect to see you here," I say as she comes around the desk to give me a hug.

"Normally true, but Kendra has a stomach bug."

"Yuck for Kendra; score for me. I need help to find a gift for Ben's mom."

"Oh, Mrs. Crawford is hilarious." Quinn grins. By the tone of her voice, she knows all about Sybil's quirks. "Let's take a look at what we've got."

Quinn and I walk around the gallery, discussing the different pieces she has on display. The place looks like it could fit in on a street in New York with its oak wood floors, brick columns, and perfectly placed pedestals showing off the different art pieces. Each one is made by local artists, which I love.

Along the walls hang a multitude of paintings. Each one seems so different from the last but fits together when looked at as a whole. Quinn is a genius, I swear.

I find a sculpture of a man and woman that, at first glance, seem to be turning away from each other, but when you shift, the piece almost moves, and the couple looks like they're embracing. It's beautiful and mesmerizing. It's also incredibly fitting for Dr. Charles and Sybil's relationship.

There were a few moments during dinner the other night when I thought they were going to get into a full-on fight. But then I'd see a little twinkle in their eye as they looked at each other, and I realized that's how they kept the spark, the liveliness, in their bond. Thinking back on the words they used, I realized they weren't really fighting, even though it sounded like it.

"This is perfect," I say to Quinn as I continue to stare at the sculpture.

"I love that piece. I'm almost sad it'll be gone, since I won't be able to look at it every day." Quinn laughs.

"I'd imagine you feel that way about most of the art in here."

"Too true." Quinn grabs the sculpture and takes it up to the counter. She wraps it up to keep it safe, and I head out with a quick hug and a *see you later*.

Dropping the box off at my car, I head back down the sidewalk to finish my errands. Things have settled since the break-in. I don't feel quite so on edge anymore, but that's probably because of Ben being at my house full time. As weird as it was to have someone in my space, I've gotten used to it. So used to it, I'm not sure I ever want him to leave. I've kept that thought to myself, though.

Digging through the decoration bin at The Treasure Trove proves to be fruitless, which is annoying. I love my small town, but there are times when it would be nice to have the bigger box stores for some additional options.

I shoot a text to Ben, giving him an update.

Me: Decorations were a bust. Any other ideas?
Ben: You in a bikini.
Me: Not exactly what I was thinking.
Ben: But it would be hot.
Me: Focus, please.
Ben: We could take a trip to Greensboro. Get you some Lucky Charms Marshmallows while we're there.
Me: I think I fell in love with you again. Is that possible?
Ben: Yes. Now, about that bikini? ;)
Me: No. Come meet me for lunch.

. . .

Rolling my eyes despite my grin, I tuck my phone back into my pocket. I can't believe he remembered my love for Lucky Charms Marshmallows. It would be kind of fun to see all his old hangouts. Although, based on his stories, I don't think it would take very long to see them all.

I head to the café for lunch. It's usually packed on a Sunday afternoon, but hopefully, I can snag a table while I wait for Ben to show up.

The smell of freshly baked bread invades my nostrils, making my stomach gurgle. The tables are packed with customers either eating or waiting on their food. I spy Levi and Hope at one of the corner tables, their heads bent together, completely oblivious to the world.

As I wait for a table to open up, I peruse the glass case of desserts. There are a couple of breakfast pastries left, three baking sheets of beautifully decorated sugar cookies, and an assortment of cupcakes, breads, and cakes.

I'm debating about getting one before Ben arrives, but a couple leaves their table, so I rush over to grab it instead of getting a cake. I read a book on my phone, willing Ben to show up soon because I'm starving, when his adorable face pops up on my screen.

"Hey, are you close?" I answer, crossing my fingers he's around the block.

"Hey, I'm so sorry. I have to take care of something really quick. Can you just do a to-go order instead, and I'll meet you back at home?"

"What do you need to take care of?" I ask, standing from my table to get in line.

"Nothing important. Just a quick errand."

"Okay, I'll see you back at the house, then."

"Perfect. Love you."

Ben hangs up after I respond, and I stare at my phone for a second, confused as to what just happened. I don't know what errand he had to run or why he wouldn't tell me what it was. It's a little suspicious, but I'll force it out of him when I get home.

"What can I get ya?" Chelsea asks from behind the counter. She has an adorably evil Yorkie that is obsessed with her and will bite anyone that comes between them. I have the scars to prove it.

"Can I get two BLTs, a bowl of chicken noodle soup, a strawberry summer salad, and two of the chocolate cupcakes to go, please?" I figure Ben can make up for his sneakiness by eating a cupcake off me. No, wait, I'll eat it off him. That's better. Torture for him, cake for me.

"You got it."

She hands me a buzzer, and I stand by the checkout counter to wait for my food. I can't wait to see Ben's face when I tell him my plan for dessert. Sometimes I wonder what I did before Ben and I got together. My life was a lot less full; I know that. Even when we stay home to watch movies on the couch, we still have more fun than when I'd do the same things by myself.

My buzzer vibrates in my hands, so I head up to the counter to grab our food. Luckily, it's only one bag, so I won't have my hands full. I head back out of the café toward my car, the smell of food wafting up and making my stomach gurgle again.

Hands wrap around my mouth and shoulders, yanking me off the sidewalk and down the alleyway between the buildings.

No. Please, not again.

I struggle against the hold as their grip tightens, willing my brain to remember my defense techniques.

Then, my body starts moving as if it has a mind of its own. I relax, dropping my weight, which loosens my attacker's hold on me. I pop my hands up to break the hold completely, sweeping my leg out to take down my attacker.

He evades my move, throwing out a punch I wasn't

prepared for as it lands in my solar plexus. I gasp at the power behind the punch, and somewhere in the back of my mind, I recognize how easy Dax's punches have been.

My attacker growls, racing forward to tackle me to the ground, using his substantial weight to pin me down.

I fight. With everything I have, I fight, trying to pull my body out from his. I gain some advantage when I get my legs loose. Using the leverage of being on the ground, I kick against his chest, careful of my foot placement. It gives me an inch of space, just enough to move my arms and punch him in the throat.

He flinches back, allowing me to get out from underneath him. I hurl myself off the ground, running toward the mouth of the alleyway. I yell out, hoping someone will find me and help me.

I'm almost out when a massive hand wraps around my face, yanking me back into his tree trunk of a chest.

"I didn't want to do this, my love, but you give me no choice."

A pinch in my neck and the burn of a liquid entering my system has my mind racing. He drugged me. I can feel my entire body slowing down as the drugs take effect. I trained for this attack. I was ready for it to happen, even though I prayed it never would. I thought I could handle anything that came my way. I was strong. I had the confidence and the skills. I was ready.

As the edges of my consciousness darken, I have one final thought.

I lost.

35

UNKNOWN

Just look at her.

I brush her silky hair off her forehead, revealing her beautiful face. I'm finally close enough to touch her, to breathe her in like I've wanted to for months. She's more than I ever thought she'd be.

I know I need to leave; I need to get out of this place, but it's so hard to take my eyes off her.

She's finally mine.

I buckle her into the seat, tying her hands to the door just in case she wakes up. I didn't want to hurt her. I really didn't. But she gave me no choice. It's imperative we leave now, otherwise, I would have had to leave her behind, and that was not an option.

So, I did what I had to do.

She'll be okay with it when we get to where we're going. She'll forgive me, I know it. I've forgiven her for all of her mistakes. That's what you do when you love someone.

I get into the car to drive back to the house. It's not the best place in the world, but it's safe, which is the most important thing to me.

Sara and I will be safe there—from everybody.

When I'm finally home, I lift Sara from the back seat, her head resting on my chest. I cuddle her closer to me, happy to finally have her in my arms. She's the one thing that's only for me. My every-thing. I can't wait to start our life together.

I lay her down on my bed, moving her hands above her head so she's secured to the headboard. I know she won't be comfortable when she wakes up, but in time, we'll be able to trust each other.

I lie down next to her, making one of my fantasies come true. She's so small next to me. I'll have to be very careful. I don't want to break her.

I run the back of my finger across her face. So beautiful.

And finally mine.

BEN

"Come on, guys! Time to go inside," I yell at the dogs. We've been hanging out in the backyard to get some fresh air. It feels like it's a million degrees outside, but the shade trees are doing a pretty good job of keeping things cooler. The dogs have been going back and forth between running around like loons and lying on the cool concrete.

Sara was probably right that soup was a bad idea, but their BLT is not the same without their chicken noodle soup. Maybe I could talk Sara into getting ice cream so I can lick it off her later.

That's a much better idea.

I open the back door for the dogs to run inside, following behind them. They slurp water like it's going out of style before plopping down on their beds for a nap. The three of them have become inseparable. They became buddies when they first met at the dog park, but ever since I've been staying with Sara, they've become more like a pack than just friends.

It's kind of crazy how quickly we all got into a rhythm of living together. There were hiccups—I'm only allowed to shower at night since neither one of us is very quick about it, and she's never allowed to cook our meals because the dish count is astronomical—but for the most part, we've settled in easily.

The decision was a no-brainer for me after Cooper told us he didn't get anything from the evidence they collected after the break-in. I wasn't about to let the love of my life live alone in a house her stalker knows how to break into. I don't regret that the situation has pushed our relationship forward faster than would be typical. We haven't been dating that long, and most people would say that moving in together this quickly would be a bad idea.

But at this point, I know everything I need to know about Sara to be sure she's who I want for the rest of my life. Dealing with all the shit with Rebecca and my job was all for her. And it was worth it. It was absolutely worth it.

My phone pings with a message.

Sara: Decorations were a bust. Any other ideas?"

About a million, all having to do with her. Instead, I go for teasing, which she doesn't appreciate.

I smile at my phone like an idiot. How can I not love a woman who is sassing me one second and reminding me why I fell in love with her the next?

She's my perfect match in every way.

I'm definitely going to do the ice cream thing. The frozen treat against her warm skin.

Shit, now I'm hard.

I swear, I'm worse than a horny teenager around her. I grab my shoes and get ready to leave the house.

When my phone rings, I answer without looking, expecting it to be Sara telling me she found a table already.

"Hey."

"Benjamin. Thank God you answered," Rebecca's whiny voice says through the speaker.

Fuck.

I've been dodging her calls ever since she came to the clinic. I have nothing more to say to her, but she's been relentless in her effort to talk to me. Being told no is not something she handles well, obviously.

I sigh into the phone, already exhausted by her theatrics. "What do you want, Rebecca?"

"Ben, please, I need your help. I rolled my ankle getting to my car, and you're the only one I know here who can help me."

"You're still in Sonoma?" I guess I should've been prepared for this after she confronted Sara.

"Yes, I just… I thought maybe I could try to talk to you one more time, but I've taken the hint. You don't want to talk to me. But I do need help."

Something in her voice has the protector in me sitting up. If she's hurt, there's no one here who would help her.

Sighing again, I agree to meet her, even though this isn't a good idea. I don't know what else to do, though.

Sadie gives me the same eyeball she's always given me when it comes to Rebecca, and I suddenly understand the look when I never could interpret it before. "What else am I supposed to do? Leave her stranded?"

A huff comes from Koda, and I roll my eyes. I'm surrounded by animals who are entirely too intelligent for their own good.

Leaving the house, I call Sara to tell her I can't make it to lunch. The suspicion in her voice makes me cringe. I don't want to keep this from her, and I won't. I'll tell her when I get home. I just don't want her to stress about it. She's got enough on her plate as it is.

I pull into a parking space next to Rebecca's car. She's

sitting on a bench across the park, her nose buried in her phone. This feels like a setup. It probably is a setup.

This was such a bad idea.

Rebecca's eyes meet mine before I have a chance to act on my thoughts of leaving. Resisting the urge to bang my head against the steering wheel, I get out of my car and walk to the bench.

"Thanks for coming. I thought it would be a good idea to go for a run, but I turned my ankle and can't make it back to my car."

"Well…let's get you to the car." Clearing my throat, I offer my hand. Rebecca takes it, wrapping her arm around my shoulders. I have no choice but to hold on to her waist as I help her to the car. My skin crawls as her body shifts against mine.

Such a bad idea…

"Have you been working out? You feel bigger than you used to," Rebecca asks as we hobble across the grass.

"Uh, yeah. I've started boxing again."

"Good for you." She pauses, a thoughtful expression on her face. "Do you… Could I come and watch sometime?"

I wait until we get to her car before responding. "What is this, Rebecca? We're not reconciling. There's no good reason for you to still be in Sonoma. Are you even hurt?"

Anger flashes in her eyes before she reins it in. "Yes, I'm actually hurt. You think I'd humiliate myself out here just to get you to see me?"

Her question is a little too on the nose. "Actually, yes. It doesn't matter, though. I'm done after this. Go back to Greensboro, apologize to your dad, and start taking responsibility for your life."

I turn to go back to my car when Rebecca calls out to me. "You're different."

"Good. Isn't that the point of life? To change? To grow?"

"I just didn't think you'd do it without me," she responds, vulnerability coloring her words.

"We spent almost our entire relationship doing things without each other. We just never noticed."

Rebecca nods. "Bye, Ben. I hope you're happy."

Surprisingly, I think she means that. "I hope you can be, too, Becks." I get into my car and head home. As much as I didn't want to have that conversation, it was necessary. Now we can both move on with our lives without feeling like we left our relationship unfinished.

Hopefully, Sara isn't too mad at me for ditching her at lunch. If I were in her shoes, I'd be pissed, though, so I'll have to make it up to her somehow. Ideas flash in my mind as I drive home. They all involve sexual favors, but I don't think she'll mind too much. Especially now that we no longer have to worry about Rebecca making any more scenes.

She's out of our lives, and we can all finally move on.

BEN

Pulling into the driveway, I'm surprised Sara isn't home yet. I wouldn't have thought it would take an hour to get our food to go, but the café can get really busy. There's also a good chance she ran into one of the millions of people who love to chat and got stuck talking to one of the gossiping hens.

Walking into the house, the dogs rush toward me as if I were gone all day. I give them all pats before plopping down on the couch to call Sara. I've got some making up to do, and I need her home to get started.

The phone rings once, then kicks over to her voicemail. Resigned to waiting, I chuck it onto the couch. The world is getting me back for ditching her. I flip on an episode of *The Office*, my mind playing over the exchange with Rebecca.

I *have* changed since I moved to Sonoma. Having such a rocky start clouded the differences I've felt since I made the decision to stay. I no longer feel the pull to keep pushing myself harder, striving for some unknown goal I'll never reach. For a long time, I thought my ambition was going to get me somewhere. It was what drove me to constantly do better, reach higher. Now, I know it was my way of filling a void inside me.

Dad was right. I wasn't happy in Greensboro. I kept striving for more in the hopes it would make me happy, but it didn't. Not until I surrounded myself with people who made happiness the goal instead of status. Hanging out with Sara's friends, analyzing Mom and Dad's relationship, even seeing the dynamic between Sara and her brothers, I realized being with people who genuinely care about me is more important than a fancy job in a fancy city.

Adjusting to small-town life still isn't easy, especially when I need something I could easily get in Greensboro that I can't here, but this feeling of contentment makes up for the annoyances. Plus, having Sara by my side makes all the difference in the world.

I glance at my phone as the episode ends; a blank screen tells me there's nothing new from Sara. I can't help the niggle of worry that forms in my gut. Even on the busiest days at the café, it wouldn't take almost two hours to get our food and then come home. We live five minutes from town.

Grabbing my keys and slipping on my shoes, I head out of the house. I know this is probably an overreaction. I can imagine her sitting at a table, talking with someone, and just losing track of time. But I can't let go of this feeling of something not being right. She was coming home to me. We were going to have lunch. She wouldn't have chatted with someone for an hour when we had plans, even if she was mad at me. If anything, her anger would've pushed her to come home sooner.

When I get to Main Street, I find her car parked a few spots from Paint and Paper. Nothing seems off about her car, so after parking next to her, I head to the café to see if she's there. When I step inside, the noise of the crowd feels overwhelming as I try to curb my panic.

I scan the room, looking for the chocolate-colored hair

I've come to love. I would think she'd be by the take-out counter, but I don't see her.

Spotting Levi and Hope, I head toward their table. "Hey, guys. Sorry to interrupt."

They both look up at me, smiles on their faces. "Hey, Ben. Pull up a chair. Is Sara here? You guys can sit with us." Levi moves to grab a fourth chair, but I stop him.

"You haven't seen Sara? She was coming by to get us lunch. I thought you might've seen her."

"We've been in our own world over here, so we haven't been paying much attention." Levi's brows furrow as he takes in my harried state. "Is everything okay?"

"Honestly, I'm not sure. She was going to put in a to-go order, and that was a couple of hours ago. Her phone goes to voicemail when I call, and her car is still parked on the street."

"Okay, we'll go check the shops and see if she had to stop somewhere before heading home." Levi stands, grabbing his crutches, and Hope follows behind him. I'm grateful they didn't immediately call me crazy for panicking.

"I'm going to go talk to Chelsea and see if she knows anything." With more people helping me find her, a little bit of my worry starts to ease. I'm praying she's just shopping and I'm completely overreacting.

I get up to the counter, grateful Sara and Michelle pushed me to improve my tableside manner, otherwise, I'd never have remembered who Chelsea was.

"Hey, Dr. Crawford. Sara was just in here." In this small town, there was no hiding our relationship from anyone. We weren't trying to hide it either, so word spread like wildfire. The new vet and his tech getting busy has been a hot topic in town.

"Yeah, that's what I'm wondering about. Did she get her food?"

"Oh, yeah, she got it and headed out a while ago. Was something wrong with the order?"

"No. Uh…thanks," I stutter. My panic is edging closer to the surface as I leave the café.

Working to keep my breathing even, I pull out my phone to call Cooper. The phone rings in my ear as I walk down the sidewalk, scanning the entire area for Sara.

"Hey, Ben. What's up?" Cooper's voice sounds distant in my ears as my gaze catches on a to-go bag splayed out on the ground.

"Oh, fuck. No. Please, no." I run down the alleyway, where plastic containers are haphazardly strewn across the ground. I carefully step around them until I see Sara's purse upended on the ground behind the take-out bag.

"Ben? What's going on? Levi's calling me now, too."

"Get down here. Bring your guys and get to the alleyway between the café and Herman's Hardware."

"I'm on my way."

Fuck!

* * *

THE ENERGY in the air is frantic as Cooper's guys scour the alleyway for any piece of evidence they can find. My entire body is tight with tension as I watch them do their jobs, wishing I could do more than stand here like a helpless idiot.

Sara's phone was found on the ground next to her purse, so we can't track it and we're still working on getting the security footage. None of the cameras face the alleyway, but Cooper's hopeful we can get something from the back of the buildings.

I don't even understand how she could've been taken. She was skilled enough to take down me and her brothers. How could someone have gotten the drop on her? It doesn't make sense.

And even though I can't prove it, I know it was her stalker. There's no other logical answer. Who else would have a motive to do something like this?

Levi's hand patting my shoulder pulls me from my introspection. "Hey, we're going to find her. This isn't the first time some asshole thought he could take one of ours."

I can only nod my head at him. He's right, and he's been through a situation similar to mine. The only problem is, they knew exactly who had Hope. We have no clue. Not a single shred of evidence to point us in the right direction.

Cooper comes walking down the alleyway, tension lining his shoulders. He looks different in his uniform, more serious, focused. I guess that's a good thing.

"We're not finding much, other than the items Sara dropped. We're going to look at the security footage from each business that has them. We might be able to catch a detail about how they got away, even if it's small." Cooper pauses, hesitation in his eyes. "Has anyone called the Ellises yet?"

"Fuck." I blow out a breath. "No. I'll do it now. They can come over to Mom and Dad's to wait since it's centrally located."

"That's a good idea. Your mom is the perfect person to help keep them calm."

I run my hands through my hair, hating the idea of making this phone call. It'll be better coming from me rather than Cooper, though.

I pull out my phone, clicking on Adam's name first. He'll be the most level-headed about everything.

"Ben, what can I do for you?" His tone is clipped, hurried, as if he's in the middle of something.

"Hey, something happened." The words dry up in my throat, and I have to force a swallow to get them to come back. "We think Sara was taken by her stalker. We found her stuff in an alleyway in town, and no one has seen her in hours. Cooper is working the scene with his guys, but they aren't getting much."

"Fuck! How did this happen? You were supposed to be watching out for her."

"I know…" I half-whisper, guilt flooding through me like a tidal wave. I never should've gone to see Rebecca. If I would've ignored her, this never would've happened. It's all my fault.

"Do Mom and Dad know?"

"Not yet. I was going to call them after I got off the phone with you."

"Don't. I'll call them," Adam says, his words coming out like a lash through the phone.

"Tell them they can come to my parents' place if they want to be closer. They can stay the night or whatever they need."

"I will." He sighs. "Look, Ben…it's not your fault. I shouldn't have said that."

"But you were right. It is my fault." The crushing weight of failure slumps my shoulders, the words drying up before I can tell him why.

I can feel his agreement through the phone, even though he doesn't say it. "Text me your parents' address. We'll be there within the hour."

38

SARA

A heaviness settles in my body, making the effort to wake up feel like I'm swimming through mud. What the fuck did I do to feel like this? God, my head is aching, and I swear I swallowed a bag of cotton balls. I try to move my arms as pins and needles buzz under my skin. A clanking noise has me looking up at my hands. They're hanging from cuffs attached to a headboard.

No wonder my arms feel like they're dead.

Oh, fuck.

Memories of the attack come flooding back into my brain, making my whole body tighten in panic. My gaze darts around the room, taking in every detail I can while my heartbeat pounds in my ears.

Shabby blinds let in plenty of sunlight, which hopefully means it's only been a few hours since I was taken. The room itself is shabby, too. Old, peeling wallpaper hangs in random places, the ceiling fan is broken, and the splintered wooden door is closed. Too many details pile on top of each other, making them blur together.

I try to pull my hands down, forgetting for a moment they're still stuck. How do I get out of this? My defense classes did not include getting captured. *Maybe they should.* Not the time to be thinking about teaching.

The doorknob turns, and fear spikes through my system so quick my vision fades for a moment.

The man who attacked me comes through the doorway. He's so big he has to turn sideways to get through the opening. Now that I'm no longer in the throes of self-defense, his features are clearer to me.

His blond hair is long, hanging by his ears that stick out from his head. He also has a long beard that's darker than his hair. He's the epitome of a lumberjack without the hipster connotation.

"You're awake." He smiles, showing me crooked teeth. "I'm so glad I can finally talk to you. It's felt like ages since you were last awake."

"You drugged me," I accuse him.

His shoulders slump. "I didn't want to, but you didn't give me a choice. I needed to make sure you came home. It was the only way."

"But this isn't my home! I don't want to be here."

"I know it'll take some time to get used to, but we're going to be a family. It's going to be wonderful. You'll remember how much you love me, and I'll just keep loving you until you remember."

"You sent me presents."

His eyes light up at my statement. "I did. That was me, Gabe." He taps his chest with his hand. "I wanted to put my whole name on there, but I was told I couldn't, so I just put 'G'. I knew you'd figure it out."

"You tried to take me before."

He bobs his head. "Yep. I did. We were always supposed to be together." His eyebrows pinch together. "That guy ruined it, though. He's been ruining everything. I shouldn't have left you that last time. Then he wouldn't have taken what's mine."

Gabe says all of this to himself, seemingly angry that Ben saved my life, and we got together because of it.

This whole situation is weird. He hasn't threatened me or hurt me. Even when he was trying to grab me, his strikes weren't meant to hurt. Just subdue me. None of this makes sense.

"What are we doing here, Gabe?" I grit out. His name feels like razor blades in my mouth.

"We're going to be a family. We're going to get a new house. I'm happy about it. I don't like this place. It's ugly. You deserve so much better."

"Where are we going?" If I can keep him talking, maybe I can figure out where we are right now. Then I'll know the best way to get out of here.

"I don't know. Somewhere better." He smiles again. If he wasn't a six-foot-five giant, it would almost seem childlike.

"Do you think you could get me a glass of water? I'm really thirsty."

"Oh, sure." He stands from the bed and steps out of the room.

Now that the drugs are almost out of my system, I do a quick inventory to figure out my injuries. My side aches where Gabe landed the punch to my ribs. My head is thumping from either the drugs or my fear, and my arms are completely numb. I need to get them out of the cuffs before I'll be able to make any type of escape. If I don't get the feeling back, they'll be useless.

Grabbing the metal ring, I attempt to pull my hand out, but the cuffs are entirely too tight. Even with my tiny wrists, I'd never be able to slip my hand through the opening.

Gabe pushes back through the doorway, a glass of water in hand. He stands there, unsure of what to do now.

"You could uncuff one of my hands and leave the other one attached to the headboard." I'm not 100 percent sure yet, but I don't think Gabe truly wants to hurt me. I think he genuinely believes we are going to be a family. If I can convince him to untie my hands, maybe I can convince him to let me go altogether.

He frowns for a minute. "Do you promise not to run away?"

"I promise."

Gabe nods his head, then comes toward the bed. My whole body tenses when he gets close, unable to control the unconscious reaction. He sets the water down on the night-stand before he pulls a key from his overalls and unlocks the cuff.

I hiss when my arm falls from the headboard, and I clench my fist in an effort to get it to wake back up.

"Here." Gabe hands me the glass, and I chug the contents. The water sloshes in my empty stomach, threatening to come back up.

I set the glass back on the nightstand, then use my free hand to adjust my body on the bed. It eases some of the tension in my cuffed arm. "So, what's the plan? If we're supposed to be moving, then what are we doing here?" At this point, refuting my involvement with Gabe would be pointless. I've seen enough documentaries on stalkers to know that disrupting his beliefs is a quick way to piss him off.

"We have to wait." He sits on the bed next to me, reaching his hand out to hold mine. It takes every ounce of effort I have not to move away from him. His hand swamps mine, making me seem tiny and fragile.

"For?"

"I'm not supposed to tell you. I don't really like keeping secrets, but I'm not allowed to tell you the plan."

"When are we leaving?"

"Soon, I think." Gabe shrugs, and it's then I realize he's not the one in charge here. Someone else is calling the shots. Probably has been from the very beginning. What I still don't fully understand is how I fit into the puzzle. Obviously, Gabe wants me to be a part of his family. As more than a sister, if my intuition is correct. What does the mastermind behind this get out of abducting me?

Gabe keeps holding my hand, a contented smile on his face as we continue to sit on the bed.

This whole thing is beyond strange.

"How old are you, Gabe?" Maybe if we talk, he'll slip up and tell me what's going on.

"I dunno. Why?"

"Um, just wanting to get to know you better. You don't know your birthday?"

He shakes his head. "Do you know your birthday?"

"Yeah, it's in April."

"Oh." His shoulders drop. "Well, we'll celebrate next year." He smiles like the idea is the best one he's ever had.

"Sure. What do you do every day?"

"I cut down trees. Then I sell them."

"Do you like doing that?"

Gabe shrugs. "I'm sorry we can't bring your animals. I know how much you love them."

I blink at his statement. "I do love them. They're probably missing me."

"You were so kind to them. I loved watching you play with them at nighttime. I got jealous of how you'd pet them. But now that you're here, you'll love me like you loved them."

Bile rises in my throat at the idea of him watching me every night. I bite my tongue in an attempt to keep my expression neutral.

"I can't bring them with me? We could stop at my house before we leave."

"No. The black one doesn't like me. He growls. He can't come with us."

My eyes close as a sigh falls from my chest. I always wondered what Koda was staring at in the backyard. He'd sit there for several minutes, unmoving, staring into the woods behind my house. He was staring at Gabe. God, I want to throw up.

"What about clothes? I'll still need to pack some things for wherever we're going."

"No, you'll be okay. We're supposed to sit here and wait. Then, we can leave."

"Wait for what?"

Gabe frowns like he doesn't understand my question. "I don't know." He lapses into silence, a frown marring his face. Why would he not know the next step in the plan? Even if he's not the leader, I would think he'd know exactly what's going on.

Except, if his only goal was to have me by his side, then his part in this plan is complete. And if my intuition is correct, the leader wouldn't want Gabe to know too much about what he's planning. Gabe's childlike mind would more than likely be a hindrance rather than an asset. The problem with this revelation is I can't figure out what happens next.

What does the leader want from me?

Gabe perks up, looking toward the doorway. He must've heard a noise outside.

My heart rate increases with the realization that his partner is here. If Gabe is being manipulated, that means the partner is the one I need to be afraid of. Gabe could hurt me just based on his size alone, but I don't think he will. As much as I hate to admit it, I genuinely believe he has no idea the consequences he's set into motion.

This partner knows. He knows exactly what he's manipulated Gabe into. There's no other way Gabe would have been able to accomplish all the things he did.

Footsteps echo from the hallway, giving away exactly where this guy is as he walks around the house. I'd had a small moment of relief with Gabe, relying on my intuition that he wasn't going to hurt me. Now, the fear is spiking, and

I'm trying my damndest to figure out how I'm going to get out of this.

At least Gabe didn't cuff my hand again.

"I'm glad you're home," Gabe says, standing from the bed, his wide body hiding the person standing in the doorway. "Are we going to leave soon?"

"Mm-hmm. Just need to do a few things before we'll be ready," a female voice says.

I frown, surprised it's a woman—one who seems familiar for some reason.

She walks around Gabe, and my whole body goes into shock.

"Michelle?"

BEN

I run my hands through my hair, pulling at the strands. It'll be a miracle if I still have hair when Sara is back in my arms.

It's been five fucking hours since I last talked to her.

Five long, tense, stressful hours and we have nothing to show for the suffering.

Cooper isn't anywhere closer to figuring out who took her. We've all watched the security footage from the alley to see if we recognized the car. The person driving was obscured, the plates were stolen, and the car was a dead end. A silver Toyota is one of the most common cars on the road, so there was no way to track it from the alleyway.

Adam and Nolan have been taking turns pacing across my parents' living room while my mom has been fussing over everyone. She refuses to sit down, choosing to bake or bring us tea or anything else we don't really want.

I don't know what to do. I go from the backyard with the dogs, to inside, to staring at my phone, praying for a call or text or anything from Sara saying she's okay.

Fuck, I just need her to be okay.

Getting up from the dining room table, I walk back

outside. The dogs are all under the umbrella, lying in the shade without a care in the world. I sit down next to them, doling out pets to each one. Without the dogs, I probably would've gone insane by now. The stack of bricks sitting on my chest would've crushed me from the guilt I carry. Every time I think about what I did, I want to punch something. Namely myself.

"I wish I were as ignorant as you guys right now. I could do with a little relaxing instead of all the stress piling up in my body."

"Same," Adam says, sitting down next to me. I didn't even hear him come out. "Sometimes I wish I could turn off this analytical part of my mind that's trying to puzzle out the answer. Trying to see something no one else has seen because I'm so desperate to find out what happened to her. It's exhausting."

"I'd really like to stop feeling like an absolute failure."

"You couldn't have done anything differently, Ben. We both know if you'd tried to lock her up, she'd have junk punched you and then ran away."

A rusty laugh falls from my chest. "That's not what I mean. We were supposed to meet for lunch, but Rebecca called me, needing help. I told Sara to meet me at home with lunch instead of waiting at the café. If I'd have told off Rebecca like I should have, Sara would still be here."

My confession is met with silence, the words hanging in the air like a brewing storm.

"As much as I want to be pissed at you for meeting that horrible human being, I can't. Ben, even if you had met Sara for lunch when you were supposed to, her stalker would've just picked a different day to grab her. This was always going to happen because he was determined enough to make it so. I know my words aren't going to ease your guilt. I've got plenty of it myself, wondering if I would've pushed her to open up sooner whether she'd be safe."

"She would've punched you if you forced her to talk before she was ready."

Adam huffs out a laugh before turning serious again. "How did he subdue her? I mean, she took down Matthew, for god's sake. How did this happen?"

"I don't know. My only guess is he surprised her and knocked her out somehow." It would've taken a really stealthy guy to do that. If the stalker is the same person who tried to take Sara from La Mensa, his bulk would've kept him from being stealthy.

Adam grunts in agreement, not liking the idea of Sara being physically attacked, either. I hate the idea of her getting hurt, but there's no other explanation for how he could have taken her down.

We sit in silence for a while, both of us taking comfort in not being alone with our fear and guilt.

My phone rings, pulling us both out of our stupors. Frowning down at Susan's name on the screen, I answer. "Hey, Susan."

"Ben, sorry to bug you on a Sunday evening. I was going over our inventory and noticed something odd."

"Why are you doing inventory on the weekend?"

"My husband pissed me off, and I needed some time away. Since Sara organized the stock closets, doing inventory is way easier than it used to be. Anyway, this inventory list isn't correct, so I was wondering if you'd be able to double-check it in case our numbers are weird."

Any other time, I'd tell her I'd look at it on Monday, but right now, I really need the distraction. With jack shit to do to help find Sara, and my guilt piling on top of me, this is the perfect thing to keep me occupied.

"I can come in and take a look at it."

"Oh, I didn't mean for you to come into the office now. We can discuss it more on Monday."

"It's fine. I'll see you in twenty minutes." I hang up the phone, then stand from my spot on the deck.

"I'll call you if Cooper comes by," Adam says, standing up with me.

"Thanks, Adam. Do you think it's bad I'm leaving?"

"No, I'd take the distraction if I had the opportunity."

Nodding my head, I turn to go into the house. I say a quick goodbye to my mom, then head to the clinic. It's early evening now, which doesn't feel quite right. This has been the longest day of my life. And I don't want it to end until Sara is back in my arms. Nothing will feel right until she's home safe.

I pull into the lot of the clinic and park next to Susan's car. Once I'm inside, I head straight for the back, knowing Susan will be knee-deep in inventory.

When I come around the corner, I find her holding a laptop while she counts glass drug containers. I wait until she turns around before I speak, not wanting to interrupt her system. She's a very scary lady when you mess her up.

"Thanks for coming, Ben. When your dad was in charge, I could only do a cursory inventory. Since nothing was in a logical place—and not always together—it made it very difficult to know how much of each item we had."

Another point in the techs' favor for putting up with my dad's ability to ruin every opportunity for organization.

"Since Sara organized, I've been able to start inventorying regularly again."

"Thank you for doing that."

Susan waves off my acknowledgment and continues. "Over the past month, we've had a steady stream of missing inventory. Mostly in our drug cart. When I first began cataloging everything, I thought it was just a mistake since things weren't in order. Now, I'm not so sure."

"Let me print off my records, and we can compare."

Susan nods her head, turning back to the drawer to finish

her counts. When I get my lists printed, I head back to the supply closet and work with Susan to compare notes.

After an hour of going through each of our lists and comparing it to the inventory, one thing becomes clear.

Someone is stealing from the clinic.

Not just stealing random things, stealing sedatives.

"Well, shit." I look at Susan.

"That's an understatement."

I run my hands through my hair. "I can't deal with this right now."

"You're going to have to. This isn't a few boxes of gloves being stolen, Benjamin."

"I know! I...I know. Susan..."

"What's going on? I haven't seen you this worked up since the day you were going to tell your dad you weren't going to North Carolina for school."

"Someone abducted Sara today. She's gone. She's been dealing with a stalker these past couple of months, and they got her. Somehow, despite the things we did to keep her safe, they got her."

"What the fuck are you doing here?"

My eyes bug out at Susan's cursing, feeling as if I'm getting in trouble with my principal. "I needed the distraction. I've been going out of my mind with worry, so I thought looking at some inventory would be a good distraction. I didn't think I'd find out someone was stealing fucking sedatives."

"Okay, that's fair." Susan crosses her arms over her chest, a stubborn set to her jaw. "Do you know anything? Has Chief Jackson found anything yet?"

"They collected evidence but found nothing so far. Until Cooper's call comes through, all we can do is sit and wait."

"So, you came here to get your mind off of things?" Susan guesses.

"Yeah, and now I have to find out who's stealing from me."

"It's one of your employees."

"Unfortunately."

Susan rubs my arm, an oddly comforting gesture coming from her. "Why don't you head back home? Let your momma fuss over you until you know what's going on."

Not exactly what I need right now, but I know if I stay at the clinic, I'll keep dwelling on the shit show that this day has turned into. "Thanks for your help tonight, Susan."

"I'm sorry we didn't have better news. Keep me updated about Sara."

I nod my head, then leave the clinic to head home. My thoughts are blank as I drive, my brain unable to focus on any one thing. It's honestly a nice reprieve.

When I pull into the driveway of Mom and Dad's house, it looks like they're having a party with how many cars are parked outside. My phone starts ringing as I get out of the car, Cooper's name popping up on the screen.

"Hey, I'm on my way to your place. Everyone still there?" he asks.

"Yeah, we're all still here," I respond, walking into the house. Everyone's head whips up, hope filling the room before disappointment takes its place when they see it's only me. I'm sure they were all hoping it was Sara coming home, or even Cooper with an update.

"I'll be there in a few minutes." Cooper hangs up.

At least I can tell them he'll be here soon.

"Cooper is on his way." My gaze flits across the many faces in the crowded room, unease lingering in the air.

"Did he say what's going on?" Cindy asks from the dining room.

I shake my head as I walk into the kitchen. I'm tempted to open a beer—Lord knows I need to take the edge off—but I grab a soda instead. I don't want to be impaired in case Sara needs my help or is hurt. I need to be ready for anything.

True to his word, Cooper comes striding into the house a few minutes later, determination lining his features. It can't be easy for him to stay professional when he's looking for someone he loves.

Sara told me after the break-in that Quinn was kidnapped last year, and Cooper almost didn't save her in time. How much harder would it be to have to methodically sift through evidence in order to find the love of your life? I can't imagine. I'm barely holding myself together right now; thinking logically is not in my wheelhouse.

"Okay, I'm going to cut to the chase," Cooper starts once we're all crowded into the living room. "We're still not sure who did this, but we do think she was drugged. We found a syringe in the alleyway that our in-house lab was able to analyze. We expected it to come back as heroin or meth, but it turns out it was a drug called..." He flips through his notebook. "Dexmedetomidine."

"No fucking way," I interject.

"What?" Adam frowns at me.

"Susan and I found out someone has been stealing that exact drug from the clinic."

"It's an animal drug?" Nolan asks.

"We use it during surgeries to keep the animals sedated," I answer. "It's not a drug people can just buy at the pharmacy, but it is safe for humans."

"Do you know who it was?" Cooper asks.

"Not yet. It was one more drama my brain wasn't able to focus on today."

"Any way we could figure it out?"

"We've got camera feeds in the clinic. But Susan only does inventory twice a month. That's a lot of footage."

Cooper rubs his jaw for a minute, the wheels of his mind turning almost visibly. "Is there any reason a tech would need to get into the drug cabinet besides for surgery?"

"More than likely. We store antibiotics and whatnot in there. But we keep everything pretty well organized now, so the only reason they'd need to get into the surgery drawer would obviously be for surgery." I glance at my dad, whose shoulders hitch at my comment. "You also need a code to open the cabinet, which means the only people with access are employees at the clinic, since the drug cabinet wasn't obviously broken."

Cooper nods. "Okay, can we access your records to find any appointments that would have required access to your drug cabinet? It'll give us a starting point so we're not running through hours of footage with no direction."

"Yeah, we can pull both the footage and records up in Dad's office." Walking from the living room, I lead Cooper down the hallway. Adam follows behind us while everyone else stays where they are.

I sit down at the desk, pulling up the records we need. "It looks like there are seven appointments that would have required the drug cabinet to be opened. Four of them were surgeries."

"Let's start with the nonsurgical appointments. Can we have multiple people logged in at the same time?"

I nod my head, pulling up the footage for the right days. "I can pull it up on my laptop for you while I watch on the desktop."

"I've got my laptop, too," Adam adds.

"Go grab it. We'll get these set up first." Cooper takes the laptop from my hands once I've cued up the feed.

For the next hour, the three of us stare at our screens, trying to find anything that could indicate who's stealing.

Cooper's voice breaks the long silence. "What drawer are the sedation drugs in?"

"Third."

"Because I think I found our thief."

Adam and I surround Cooper's chair, leaning over to watch the screen. Sara is grabbing supplies from the closet while Michelle is standing by the drug cart. They're chatting and smiling at each other before Sara walks down the hallway and into an exam room. Michelle opens the top drawer, pulling out antibiotics as would be appropriate. Then she opens the sedative drawer, grabs one of the glass bottles, and slips it into her pocket. It happened so fast, you'd never have noticed she did it if you weren't looking for it.

"I don't understand. Why would Michelle be stealing drugs from us?"

"You can make quite a bit of money on black market drugs," Coopers responds.

"But it's a sedative, not a narcotic."

"You'd be surprised." Cooper raises an eyebrow.

"Was enough stolen to knock out an adult?" Adam asks.

"More than. But you'd need to know the right dosages to knock out a human without killing them." I shrug my shoulders.

"And Michelle would likely understand the dosage required," Cooper says, continuing Adam's thought. "Can you pull up her employee file?"

After pulling the file, I hand the laptop back to Cooper. "None of this makes sense. If Michelle is the one who abducted her, is she also the one who's been stalking her?"

"Potentially. I've got my guys running her information now." Cooper slides his phone back into his pocket.

"But it was definitely a man who attempted to take her the first time. I know that for a fact." The dude was jacked; there's no way that was Michelle.

"Maybe we're dealing with two different people," Adam suggests.

Cooper's face turns grave. "Or they're working together."

SARA

"Surprise!" Michelle grins, sauntering over to the bed. She sits down next to me while Gabe stands at the foot of the bed, happy as can be.

"I…I don't understand," I stutter.

"What do you mean? We've been planning this for ages." Michelle frowns, as if I'm missing something obvious.

"Planning what?"

"Ohhhh. How silly of me. Those drugs probably muddled your mind." She glares at Gabe, who flinches under the scrutiny. "I didn't want to use the drugs on you, but Gabe insisted. Said it was the only way to get you here." She rolls her eyes. "Boys. So illogical."

Now my brows furrow at her words. From our conversation before, I highly doubt Gabe was the one who insisted. Instead of contradicting her, I go with her crazy pants idea. "I do feel pretty cloudy right now."

"Gabe, go get her a glass of water."

He dutifully leaves the room, leaving the two of us alone.

"Such a little puppy, I swear. Anyway. You and I have been planning this escape for a while now. We're going to be a family, the three of us. You're my sister, my best friend. Gabe loves you, too. We'll have the best life."

My jaw starts to drop open, but I catch it before I give away my shock at her words. She sits there smiling at me, completely unfazed by this whole situation.

"What about my fam—my other family? My brothers? They're all going to worry about me."

"Psh. They don't care about you." She grins. "Only I do, remember? Your brothers are a bunch of idiots. They only care about themselves."

Her statement echoes words I've said when I was at my peak annoyance with them.

Does she really think because I complained about my family to her, that they don't love me?

"What about your family?"

"You know I only have Gabe. Obviously, he's not a state away from me. That was a lie. My parents are dead, though. They sucked, so I made sure they couldn't do anything bad ever again." She shrugs her shoulders.

Oh, fuck. Did she just imply she killed her own parents? Who the hell have I been hanging out with?

"So, we're going to be a family, then?"

"Of course, we are. You're the only one who hasn't let me down—*yet*." Michelle looks at me as if she's waiting for me to turn on her. Does that mean there were others before me? People she wanted to be a family with that didn't meet her standards like her parents?

"What about Ben?" My question has hatred burning in her eyes, making me flinch away from her.

She schools her expression, then pulls out her phone from her pocket. "That asshole didn't deserve you, sis. He was nothing but hateful. I thought about putting him down like the dog he is, but it turns out I don't have to."

She turns her phone toward me, a picture of two people walking across the park, their arms around each other. She flips to the next picture, where I can see Ben's profile as they walk to a car. The final picture is of Ben and Rebecca, standing close to each other, serious looks on their faces.

Ben is in the same T-shirt and shorts he was wearing earlier today, so these must've been taken when he told me had an errand to run. Why wouldn't he tell me he was meeting Rebecca?

"They look awfully cozy, and I mean, good for them. They deserve each other's bitterness, am I right?" Michelle ribs, smiling at me. "I'm sorry he tricked you, but I'm not sorry he's out of the way. Makes our lives so much easier. No one will be looking for you now!"

Is she right? Did Ben get back together with Rebecca? She's gorgeous, sophisticated, and loves city life. She's the complete opposite of me in every way. What if Ben decided he was tired of living in a small town and took Rebecca up on her offer to get back together?

No.

That's ridiculous. She may look put together on the outside, but her insides are filled with darkness. I know Ben on a much deeper level, and what she represents isn't what Ben wants anymore. He wants me.

But the idiot still met with her behind my back, and we will be having words about it.

Anger must show on my face because Michelle's eyes sparkle.

"Want to go hit him where it hurts?" she asks, completely misinterpreting my anger.

Shaking my head, I tell her no. "He doesn't deserve our attention."

With a pat on my head and a pitying look, Michelle stands to pace the room. I have to figure a way out of this. I can easily take Michelle down, but with my hand still shackled to the bed, I have no hope of winning that fight. Could I convince her I'm ready to be a part of her family? It's not going to be easy. I already feel bile rising in my throat at being kind to her.

Gabe walks into the room, interrupting my plans. He hands me the second glass of water, and I chug it down. It helps to clear my head of any lingering fuzziness, sharpening my focus on my next steps.

I can't take down Michelle and Gabe at the same time. There's no way. But, if I can somehow get Michelle on her own, and my handcuffs unattached from the headboard at the very least, I might have a chance.

"So, what's the plan now?" I ask, setting my empty glass next to the other on the nightstand. "Gabe mentioned we're moving?" If I use the same tactic I did with Gabe, I might be able to keep up this charade.

"You don't want to live in this shack, do you?" Sarcasm drips from Michelle's voice.

Gabe shakes his head no, sitting down next to me on the bed.

"Where will we go instead?"

"Don't you worry your pretty little head about those details. I've got everything covered."

If we all leave at the same time, I'll have no chance of getting away. But how can I separate them? Suddenly, an idea pops into my head.

"Um, Gabe, could you give Michelle and me a minute alone? I need to discuss some rather delicate matters, and I'd prefer not to say it in front of you since you're a boy."

He furrows his brows, not quite understanding my words.

"Go on and pack our stuff, Gabe. We'll meet you outside." Michelle nods her head toward the door. He follows instructions, lumbering through the doorway and down the hallway.

"What did you want to talk about?" Michelle asks, sitting next to me. She reaches out to grab my hand, gently holding it until she squeezes tight enough to become uncomfortable.

"I just…" I swallow the bile rising in my throat. "I'm just grateful for all the things you've done. I didn't want to say it in front of Gabe because I was worried he'd be jealous, but I'm glad you brought me here." The words taste like acid against my tongue. I hope they were convincing enough.

Michelle's stare tells me she's not sure if she believes me or not. I can't do anything more than that. If she doesn't believe me, I'm screwed.

"Let's get you ready to go." Michelle leans forward to uncuff my hand from the headrest. She holds them both in her own hands, then with a squeeze, she clamps the loose cuff to my free hand.

"Michelle?"

"Just don't want you getting any ideas," she says, an air of nonchalance surrounding her. It feels fake, like she's suddenly suspicious of my motives. If she doesn't trust me at this point, it's only going to get worse. I won't be able to keep this charade going for much longer.

Now or never.

I slam my head forward, smashing the crown of my head into Michelle's nose. Her ear-piercing scream reverberates through the room, magnifying the pulsing pain in my head tenfold.

Fuck, that hurt. I spring from the bed, still dizzy from the hit, but determined to get away. My hair is tugged backward right before I get through the door, pain singing through my scalp.

"You bitch!" Michelle screams. "You were supposed to be my best friend. My family. What the fuck have you done?"

She slams me to the ground, cocking her fist back and landing a blow to my face. Another one lands in my stomach before I can recover. Rolling across the floor, I barely avoid her next punch. I get her in my sights, analyzing her potential moves, my training roaring through me as I figure out a plan of attack.

I've fought people much bigger and stronger than me, but none of them were trying to kill me. We were only sparring. Michelle has nothing left to lose now. I've ruined her plan for our life, for her family.

I react before she does, choosing the offensive side since I have the skill. Dropping my shoulder, I slam into her midsection, forcing us deeper into the room. She gets her hands linked through my bound arms and tugs me around so we're tangled together. Before she can wrap her arm around my neck, I use my foot to stomp on her instep, then throw my elbow back into her ribcage.

Michelle buckles, almost taking me with her as she drops. I twist just in time, untangling my arms from hers as she goes down. I bring my elbow down again, this time to the side of her head, disorienting her. With one more front kick, I send her across the room in a heap. It gives me just enough time to sprint out of the room, adrenaline surging through me, making me feel like superman.

The short hallway leads into a bare living room and outdated kitchen. Everything about this place screams criminal hangout, and I slow my steps, glancing over my shoulder to make sure Michelle isn't following me.

I know I'll have another fight to go when I get outside. Gabe won't let me go easily, so I either need to prepare to run away or find a weapon to use against him. It's the only way I'll win a fight against the giant. Especially with my hands still cuffed.

The only thing within reach is a fire poker, which feels oddly cliché, but I don't have time to think about it.

Picking up the heavy metal, I walk to the windows facing the front yard. Gabe is loading Michelle's car, about to add the last bag to the trunk. How he didn't hear Michelle's screams, I'll never know. There's a side door in the kitchen that will hopefully allow me to get outside without alerting Gabe to my presence.

I cringe when the door creaks open, but I can't stop now. If I've been made, I need to be ready. Once I'm outside, I take a deep breath of fresh air, hope flickering to life with my inhale.

Creeping around the side of the house, Gabe shuts the trunk of the car, done with loading the bags. I pull back from the corner, listening for Gabe's steps as they go from crunching on gravel to pounding up the wooden porch steps. The door opens, then slams shut again, and I know I have only moments to make a break for it.

My body reacts, sprinting across the gravel, my hands bouncing back and forth in front of me as I try to run with them bound.

Shouts behind me have my steps faltering, but I recover, my chest heaving with the exertion. I have no fucking clue where I am; I can only hope to find a place to at least hide until I make my way back into town.

At the end of the long gravel driveway, I sprint across the pavement and into the forest. If I stayed on the road, Michelle would likely be able to find me in her car. Instead, the trees are thick with summer growth, offering plenty of places to hide.

I get into the thickest part of the woods, hoping it'll keep me safe.

41

BEN

"Now we have to find *two* people?" I pace around Dad's office, unable to keep my body still.

"They're more than likely related, and since we've got Michelle's name, we have a starting point," Cooper says, turning back to his laptop. "What do you know about Michelle?"

"Not much. Let me get Dad. He knows her better than I do." I walk out of the office and toward the living room. Everyone is still gathered on the couches, doing their best to stay calm. The tension in the air is heavy with uncertainty, no one quite knowing what to do while we wait.

"Hey, Dad, can you help us?"

"Did you find something?" Mom asks from the couch, her hands wrapped around Cindy's.

"Potentially. We're still looking, though." I look across the room. "Dad?"

He nods his head and follows me back to his office. I lean against the desk as Dad stands next to me, his hands on his hips. "What can I do?"

"What can you tell us about Michelle Graves?"

Dad's eyebrows wing up. "Uh, well, she started at the

clinic a few years ago. Pretty shy at first, but she and Sara became good buddies. Seemed like a nice enough girl. Was she the one stealing?"

"We think so, yeah," I answer. I probably wasn't supposed share that, but at this point, we need every bit of information we can get.

"Huh. Never would have thought she could do something like that. I guess it just proves you never really know anyone as well as you think you do."

"Was she pretty open with her history? Her past?"

Dad looks down at the floor. "You know, now that you mention it, I don't think I knew a single thing about her besides her employment history. I don't even know if she has any family."

"That's not a surprise. She was probably really good at making it seem like she gave you a lot of information, but in the end, she gave you nothing of substance," Cooper explains.

"That's exactly what she did. We chatted all the time, but it was usually about things happening in the town or random chit chat, nothing of consequence."

"If she's the mastermind behind Sara's kidnapping, I'd wager to bet she's a sociopath in need of complete control over her environment. How that factors into why she'd take Sara, I have no idea." Cooper's cell phone starts ringing, interrupting his musings. He answers it, his persona morphing into police chief within a heartbeat.

"Send me the address," Cooper says, hanging up the phone. "We've got an address for Michelle. Some beat-up farm out on Highway 17." Cooper slips his phone back in his pocket, giving me a serious look. "I can't let you come with me, Ben. It would go against protocol."

My teeth clench. I know Cooper's just doing his job and not trying to be an asshole. It doesn't make it any easier. "I understand. Bring my girl home. Please."

Cooper nods, then leaves the office.

"Do you think Sara's there?" Adam asks, taking Cooper's now-vacated chair.

"I fucking hope so. I'm not sure how much longer I can take the waiting."

Dad's hand on my shoulder is a balm for my nerves. "She's a fighter, son. She'll come back to us."

In the quiet moment, an idea pops into my head, and I grab my phone to dial the number.

"Hello," Dax answers.

"Hey, man. I have a big favor to ask."

"Ooookay," he drawls, hesitancy clear in his voice.

"Long story short, Sara was kidnapped by her stalker, and we think Michelle Graves, one of my vet techs, had something to do with it. Is there any chance you know someone who could get us information on her? I'm dying here. I can't wait for Cooper to come back with an update."

"Jesus. I'm sorry, Ben. Let me...I've got a buddy I can reach out to; just send me everything you know about her."

"Thanks, Dax." I hang up the phone and look back at Adam. "Dax was a Navy SEAL before he came to Sonoma. I figured it wouldn't hurt to ask."

"Good thinking. Let's hope he can find something quick before we both lose our minds."

For the next ten minutes, Adam, Dad, and I sit in silence, hoping Dax can get back to us soon. I wish I knew more about Dax to know if this is going to pan out or if it's going to end in disappointment. I can't even think about what Cooper's doing right now.

The sound of my ringtone breaks the tension mounting in the office.

"Anything?" I ask Dax when I answer.

"Just an address so far, but he's working on more."

"Send it to me and anything else that comes your way as soon as you get it." My heart starts to pound. I'm going to find her.

"Will do."

"And thanks, Dax. This means a lot."

"No problem."

I hang up the phone and tell Adam we've got an address. He's out of his chair and through the doorway before I can even ask if he wants to go.

"I'll update everyone on what's going on," Dad says from behind us. "Be careful, guys."

I nod at him before leaving the house with Adam. We get into my car, and I have Adam give me instructions on where to go.

"She's going to be fine." Determination rings through Adam's voice. "Your dad was right. She's a fighter, and she won't give up just because this asshole managed to sneak up on her."

"What if she isn't there?" My grip is tight on the steering wheel, turning my knuckles white. I'm doing my best to keep my hope in check. The disappointment may crush me if she's not okay.

"Then we'll keep searching until we get her home. No matter how long it takes."

We're silent as I drive, worry blanketing the car and keeping us both in our heads. With dusk settling in, the trees lining the two-lane road feel ominous. A heavy weight settles in my gut the closer we get to Michelle's house. We're one step closer to finding Sara, but it doesn't feel like this is the end of the nightmare.

Flashing red and blue lights bounce off the trees down the long driveway. I start to slow down my car, unsure of where to park, when a figure comes striding out of the woods on the other side of the driveway.

"Fuck!" Adam yells, opening his door before I can stop the car.

Sara's brown hair is a mess around her head, a bruise is forming around her eye, and her clothes are disheveled. She's a mess, but she's never looked better to me. I throw the car into park, jumping out without even turning it off. Adam and I run toward Sara before she gets to the road, but someone grabs her from behind, yanking her back from the road.

Sara's yell makes my stomach drop to the ground. There's a knife glinting at her throat while Michelle's arm is wrapped around Sara's shoulders.

"Come any closer and I kill her," Michelle says, her tone calm and determined. Her threat is not an idle one.

Adam and I both hold our hands up in surrender, freezing on the side of the asphalt. We're only feet away from Sara, and I've never felt like she was further away from me. "What do you want, Michelle?"

"You to leave."

Adam glances at me, silently communicating he'll go find Cooper. I nod at him, then turn my attention back to Michelle. She's cooing in Sara's ear, something about how they can still be together and not to worry. She doesn't even notice that Adam's no longer standing there.

"Can you at least put down the knife?" I plead. My whole body is tight with tension as a small bead of blood pools around the knife tip.

"Aren't you supposed to be on your way back to Greensboro?" Michelle's question throws me off for a minute.

"Why would I go back to Greensboro?" I glance at Sara, and her steady gaze on mine is enough to allow my body to lose some of the tension. It's hard to remember how strong Sara is sometimes. My protective instincts want to push her behind me while I take the blows, even though she's fully capable of handling herself.

"I caught your little tryst with Rebecca, Ben. You're just a snake who hoodwinked my Sara into dating you. You shouldn't be here."

"I'm not dating Rebecca behind Sara's back," I respond, my gaze locked on Sara despite answering Michelle's question. I need her to know I'm with her all the way. "I'm in love with Sara. She has my whole heart in her hands."

"You lie! You don't love her like I do. You can't protect her like I can," Michelle screams.

"Michelle, you're hurting Sara right now."

"She deserves it. She tried to run away from our family. You don't get to do that without punishment." The knife digs a little deeper into Sara's neck. She hisses in pain as blood streams down the column of her throat.

"Okay, okay." I hold my hands up with my palms out, trying to keep her calm.

Michelle's wild eyes fixate on something over my shoulder as feet pound across the pavement.

"Michelle, put the knife down." Cooper's authoritative voice rumbles across the ditch.

Desperation starts to leak out of Michelle, her gaze bouncing between the deputies surrounding Cooper. "No. We're supposed to be a family."

"I understand, Michelle. I do. But holding a knife to your sister's throat isn't the answer," Cooper says, putting his gun back into his holster. I want to scream at him to take it back out, to keep Michelle in his sights, but I have to trust he knows what he's doing.

"Sara, are you okay?" Cooper asks.

"I'm okay, Coop," Sara responds, her voice even, calm. Something passes between them, a silent communication no one else is privy to.

"I want to help you, Michelle. How can I make sure you get your family back together?" Cooper steps forward, inching closer to them.

"I need you all to leave so that I can take my brother and sister away from this place. It's filled with people who pretend to care." Michelle's eyes bore into me, her point obvious.

"Okay, we'll back away and let you go."

I bite my lip so I don't scream out *no*. Cooper won't let them get away, I know that, but it doesn't make hearing those words any easier.

"First, I need you to lower the knife, okay? You don't want to hurt your sister before you can leave, right?" Cooper takes another step forward, positioning himself right in front of the two women.

Michelle starts to lower the knife, and the minute it's pulled away, Sara drops her body, swinging her leg out to take Michelle's weight out from under her. Michelle drops like a rock as Cooper jumps forward, flipping her over to slap cuffs on her wrist.

"Michelle's brother, Gabe. He's here, too." Sara frantically looks around as if he's also going to pop out of the woods.

"We got him. He's in the back seat of one of the cruisers," a deputy tells her.

She nods her head, watching as a couple of officers pick up Michelle and walk her across the highway. Cooper pops the cuffs off Sara's wrists, then follows behind his officers.

When he's gone, a paramedic guides Sara to sit down on the pavement and starts checking her out.

I can't take my eyes off her. She's safe. She's here. It doesn't feel real.

The minute the paramedic walks away, Sara turns toward me and barrels across the grass. She slams into me, her arms wrapping around my waist as I tighten mine around her shoulders. I've never felt anything better.

"You're safe. I've got you." I continue whispering more words of safety to her until her body begins to relax against me. She pulls back, her hazel eyes filled with tears. I take her mouth with mine, unable to hold back anymore. I need to ensure she's truly here. That I'm not making this up in my head only to wake up and realize it was all a dream.

Our kiss is healing, filled with the longing we've separately shared this whole night. It's everything we need to reconnect with each other.

Adam clears his throat, reminding us both he's still standing there.

Sara pulls back, a grin on her face as she looks over at her brother. I set her on the ground, and she steps toward Adam as he wraps his arms around her. "It's good to have you back, sis," he whispers into her hair.

"Thanks for coming for me." She pulls away from him, her gaze meeting mine.

"We always will," Adam responds, since I can't. Too many emotions are clogging my throat as I stare at my beautiful girl.

Seeming to understand my needs, she steps back to me and leans against my chest.

"When Cooper comes back, we can figure out what to do next. Are you okay? Do you need to go to the hospital?" Adam asks, already going into analytical mode.

"I'm fine. The paramedic cleared me to go home."

Cooper comes walking back across the highway as two of the three cruisers parked in the driveway leave the house.

Sara steps toward Cooper and wraps her arms around him in a tight hug. He takes a deep breath as he holds her, seeming to finally relax. "Glad you're okay," he says as they separate.

"Glad you found me," Sara responds.

"Michelle and Gabe are on their way to the station. We'll put them in cells until we can get them transferred to the county jail." Cooper puts his hands on his hips, looking every bit the police chief.

"Cooper, please be kind to Gabe. I don't think he truly understands what's going on or that what he did was wrong. I think he has a mental disorder of some sort."

Cooper nods. "I'll ask for an evaluation when we get to the station."

"Thanks."

"We'll need to get your statement for the report. Are you up for that right now?"

"Yes. I want to get it all done and out of the way so I can move on."

I wrap my arm around Sara's shoulders, unable to keep myself from touching her.

Cooper gestures to our car still parked in the middle of the road. "Let's go end this."

42

SARA

The pop of a cork makes me look up from the notebook I'm staring at. "Really, Nat? Champagne?"

She quirks her eyebrow at me from across my kitchen, then proceeds to pour a massive amount into a glass tumbler. She splashes some orange juice into the glass before handing it to me. "Drink up, buttercup. In the last two months, you've been attacked, had your house broken into, been kidnapped, and then almost killed. I think of anyone, you deserve this the most."

"When you put it like that, I can't really argue with you." I lift the glass into the air, toasting Natalie for her brilliant thinking, then take a drink. The ratio of champagne to OJ makes me cough.

"You want one, Cindy?" Natalie asks as my mom comes to stand next to me at the island.

"Please. We've got some celebrating to do." Mom wraps her arms around my shoulders to give me a squeeze.

It's been two weeks since Michelle and Gabe kidnapped me, and it feels like it was both yesterday and a lifetime ago.

Michelle is awaiting trial in jail after the judge deemed her to be a danger to society. My statement spurred police to investigate other murders in the areas Michelle has lived, and it turns out, my hunch was correct. She's killed other people who went against her idea of family, not just her parents.

Gabe got transferred to an institution when his psych evaluation indicated he was not capable of understanding the difference between right and wrong. I'm not sure what will happen to him now, but I hope he can get the help he needs.

I've been trying to work through my own emotions about everything that's happened, but it hasn't been easy. It all feels like a hazy dream at this point. Like a nightmare I'm still trying to shake off. I imagine it's my brain's way of coping with the trauma of almost dying. If the memories are cloudy, it makes them easier to ignore.

I don't want to ignore them, though. That's what I did the first time I was attacked, and it only compounded my issues. I made everything worse by choosing to shove down the feelings I was experiencing. I'm determined to address every reaction or trigger that happens instead of pushing them away as if they aren't actually happening to me.

"What are you working on?" Nat asks, coming to stand next to me with her mimosa in hand.

"The fundraiser is a week away now, so I'm going through our final to-do list to make sure everything is ready. Ben's in Greensboro today, picking up the rest of the stuff we couldn't get here."

"Why didn't you go with him?" Mom asks.

I take a deep breath, recognizing this moment as my chance to start being open with people who love and support me. "I'm not quite ready for a big outing."

"That's fair." Nat slips her arm through mine and leads me to the living room. We sit on the couch while Mom sits in the chair next to me. Koda jumps up next to me and snuggles into my side. I have no idea how he knows something is wrong, but he's stayed close to me from the minute I got home.

"There's going to be a lot of things you'll have to say no to for a while," Nat says, taking a drink from her glass. "It's going to be important for you to know when to say no and not feel bad about doing what's best for you. The guilt is going to make you want to push through, but don't. It's not worth it, trust me." Nat squeezes my hand.

This is why I invited her and Mom over today while Ben was gone. I needed some perspective on how to navigate my responses to things. Since Natalie had both gone through a traumatic experience and is my best friend, I knew she'd be the perfect person.

"Thanks, Nat."

"You might consider talking to someone, a counselor maybe, about what happened," Mom suggests.

"You definitely should check into it. It made all the difference for me, and you already know how much Quinn and Hope benefit from it," Nat reminds me.

"I've been making a list of names, and I've even gotten on a couple of waiting lists. I'm working on it."

"Good. Now, can we please talk about Ben?" Mom's face is pleading and teasing at the same time, making me laugh. Which, if I had to guess, was her goal. She's always known when I needed help to get out of my head.

"Did you hear he's the best sex she's ever had?" Natalie stage-whispers, much to my mortification.

"Natalie!" My face is flaming.

"What? I'm just saying…it's an important factor."

"A very important factor. I knew the minute I met him he had some moves." Mom winks at Natalie.

"You two are ridiculous. Let's not talk about Ben's sexual prowess. How about you help me decide what to do about the fact that he went to meet Rebecca behind my back."

Natalie's nose turns up at that. "The she-devil deserves to have all of her eyebrow hairs plucked out."

"Interesting choice, Nat." I laugh.

"Well, she needs to be punished but not, like, harmfully… You know what I mean." Natalie waves her hand in the air.

"What's the actual issue here?" Mom asks, focusing our attention back on the problem.

Is it even a problem? My brain says it is, but my heart says I need to move on. He's been so great these past couple of weeks, doing everything he can to help me heal. It's made me feel crazy for still being upset about this. My uncertainty has created some strain between us that was never there before. It's another reason why I didn't want to go to Greensboro with him. I needed some time away to figure out if I'm being petty or if there's genuinely an issue here.

"I just…I don't know. Why wouldn't he tell me he was going to meet her?"

"If I had to guess, he probably thought he was protecting you from stressing out. And while I know it was stupid, can you understand why he would want to protect you?"

"Maybe…" I say sullenly. "Doesn't really make me feel better about it, though."

"No, it doesn't," Mom concedes. "Let me give you a bit of advice. Men are idiots. They don't always use their common sense the same way women do, so there are going to be many times where you'll want to wring his neck for some of the stupid stuff he'll do."

"Amen," Natalie says, raising her mimosa in the air.

"But the important thing here is to communicate when something he does pisses you off. Because the other thing men are not are mind readers. And don't forget, you're going to do things to piss him off just the same. The only way you'll make this relationship work is by telling each other what's going on. Which means you also need to be open with him about your struggles when you're not feeling yourself."

"We've already had that conversation," I tell Mom. "I'm not good at having the spotlight on me; it's easier to just figure it out on my own. But Ben brought it to my attention that I was actually making things worse."

"Good. Sounds like you two are already on the right track." Mom nods her head, leaning back in her chair.

"So, am I'm being irrational by being angry he met with her?" I ask. I don't really like that idea.

"Absolutely not," Nat starts. "All your mom is saying is to make sure you talk it out with him. You have a right to be angry, but holding on to it and letting it fester isn't going to get you anywhere."

I wince. That's exactly what I've been doing. "I've got a long way to go before I'm any good at this relationship stuff."

"You'll be just fine. If I can make a relationship work with how sassy I am, you definitely can." Natalie grins at me while Mom laughs.

"How about another round, Nat?" I ask, incredibly grateful to have her as my best friend.

"On it." She gets off the couch while Mom and I keep up a steady stream of chatter.

After talking with my mom and Natalie, I'm ready for Ben to be home. I want us to finally be settled, to be on a path moving forward instead of stuck in this holding pattern we've been in since Gabe tried to kidnap me the first time. In order to do that, I'm going to have to open myself fully to Ben.

I think I'm finally ready.

* * *

Keys unlocking the front door alert the dogs to Ben coming home. They scramble toward the door, ready to greet him as if he's been gone for a week. He comes inside, bags weighing him down.

"Did you bring home all of Greensboro?" I ask him, grinning as he tries to say hello to three dogs who each want his utmost attention.

"It feels like it," Ben says, finally giving up on the dogs and walking toward my spot on the couch. He places his hands on the back of the sofa, trapping me between his arms. "Hi." He bends down, giving me a long, slow kiss. He's been so gentle with me since the attack, and while I have enjoyed this side of him, I'm ready for things to go back to the way they were. To when he was my dominant, passionate guy.

Mom's words remind me that, in order to get there, I have to be open with him about all the things that have been bothering me recently. He isn't a mind reader, and I can't expect him to know how I feel if I don't tell him.

"Hi." I smile when he finally pulls away from me.

"How are you?" Ben sits down next to me, wrapping his arms around my shoulders.

"Ready to talk."

Ben's eyebrows wing up. "Yeah?"

I nod. "I talked with my mom and Natalie today, and they reminded me that, in order to heal, I need to be open with you."

"You know I'll listen whenever you need to talk things out."

I take a deep breath, giving myself a minute to gather my thoughts. "I know I'm not quite 100 percent yet. But I feel more like myself than I have in…weeks. Even before the attack. And I'm ready for us to be back to normal. In fact, I *need* us to be back to normal. I don't want you to treat me like I'm fragile anymore."

A small smirk pulls at the corner of Ben's mouth until suddenly, he's grinning so widely I'm afraid it may take over his face. "I can do that, Shortcake. Anything else?"

"I want to talk about Rebecca."

Ben's smile dims just a bit, but he nods his head in understanding. "Yeah. Look, I know I was an idiot. I knew it the minute I showed up there that I had done the wrong thing by not telling you, and I'm sorry. I'm sorry for assuming you couldn't handle it, and I'm sorry it's been bothering you."

I open my mouth, but then close it again. His apology takes the wind right out of my sails. Which is probably why Mom suggested I talk with Ben about it. "Why didn't you just tell me in the first place?"

"At the time, I thought I was protecting you. I had a feeling she was using her injury to convince me to get back together, and I didn't want you to worry. I showed up at the park, where she'd genuinely hurt her ankle, and helped her to her car. I told her there was no chance of reconciliation no matter what she did, and I think she's finally accepted that." Ben pauses, his gaze locking on mine. "It's always going to be my goal, you know. To protect you from having to deal with shit you don't need to. But what I forget sometimes is how capable you are of protecting yourself. I'm not always going to make the right decisions, but I am going to do my best to remember how strong you are."

"And I will try to let you take care of me more often. I know I don't have to do everything on my own anymore."

"I think as long as we talk to each other, we'll figure it out." Ben tucks a piece of my hair behind my ear, leaving his palm resting against my cheek. I nuzzle into it, happy to have that heavy weight off my chest.

"You know, it's not always going to be as easy as having a conversation like this," I say, snuggling deeper into his side.

"Nope, we're probably going to fight like my parents. Between your sass and my tendency to be an asshole, we're going to get on each other's nerves."

A laugh bursts from me. "Completely accurate, you broody bastard."

"Oh, you're going to pay for that one." Ben throws me over his shoulder, making me squeal. He slaps my ass as he walks into my bedroom, my laughter flowing behind us.

When he dumps me on the bed, I feel all the worry and stress from the last couple of weeks melt away. With one look from Ben, I know we're going to be okay.

"Don't you move a muscle," Ben demands, pointing a finger at me.

"Yes, sir." I salute him, grinning when he narrows his eyes. He leaves the room but is back within a minute, holding something behind his back.

"I got you something while I was in Greensboro. Something that I hope will make up for my idiocy. At least this time." Ben looks adorably chagrined, like he knows bringing me a present isn't exactly going to make up for him keeping things from me.

He pulls the item from behind his back, and it takes me a second to understand what he brought me.

"You brought me Lucky Charms Marshmallows?" Sitting up in bed, I reach for the box he's holding out.

"They're your favorite." Ben shrugs.

Tears swim in my eyes at the gesture, unable to contain my happiness. "I love you so much, Benjamin."

"I love you, too, Sara." He plucks the box out of my hands, despite my protest, then pounces on me, throwing me back to the bed.

I am going to love this man for the rest of my life.

I can't wait.

43

BEN

Sliding my pen across the page, I scratch off the next item on my list. Is it growing? I'm pretty sure it's grown in the ten minutes it took for me to stock the water bottles.

"How are the—" I look over my shoulder, but no one is standing next to me anymore. I thought our intern was still helping, but apparently not. There are several people buzzing about the park, hanging up banners and setting up tables. Everyone is busy preparing for the fundraiser.

And I'm an absolute fucking disaster.

I've never been so nervous about anything in my entire life. Not even during my boxing tournaments, where I was outmatched. This event is my first statement to the town saying, *I'm here to stay, and I want to do something good.*

What if no one shows up? What if the whole town shows up and I make an idiot of myself?

Oh, God, this is not going to go well.

Sara comes up beside me, taking in the madness of the park. "Take a deep breath."

"I am breathing!" I snap.

Sara quirks an eyebrow at me.

"Sorry." I take a deep breath as suggested. It helps release some of the pressure in my chest.

"It's okay to be nervous. But just so you're prepared, the whole town will be here."

"That's what I'm afraid of," I mutter.

"It's going to be great." Sara wraps her arms around my waist and squeezes me tight. I know she's right. It's going to be fine. I might throw up, but it's all going to be okay.

Get yourself together, Benjamin. Jesus.

Clearing my throat, I straighten my spine. It's time I grow the fuck up and get this done.

"Okay, we're still waiting on the catering delivery, and we need to finish putting together the silent auction table and make sure the band is good to go."

Sara grins at me. "The silent auction table is done. Your mom finished that one. I talked with Chelsea, and she's on her way with the pastries, and Nolan is currently chatting with the band to make sure everything is good to go." She points across the park where her brother is standing next to the lead singer of the local band. "I even called Margie at the animal shelter, and she said they'll be here soon."

"So, basically, everything is done."

"Everything is done."

"Good, that's…good." Without anything else to focus on, I'm not sure how I'm going to expel the rest of my nerves.

"Come on, I want to show you something." Sara pulls on my hand, dragging me away from the center of the park. She ducks around a couple of trees where we're out of sight of anyone milling about the park.

I frown at her, confused as to what she would need to show me here. "What are we doing?" I whisper.

"Why are you whispering?" Sara grins at me.

"I don't know. 'Cause you're being secretive."

She laughs, making her eyes light up. It's so good to see this lightheartedness return to her. After the kidnapping,

Sara started withdrawing into herself. I wasn't sure if it was the trauma or something I was doing wrong. She barely talked to me, and it was killing me. When she told me all the things going on in her head last weekend, I wanted to punch myself with how stupid I'd been. I won't ever keep stuff like that from her again. Especially since I know she can handle it.

Lately, she's been a lot more open with me about when she's struggling more than usual. She's also started talking about her nightmares instead of holding it all in. I hate the images in her head, but I'm glad she's opening up to me finally. I've been worried the event will be too much for her, even though she's told me it won't be. She said it's given her something else to think about so she's not dwelling on the negative, and being surrounded by people she loves will help keep her grounded.

Her awareness of her triggers solidified how far she's come in dealing with her trauma. I'm incredibly proud of her.

Fisting my shirt, Sara pulls me closer, my hands landing on the tree behind her and caging her between my arms. Before I can say anything, she takes my mouth in an all-consuming kiss, rendering me completely stupid. Bending my elbows, I lean into her, twining my tongue with hers as I duel for dominance.

I slide my hand into her hair to cushion her head, while also pulling it back to gain more leverage. The little whimper from Sara has a growl rumbling through my chest.

"Benjamin Charles Crawford! You quit necking and get out here." My mom's screech can be heard across the entire park, effectively acting as a bucket of cold water.

I pull away from Sara, biting my lip to keep from laughing. Her wide grin and shining eyes tell me she's having just as much trouble as I am.

"Coming, Mom!" I shout back. Running my thumbs

across Sara's cheek, I realize exactly what she did for me. My nerves have settled into excitement all because she knew I needed a distraction. "I love you, Shortcake."

"Love you, too."

After a quick peck on her lips, I take Sara's hand and lead her back to the park. There are way more people here than there were ten minutes ago. The volunteers from the shelter are here, setting up crates and playpens for the animals. People are already cooing over the puppies and kittens, checking out the auction items, and mingling with the other attendees. The event doesn't start for another half-hour, and there are more people in attendance than I ever imagined there would be.

"Are we prepared for this many people?" I murmur to Sara.

"Yep. I upped your catering numbers because I knew more people would show up than you thought."

I squeeze her hand. "I am falling in love with you all over again."

"Good." She grins, then leads me over to a mangy-looking pup, cooing at the little guy.

"Absolutely not. We have six animals as it is!"

"Oh, stop. I'm just looking," Sara grumbles.

"That's all it takes, love. One doe-eyed look and he'll have you taking him home in a heartbeat." I pull Sara away from the temptation and closer to the food table, hoping a cookie will distract her long enough that she'll forget about the dogs.

"I know you're trying to distract me," Sara says around a mouthful of sugar cookie. Her glare would be deadly if she wasn't so cute.

I lean in and kiss her forehead. As the fundraiser hits full swing, I realize Sara was right: Nearly the whole town has shown up for the event. There are so many people here, milling about and chatting with each other. I can't quite believe they'd all be willing to support this event—support me.

"Hey guys," Dax says, walking up to us. "Quite the turnout. Congrats."

"Thanks." I reach out to shake his hand.

"How you holding up?" Dax asks Sara.

She shrugs her shoulders. "As good as you'd expect. I heard you helped get the information needed to find me."

Dax nods his head, but doesn't say any more about it.

"Seriously? That's all I get? A head nod? I mean, you'd think getting kidnapped would allow me some secret information, but noooo. Not with this guy." Sara shakes her head, fighting a grin.

Dax busts out laughing and rolls his eyes. "No amount of whining will do it either."

"We'll just have to get him drunk," she conspires, leaning in close to me as if Dax can't hear her.

"That won't work either." He grins.

"Ugh. Fine. Whatever. I'll just force you to be my friend, and eventually, you'll tell us something about you."

"Sure. You get right on that." He shakes his head before growing serious. "I am glad you're okay, though."

"Thanks for helping with my rescue."

"Yeah, we really are grateful for your help," I add.

"Happy to be of service. And hey, if you want to come by next week and talk about starting a self-defense class, let me know." Dax's change of subject doesn't go unnoticed, but Sara lets him get away with it.

"I'll give you a call."

We say goodbye and start moving through the crowd, each person stopping to say hi and how much they're loving the event. Some of them are even asking when we'll do another one.

"Dr. Crawford!" Margie calls from across the park, her green animal shelter polo making her stand out from the crowd.

"How's it going?" I ask when we finally make it to where she's standing.

"Every animal has been spoken for." She grins, excitement brimming out of every pore.

"Seriously?" Sara's jaw drops, mirroring my own surprise.

"I can't even believe it. We've never had this happen before," Margie says. One of her volunteers comes up to ask for her help, so she says goodbye before taking off in the other direction.

"Well done, my love." Sara wraps her arms around my waist, leaning on to her toes to press a kiss to my lips.

"I wouldn't have been able to do it without you. You know that, right?"

"You could've. You probably would've run out of food ten minutes in, but you could've." Sara winks at me as I throw my head back in laughter.

Mom comes up to my right side with a microphone in hand. "Ben, it's time to announce the winners of the auction."

I take a deep breath, my nerves returning in full force. Sara squeezes my hand, then shoves me forward.

Shaking my head at her, I walk up to the stage, a huge smile on my face. "Hey, everybody! Can I have your attention for a few minutes?" The microphone echoes across the park, making the crowd turn toward the stage.

"For any of you who don't ride the gossip train, I'm Benjamin Crawford, the new vet at the animal clinic in town and host of this event." The crowd laughs, easing the rest of the tension in my shoulders. "First off, I want to say thank you to all of you here today. As the new guy in town, I really appreciate your support of the clinic and helping me achieve this goal. I am incredibly lucky to call this place home and can't wait to see what else lies in store for both me and the clinic." A round of applause meets my words, making me grin.

"Now, on to the fun stuff. I was just told a few minutes ago that every animal has been spoken for and will be going to their forever homes at the end of the event today!" A loud chorus of cheers echoes across the park. When it dies down, I continue speaking, telling everyone about the baskets and who donated what, as well as the winners of each one. It feels like I've been up here for an hour before I'm able to hand the mic off to the band again.

"Well done, Dr. Crawford," Sara says when I meet her back at the drink table. She hands me a water bottle, and I chug down the contents before I respond.

"That was the most nerve-racking thing I've ever done." I sag against Sara, my arms around her shoulders. "When do you think we can get out of here?"

"Not for a while. We still have to take everything down."

I groan; all the adrenaline pumping through me has finally dissipated, and now, I want to go home and take a nap. "How are you doing? There's been a lot of people here today."

"I'm doing okay. Hanging out with my brothers has been good. They actually haven't let me out of their sight."

"They're still worried about you."

Sara sighs. "I know, but it doesn't make it any easier to deal with their hovering."

"Just give them some time. The same way you're giving me time to stop hovering over you, too." Sara grins at me, nodding her head.

I look across the crowd of townspeople gathered in the park. All the animals are now either on leashes or headed to their new homes. The playpens have been taken down to make more room for everyone to mill about, and the band is in full swing, playing all the best pop covers while people dance. The whole park has turned into a party.

"We're going to have a good life together, aren't we?" I ask, keeping Sara tucked into my side.

"Yeah, we are."

44

SARA

The muscles in my arms quiver, but I try to ignore the ache. When I get in the house, I set the box down in the kitchen, breathing out a deep breath. That one was heavier than I anticipated.

Looking around, I can't help but smile at the beautiful space. The farmhouse-style kitchen with its white cabinets, butcher-block countertops, and silver fixtures turned out incredible. The rest of the house has a similar vibe since Levi was in charge of picking out the materials—thank goodness.

It's all perfect, and I still can't quite believe we're going to live here. The four-bedroom house feels huge compared to my little cottage. But the dogs have so much more room to play, and Ben and I are making the house into a space for both of us.

The day Ben asked me to move in with him will forever be one of my favorite memories. We had finished finalizing the details with Dax for me to start teaching a self-defense class when Levi called him to say the house was ready for a final walkthrough.

When we got there, Levi was standing at the front door to

hand over the keys. They were done with everything, and the house was officially ready. As Ben and I walked through each room, I just kept thinking, *what happens now?* He wouldn't need to live with me anymore. He could finally move out of his parents' house and have the space he's needed since he moved to Sonoma. And I was trying to keep my disappointment shoved down into a corner of my heart.

I didn't want him to leave, but I also didn't want to tell him what to do. So, I just followed him around, pretending to be excited about the beautiful space.

And then we walked out into the backyard, where all three dogs were racing around the fenced-in area, wrestling and having a blast.

"Looks like they like it here," Ben had said to me while I tried to figure out what was going on. "Do you think you could like it here, too? I know it's not as cozy as your cottage, but I figured we could make it into our home. If you want..." His hesitancy melted every ounce of worry I'd been holding on to, and I ended up launching myself at him.

When we fell into the grass, the dogs piled on top of us, cementing my decision to say yes.

That was a week ago, and it's been a whirlwind of boxes and take-out breadsticks ever since.

I walk back out to the front as Ben and Adam lift my couch from the moving truck. We've been going at it for most of the day, despite the early September heat. Between Ben's packed storage unit and my house, we have a lot of stuff.

"Think you could tone down the ogling?" Nolan asks, wrapping his sweaty arm around my shoulders.

"Nope." I send an elbow to his ribs, making him grunt. He drops his arm, rubbing his side while grumbling about having to watch his sister salivate over a guy.

I wasn't staring at Ben, but since Nolan mentioned it, he does look pretty fucking hot right now. His cutoff shirt is highlighting his biceps as he carries the heavy couch inside. Makes me want to lick him.

Shaking myself out of my stupor, I grab another box from the truck. It takes us about an hour to finally get everything unloaded. And thanks to my mom and Sybil, all the boxes have been organized into their respective rooms. It'll make unpacking everything much easier.

Everyone is gathered around the island, eating pizza and chatting. I step up next to Ben, wrapping my arms around his waist. He kisses my temple, then goes back to eating.

The past few weeks have been...hard. The fundraiser was an excellent opportunity for me to distract myself from all the things that happened, which was great. Until it was over. Then I didn't have anything to focus on besides the recurring nightmares, my inability to go anywhere by myself, and the undercurrent of panic that doesn't ever seem to go away.

It's been frustrating to say the least, but my therapist has encouraged me to focus on the progress I've made instead of focusing on the negative. The panic has eased significantly, I no longer feel like someone is watching me all the time, and I'm more in love with Ben than I've ever been before.

The man is a saint for putting up with everything. He's been patient with my triggers, understanding of my need for space while also never letting him leave my side, and willing to do whatever I ask of him when I ask it. I couldn't have gotten luckier.

I also think moving into his new house will be beneficial not just for us as a couple, but for me to be in a new environment that isn't tainted by all that happened. I already feel like I can breathe easier, and we haven't even spent our first night in the house.

"What do you mean, you're going to get someone else? It's only been a couple of weeks." Nolan's question has me tuning into the conversation.

"It means exactly what I said. She doesn't take anything

seriously. I need an assistant who is going to focus on the tasks I give them, not try to find ways to *spice up my life.*" Adam quirks his fingers, using air quotes. They must be talking about Adam's new temporary assistant while Tessa is on maternity leave.

"Is she doing a bad job? Not getting things done?" Matthew frowns. As the CFO of Sidelines, he's probably wondering if they're paying someone when they don't deserve it.

"No, she's staying on top of everything, but the woman uses a purple, sparkly pen, for god's sake. And she keeps putting these affirmations on my computer every morning."

Adam's statement is met with silence. Everyone looks at him like he's crazy until we all bust out laughing.

"Seriously? That's why you want her gone? Because she uses a purple pen?" Matthew asks.

"No. I just… She doesn't take anything seriously. She's too happy." Adam sulks.

"So, you can't be happy and work in an office?" I ask, enjoying Adam being in the hot seat for once.

"That's not what I said."

"Sort of is, bro." Nolan grins.

"Whatever. I'm out. You guys are on your own to find a way home." Adam stalks out of the house, the front door slamming behind him. We all start laughing again, unable to contain it.

"I'll go make sure he's okay." Matthew walks out of the kitchen, the sound of the front door opening and closing again ringing through the kitchen, only softer this time.

"We should all head out. Let these two settle into their new home." Mom gives me a big hug, then turns to Ben to do the same. Everyone follows suit, saying goodbye and giving out hugs. When they're all gone, Ben and I collapse onto the couch. The dogs, having already given up on the day, are sacked out in their beds.

"Why is moving so exhausting? We work out regularly. I should not be this tired," Ben asks as he leans forward and picks up my feet, swinging them onto his lap to start massaging them.

I groan, the pressure feeling incredible. "Because instead of doing only an hour of focused exercise, you're lifting and moving for an entire day. You don't realize how much you've done until you finally relax and can no longer feel your arms." I relax into the throw pillows on the couch, enjoying the constant pressure Ben keeps using on my arches.

"I never thought about it that way, but you're right."

"Mm-hmm," I mumble, trying not to fall asleep.

"Come on, you. Let's go get ready for bed."

"But it's only eight-thirty." My attempt at arguing is half-hearted. I'm exhausted.

"How about we shower together, then see how you feel." Ben picks me up, my legs dangling over one arm, while the other is wrapped around my back. I snuggle into his neck, breathing in his masculine scent. I don't even mind the sweat. Much.

When the hot water is streaming over both of us in the massive grey stone shower, I don't feel quite so tired as my hands slide across Ben's wet skin.

"I'm never going to get enough of you," I tell him, leaning in to place a kiss on his chest.

"Good. Because I'm keeping you forever."

"Forever, huh?" I quirk my eyebrow at him, pretending like that's not exactly what I want from him, too.

"Forever. My heart is yours, Sara. And it always will be." He presses his lips against mine, his kiss searing into me as our bodies slide against each other.

"I'll protect it with all that I have, just as you'll protect mine," I whisper against his mouth.

He's the one I've waited my whole life to find. The one I wasn't sure was out there until he stomped into the clinic with a storm cloud raging over his head. He's everything I dreamed of and nothing like I expected.

He's my happily ever after.

EPILOGUE

BEN

"Should you chew some gum? Bad breath could ruin the whole moment," Mom asks, fussing with my tie. I'm pretty sure if she tightens it anymore I'm going to pass out from lack of oxygen.

"No, I don't need gum, Mom. I brushed my teeth." I gently push her hands away from my neck.

"Charles, can you get him some gum? There should be some in my purse." She continues ignoring my refusal. I glance at my dad, his eyes rolling like a teenager. I hide my smirk, knowing he'd never have done it if Mom's back wasn't turned to him.

She keeps fiddling with the lapels of my suit, the boutonniere pinned perfectly in place, anything else to keep busy. "Mom." I grab her hands, forcing her to look up at me. "Stop fussing. Everything is perfect."

"But you're my baby boy, and it's your wedding day. I can't help it." Her eyes get a little teary as she cups my face.

"Well if you keep tightening my tie, I won't be alive long enough to actually get married."

Mom swats my shoulder, fighting a grin. Dad comes over

and wraps his arm around her shoulders, kissing her forehead as he pulls her away. Mom melts into his side, and I just smile at the two of them, the best example for me to strive for in my own relationship.

Adam pokes his head into the guest bedroom. "She's about ready. It's time to head out there."

A bout of excited nerves filter through me as I walk out behind him, my parents following me.

We're getting married today. Finally.

I asked her to marry me about six months after we moved in together, which was answered with an emphatic *yes*, but it's taken us over a year to get to this day.

At first, neither one of us were in a huge hurry to get down the aisle, but when people started questioning why we felt that way, we both realized there was more to it than just not wanting to rush.

A few months before I asked Sara to marry me, we found out Michelle had been charged with two counts of murder in South Carolina. At the time, we thought it was a great thing because it meant Michelle would likely receive a much longer sentence in the end. But what ended up happening instead was a long, drawn-out trial that lasted almost a year before any sentencing happened.

The defense attorney tried to get a plea deal, but Michelle refused to sign it, maintaining her innocence, and sending them to a full trial.

The evidence against her was irrefutable, so we were confident she would be sentenced, but Sara and I couldn't move forward with planning our wedding, knowing there was even a small chance Michelle could get off. We needed that part of our lives to be settled before we felt ready to move forward.

The day the jury came back with a guilty verdict, both of us were able to breathe a huge sigh of relief. Michelle was charged with three counts of first degree murder which resulted in her being sentenced to life without parole. Since we knew she was never getting out of prison, we opted out of going through a trial for Sara's kidnapping. We just wanted it to be over.

Then when we started discussing the wedding, our mothers began planning this over-the-top, froufrou event that wasn't even close to what the two of us wanted for our day, and we finally had to threaten a courthouse wedding to get them to back off.

Now, we're about to get married in our backyard with our best friends and family holding beers and their kids running around like banshees, all while our dogs chase butterflies, dodging the high-top tables set up under the canopy.

It couldn't be more perfect.

"Is she okay?" I ask Adam as we walk under the tent where Cooper is standing, waiting to marry us. We didn't want some random pastor that barely knew us to officiate our wedding, so we asked Cooper if he would be willing to do it instead.

"She's beautiful." Adam's voice catches, emotion written all over his face. Fuck, I'm going to cry just looking at him. There's no way I'll be able to keep my composure when Sara gets here.

* * *

Sara

"One more pin and you're ready," Megan says, shoving another bobby pin into the bun at the back of my head. Once it's secured, she squeezes my shoulders. "Beautiful."

I smile at her through the mirror, beyond grateful for her

lifelong friendship. After all of these years of doing each other's hair, I couldn't imagine anyone else doing it for me. And in all honesty, my attempt to do it myself was pathetic.

"Okay, Cinderella, it's time to get your happily ever after." Natalie pulls me out of my chair, not giving me a second to take a breath.

I squeeze her hand, pulling her to a stop. All of my best friends are in my bedroom, helping me get ready, and all the emotions I've been feeling start bubbling to the surface.

"I am the luckiest woman in the whole world to have you girls as my best friends." I look at Lucy, Megan, and Natalie, the three of them standing together in their adorable sundresses. "I wouldn't be me without you three, and I am so grateful to have found such loyal friends from the very beginning." I hold my hand out to Quinn and Hope, beckoning them closer. "And you two. It's as if you've both been a part of the group the whole time. We got so lucky when you came into our lives and accepted us as we are. I love you guys."

"Bitch," Natalie whispers, swiping the tears from under her eyes. We all bust out laughing, sniffling as we try to contain our emotions. A group hug ensues because we can't help ourselves, giggling as we love on each other. This is why they are my best friends.

"Come on, ladies. It's time to get going," Adam hollers from outside the door, interrupting our moment.

The girls all throw their shoulders back and head out of the bedroom. I hear Natalie tell Adam to come say hello, and a minute later, he's standing in the doorway, an awestruck expression frozen on his face. His eyes take in my sleeveless, satin, mermaid-style gown, tears welling as his emotions get the better of him. He clears his throat and wipes his mouth as he tries to get himself under control.

"You look beautiful, sis." He walks toward me, and I meet him halfway, wrapping my arms around his waist.

"Thanks," I whisper into his chest, overcome with happiness.

Adam clears his throat again before pulling away. "I'm going to go get your groom. Then I'll send Dad up when we're ready for you to come down."

I nod my head, smiling at him. It's still a little hard to believe that Ben and I are finally getting married. It felt like this day would never come, and now that it's here, it doesn't quite feel real.

But I get to marry the love of my life today, and that's as real life as it gets. To be able to choose the one person I want by my side through all of life's ups and downs is the most human part of our existence. It's beautiful.

A few minutes later, Dad comes bounding up the stairs, grinning from ear to ear. He and Mom stuck around for the majority of the morning, getting a sneaky first look at my dress before the girls came up to fix my sad attempt at doing my own hair and makeup. "It's time, baby girl. Are you ready?"

"Beyond ready." I grin. He leads me down the stairs and toward the backyard, where everyone is gathered. I immediately find Ben through the windows, looking devastatingly handsome in his navy blue suit.

Dad opens the back door for me, then holds out his arm to escort me the rest of the way. My gaze locks onto Ben as he starts to get choked up, his eyes welling and his smile as bright as the afternoon sun. Naturally, my eyes tear up in response, and the rest of the walk is blurry as I try to fight them back.

Ben takes my hand in his, kissing the back of it as he pulls me in close. He swipes under my eyes, helping to clear the remaining tears. "You look gorgeous. I can't believe you're mine."

"Believe it, baby. My heart is yours." I smile at him.

"Just as mine is yours. Forever."

THE END

*Keep reading for a bonus epilogue and a sneak peek into
Dax's book, Reckoning*

BONUS EPILOGUE

DAX

Fists smacking into punching bags echo through the room, the sound filling me with satisfaction. After six years of being open, it's still a little surreal that the gym is still going strong. I didn't have much in the way of expectations when I first opened the place, but seeing the success I've had since I opened has been pretty great.

"Dax!" Sara calls from across the room. She's been teaching classes for the last two years and even added an advanced self-defense course to her roster when the women in her beginner class wanted to learn more advanced skills. Her classes are popular enough she could teach full time, but she still loves working at the clinic with Ben, so she only teaches the two.

"What's up?" I ask when she gets close.

"Quinn has a friend in town who wants to join our class tonight. I wanted to make sure that was cool with you before I said yes."

"Sure, just have her sign a waiver first."

"Will do! And I may need you to help me teach if we're short a partner."

I nod. "Just let me know."

Sara swats me on the arm in thanks and jogs back over to the mats, where Ben is still working out. The two of them have basically forced me into friendship. Any time they invited me over for dinner or out with their group, they always made sure I didn't have a choice in whether I was coming or not.

If I didn't like them so much, I would've been annoyed. Instead, I sort of enjoy being their friend. Not that I let them know that. I have a reputation to maintain.

An hour later, I find Ben and Tucker chatting by the weights as Sara and the girls start setting up. Most of the people in the advanced class are Sara's friends, but there are a few others that join regularly, as well.

"Hey, guys. All good?" I ask as I stand next to Tucker.

"Hey, man," Ben greets me. "We're great. How are things for you?"

"Can't complain."

"You never do," Tucker teases.

I smirk, nodding my head. It's true. I don't talk about myself very often around these guys, even though I know they'd welcome me with open arms if I shared any part of my past with them.

Before we can say anything else, Sara comes over. "Hey, turns out, I'm one partner short tonight. Do you mind sparring with Quinn's friend, Hailey?"

"No, that's fine. Has she taken any classes before?"

"She said yes but didn't elaborate, so I have no idea what her skill level is."

"Okay. It doesn't matter either way. Just wanted to know." I follow behind Sara after saying a quick *see you later* to the guys.

When we get close, I spot the woman in question. Her tight leggings highlight every lithe curve she has, while her sports bra demands you notice her toned shoulder blades and arms. Damn, this woman is fit.

Her white-blonde hair is up in a messy bun, and the second she turns toward Sara, I swear every ounce of air in my body leaves. Her round face and crystal-blue eyes send shock waves through my system.

In all honesty, it sort of pisses me off. I have more control over myself than this. I'm not some horny teenager seeing his first pair of tits. I'm a grown-ass former Navy SEAL for Christ's sake.

Before I can fully get myself together, Sara makes the introduction. "Hailey, this is Dax Pierce. He owns the gym and helps hone my skills. Dax, this is Hailey Adler. She's here visiting for a couple of weeks."

"Nice to meet you," Hailey says, reaching out her hand. It's soft and delicate in mine, making me feel like I need to shake it gently.

"You, too. You've taken classes before?" I raise my eyebrow in question, trying to figure out if the woman is actually as delicate as she seems or if that's a front she puts up so others will underestimate her.

"Yeah, I've got some skills." Her cocky grin has my body stirring, and I can't help the smirk that tugs up the corner of my mouth. I turn toward Sara, ignoring the pull I'm feeling, as she gets the class started.

"Okay, everyone, we are going to work on an armbar to finish out our chokehold defense lessons, and if there's time, we'll start on the next segment." She demonstrates the different positions they're working on and provides refreshers for anyone who needs them. While everyone's focus is on Sara, I take in the tiny woman next to me, my eyes lingering on the curve of her ass.

She may look like a pixie, but I have a feeling she's ferocious. My eyes snap back to her face when I realize she's caught me staring. Her smirk tells me she doesn't think I'm a creep, so there's that, I guess. "Have you done this position before?"

She raises an eyebrow. "I've done several positions. This one is very familiar to me."

Fuck, she's a spitfire. I cross my arms in an attempt to keep my cool. "Good. Let's get started, then. You can show me what you're made of."

"Shit talking and sarcasm. And a lot of sass." She grins.

I huff out a laugh, unable to hold it in, and nod my head at her to get into position. She lays flat on her back while I hover over her, my hand at her throat to simulate an attack. "I usually prefer a guy buy me a drink before he gets me on my back, you know."

I growl at her comment, annoyed at the instant affect her words have on my body. "Shut up and take this seriously." I squeeze her throat, prompting her to focus. And maybe myself a little bit, too.

She positions her feet almost perfectly, tightens her muscles, then suddenly flips me onto my back, my arm pinned between her thighs in a strangle hold.

Fuck me, that was hot.

"Does that work?" she asks, a huff to her voice.

Not wanting to show my lust, I go for critical instead of praising. "Not quite. You need to tighten up your leg placement, otherwise an attacker could get the upper hand."

She narrows her eyes at me, determination seeping through every pore.

This is going to be fun.

ALSO BY SHELBY GUNTER

The Sonoma Series

Forever, Always (Todd and Megan prequel novella)

Guarding Her Love (Cooper and Quinn)

Breathing Her Fire (Natalie and Tucker)

Finding Her Strength (Levi and Hope)

Protecting Her Heart (Sara and Ben)

The Metamorphosis Series

Catalyst (Adam and Ellie)

Blindsided (Matthew and Tilly)

The Shadow Series

Reckoning (Hailey and Dax)

Relentless (Lizzy and Isaac)

Resurgence (Thia and Jackson)

ACKNOWLEDGMENTS

I feel like I should be singing the song *Closing Time* by Semisonic right now as I write this note. It's hard to believe that this is the final book in the series. I feel like these characters have lived in my head for years and I'm not quite ready for them to move on with their lives. Hence why they're probably singing that song to me right now.

I started writing this series when I was in desperate need of an escape from reality. Cooper and Quinn came to me first and their friend group grew until I had all these characters fighting me for attention. And after writing Sara's book, I have even more people in my head whispering their stories. Can we finally talk about the Ellis brothers??? Those boys are something else let me tell you.

There are what feels like a million people who deserve credit for helping me make this series into what it is but first I need to thank you, dear reader. Without you, I wouldn't be able to keep doing what I love and for that, I will be eternally grateful.

Another huge thank you goes out to my husband and family. I am incredibly lucky to have their constant support and encouragement in my life. I love you all with everything.

My editor Jaime Ryter is one of the best people I've ever known. She kicks my butt into gear and makes me laugh while she's doing it. I love her dearly.

I would be remiss if I didn't mention my beta readers, Robin, Emily, and Tina. You are the freaking best and I have no idea what I would do without you!

To Clarise Tan at CT creations for dealing with the constant back and forth on this cover. It's exactly what I wanted and I'm so grateful for your patience.

And finally to my online family. My pocket friends who make me laugh and send me virtual hugs when I'm in need of encouragement. You guys are my people and I love you!

ABOUT THE AUTHOR

Shelby Gunter is a romantic suspense author who loves to write twisted endings you'll never see coming. She lives in Kansas City with her husband and fur baby and is either writing, reading, or drinking coffee. Sometimes all three at the same time.

You can find Shelby on all social media sites as well as join her Facebook group, Shelby's Shameless Book Sirens for exclusive content.

Visit authorshelbygunter.com to stay up to date on Shelby's latest releases.

www.ingramcontent.com/pod-product-compliance
Lightning Source LLC
Chambersburg PA
CBHW051217130726
47988CB00001B/124